Masala Wedding

Sonny Singh Kalar

This book is published by
Grosvenor House Publishing Ltd
28-30 High Street, Guildford, Surrey, GU1 3HY.
www.grosvenorhousepublishing.co.uk

A CIP record for this book
is available from the British Library

ISBN 978-1-906210-63-2

Dedicated in memory of mum
You were truly an inspiration to us all.
A very special, warm, and loving
person - we will never forget you.
We pray that you are always close to guide us
through the rest of our lives wherever we are.
We love and miss you so much – RIP

A note from the author...

There will always be successes and failures in life,
but it is in the joy of creating and performing
your chosen craft that you truly savour
the sweet taste of satisfaction.
As a life long student and aficionado of the written
word, I have an unquenchable verve and passion
to pursue my hobby of writing. I find it
edifying and deeply therapeutic.

Remember, if you believe in something
with a passion then YOU will succeed.
It takes perspiration, commitment, tenacity and
above all desire, but the fruits of your labour will be
worth the blood, sweat, and tears it took to achieve.
You need to have tremendous self belief in
yourself – this is the essence of success.
I hope you enjoy my book as
wonderfully as I have had creating it.

Reader I salute you...your humble author...

www.masalabooks.com   masalabooks@yahoo.com

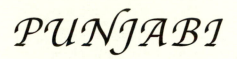

"PURE

—

PUNJABI

—

PASSION"

Contents

Chapter 1

Profanity parents

Telling your parents to *'fuck off'* is not one of those moments you want to remember and cherish with any fondness. It was the day of reckoning about six months ago when they finally nailed my dark secret, exposed my downtrodden existence and discovered exactly how my life had become a total disaster movie, an unmitigated crash site. At the time I felt on top of the world, untouchable and like a veritable God. I had just taken a heavy shot of the white stuff in the toilet at work. This was my unique, tried and trusted way of escaping the mundane and stupefying groove of life's chores. It had been a long and gritty day and I was getting ready to go home, get shit, shaved and showered and then hit the local pub with my brethren Dev. I needed this fix, just one last time, a trusted stimulant to get me in the party mood.

My year long affair with my seductive white powdered goddess, a kind and dependable angel was full of incident. At the time it was simply a nightmare born of necessity as I had continually struggled to find my way through the circus of life, to find parity and excitement

1

in the oubliette of my mind, to make sense of my myopic view of life and its tribulations.

However, today was to be my last day of taking drugs, the gravy train was very much hitting the buffers despite the euphoric feeling dancing through my body. My moralistic arbiter with all its unalterable resolve had already decided that this was to be my last drugs hit...EVER!

Sneaking around and taking the odd drugs fix had become a paradigm for my life, as a young mid twenties Punjabi guy, hiding away in the toilets taking drugs, doing loose women and generally indulging in anything and everything villainous that was socially and culturally taboo in my circles, but hey – it is my life, my bed of nails, my tunnel of escape from my cloistered existence. I knew I had to stop myself though, to prevent myself from spiraling down this journey of self destruction before I reached the point of no return.

I stood in the end cubicle, my usual hideaway spot, on the second floor men's toilets in my office block. My nostrils sucked up the crisply laid out line of demonic white powder nestling incriminatingly on the toilet seat through a tightly rolled twenty pound note. Using a note was easy; it picked up the charlie (cocaine) without quibble and was just the right size to feed into one of your nostrils. I had read somewhere that ninety nine per cent of twenty pound notes circulating throughout the UK have traces of cocaine on them. This was a disconcerting statistic: and timely reminder of how widespread drug use has become throughout society.

I leaned against the cubicle wall and immediately felt the surge of adrenalin go through my body like a bolt of electricity.

My hands felt like hammers, heavy, immensely powerful and gorged with blood. I gritted my teeth, bracing myself as my heart began to beat furiously, almost uncontrollably. The endorphins were coursing around my body, skipping the light fandango with unbridled freedom. This wasn't my first time and as a seasoned professional druggie I knew what the effects would be and how long they would last.

I wiped down the remaining traces of powder from off the toilet seat. I had to remove any traces of evidence as the bosses at work were getting suspicious with the amount of time a lot of the lads were spending in the toilets. They had even got hold of special wipes which they would wipe the toilet seats with in order to test for traces of drugs.

I worked in a computer firm in Hounslow. I would provide advice over the phone in my consultancy position to muppets out there who would whinge and moan about their computers not working. I would find myself biting my lip, stopping myself from telling them to shove the keyboard where it doesn't shine. Most of these simpletons merely had to reboot the computer to get the darn thing crackling into life again, the nonsensical twats. I had been at the firm for over five years, it was a deadbeat position, the office gossip, the broken air conditioning, the bosses body odour, the stream of morons phoning the customer service line had sucked the energy and verve out of me, but it put bread on the table, let me earn a crust and allowed me the freedom to live a swanky lifestyle.

I took a deep breath, straightened my tie and dusted down each shoulder of my suit as I opened the cubicle door and walked towards the basins.

I was super charged, primed and raring to get amongst them.

I left the toilets and walked down the hall and out into the car park, it felt good leaving the depressing hell hole for the next few days. I had a spring in my step and felt alive, ready for the evening ahead.

I called Dev, he answered; 'what you doing bruv, not having a cheeky 'mutt' (wank) were you?'

He laughed. 'Pick you up in an hour my friend, just going to pop home and sort my shit out.'

He was always perfectly relaxed 'yeah Kam, no problem see you soon bruv.'

I negotiated the ten minute journey from my work place to my des res in Southall, a three bedroom semi detached house in Burns Avenue. We had lived there for over twenty years and it was home. I lived with my parents and as the only child I had the veritable run of the household. I got home that evening in record time and without too much fuss. My mind anticipating the drink fuelled evening ahead and a long, overdue reunion with my tempting mistress Stella, or Miss Artois for the less discerning of you. I parked up, and bounded up the drive like an antelope sweeping in majestic fashion to my house, still intoxicated from the euphoria of the hit I had taken before.

I felt good and wanted to share my secret with mum and dad, a secret that I had been hankering for some time now – my wish to settle down and get married and personally to leave the world of drugs behind me. I was excited at this prospect of telling them as I knew that mum would be getting the ludoo's (orange balled sweets) out and kissing me. Dad would shake my hand and tap me on the back – being careful not to show too much emotion as dad's do, and later that evening I was certain mum would be wading through her hordes of suitcase containing about forty six thousand Asian suits just to be prepared for when the big day arrived. It would make their day. I was literally bursting with perpetual pride. I turned the key in the lock and pushed the front door open.

Although I had been on the *'stuff'* for about one year prior to this day, I knew that I was wasting my life and there would come a time when I simply had to wean myself off of them altogether. I would reduce my fix to once every few weeks and gradually stop. This was the mapped out game plan and although I had just taken some, I knew within the next few weeks I would stop as simple as that, telling my parents that I wanted to settle down tonight was to be the watershed in my life.

This was going to be a cracking evening for them, for us, the thoughts percolating in my mind. I closed the front door behind me and walked up the hallway taking my coat off. I could immediately smell the air thick with the aroma of incence sticks pervading throughout the house where mum would strategically place them in various rooms. This was always a refreshing way to lift your flagging and dejected spirit after a hard days gruel at work in the same way that smelling essential oils such as jasmine, lavender and sandal wood to name a few would have the same uplifting effect on a persons soul. I was closest to mum, *(Harjit Kaur Gill),* her gentle nature, her fragile fifty eight year old frame, a cute five foot two inches (all Asian mums were this standard size – small and cuddly) with a round face punctuated with warm and soft features, her greying hair always covered by a chunni (head scarf) her petite, cuddly body akin to that of the fluffiest teddy bear in the fluffiest toy store in the world: all gently accentuating the natural warmth and refined grace she exudes.

She would often knit jumpers, jackets and all sorts of garments for the local biddies from the gurdwara with resolute adherence. She was very adept at knitting and I had often teased her that she would be the new Indian Versace. She would laugh and hit me. The teasing would continue, amongst all the plaudits and adulation she would receive from her own clothes range, she would also have the biddies modeling her jumpers and jackets on the catwalk, strutting their stuff with attitude and panache. This teasing would often be followed by a slap on the back and 'chup kurr kuttiya' (shut up you dog) – said and translated as a term of endearment in Punjabi.

The gurdwara was mums' sanctum, the place where she was at one with god. She was deeply religious and knew everything there was to know about her faith. She would constantly pray for happiness and prosperity for our family and recite and whisper the hymns as she dutifully carried out the housework around the house. The gurdwara was also a fantastic place to catch up on the latest gossip within the community. Her stories were cracking, ranging from someone's daughter running off with a 'cala' (black guy), or another old dear's son kicking her into an old peoples home. She would tell me about these stories with great fervency and enthusiasm. When I was a lot younger she would often tell me stories of the hardship she had suffered growing up in India back in her salad days. As her only child she loved to educate and steer me to live my life with a guiding map of beliefs and principles. A kind of abc to refer to when I was at any kind of fork in the road throughout my life. She had a wonderful knack of saying things to me, reciting memorable stories, painting tangible pictures of her childhood and catapulting me back to the homeland and to the lush corn fields of her village amongst other wonderful places she had visited. This nurturing and invested time in me had been well spent, to a degree. I had picked up valuable lessons through these interactions and she gave me the belief to do things, be an achiever in life and be successful. This was character building and I loved it: As they say *'character is like a good curry, it is best made at home.'*

Despite this, I still had my fair share of near death chappal (flip flop) moments with mum wielding these weapons of mass destruction with defining aplomb, chasing me around the living room when I was a youngster striking with unerring efficiency, as I bobbed and weaved deftly from every swipe and slash of the chappal. She was the mystical grandmaster of Chappal Fu – only taught to the most talented disciples in a secret mountainous location back in Punjab. She was accurate, determined and a wily fox when armed to the teeth with these fearsome tools: the true nemesis of every adolescent Asian boy growing up. All in all she was the best mum ever, really lovely.

Dad, *Karnail or Kevin* as he was known to his English mates on the other hand was a tougher, stricter cookie than mum. He was in his early sixties and at five feet ten inches, he had a good physique for his age, and had hands of steel. His greying and receding hair pushed back over his head, his sharp features on his face, with his no nonsense brown eyes full of stories of hardship. He had served in the Indian army and had been working in a factory since coming to England when he was younger. He had retired last year and was eking out his well deserved retirement relaxing at home, doing the odd bit of DIY and helping out friends and family with odd jobs when he had the time. Dad spoke good English and had settled in well after weathering the usual storm of racism that every Asian parent faced throughout those early turbulent times from neighbours and the general hoi polloi. However despite his well grasped command for the English language, he would often ramble on humorously in Punjabi after he had necked a few whiskies too many of an evening. This was the time when the classic Punjabi proverbs would come out in all their confusing and jumbled up glory. Now over the years I had read many famous Chinese proverbs, fortune cookie sayings and wise words from past masters like Sun Tzu. I mean at university I was quite fascinated by the wisdom of the Chinese. However nothing could have quite prepared me for dad's Punjabi proverbs. They never made sense, were overly profound and nine times out of ten had no resemblance to the conversation that was taking place.

Another annoying, but similarly endearing foible that dad would display with relish was the incessant use of the word 'you people.' Everyone, you, me, the neighbour, the flaming cat were – 'you people.' Every god damn sentence would amusingly start with 'you people...'He was a great guy though, straight as a die, and I loved him. I mean don't get me wrong things haven't always been rosy, and like any Asian lad growing up we have crossed swords on the odd occasion. I would normally be on the wrong side of a tongue lashing from dad for attaining mediocre results in my school exams, staying out late, going out with a white lass who lived down the road, you know the usual, but one thing was that he was always fair with his assessment of the situation, if he had to dish out a beating then I kind of had it coming.

My parents have always been proud of me throughout my life; they have been there for me from the halcyon school days, to supporting me through University and all the other fun times together. They were good eggs, the standard bearers of a typical happy couple, always smiling and dutifully going about their business and helping others where they could.

As I hung my coat up on the stand I immediately sensed something, I could not understand what, but something wasn't quite right. My grinning and self confident demeanor turned to an uneasy feeling, one of trepidation and uncertainty. I could sense an air of malevolence pervading, redolent of the crying gallows of death row. Today the house was quiet, almost too quiet, my canine like instinct immediately sensed that the atmosphere was bleak, what was waiting for me behind the living room doors I cogitated as I pushed open the door, it was to be the gateway to hell.

I walked in and quickly scanned the room. Dad was by the window with his hands clasped behind his back, staring pensively into the street and mum was sat on the sofa weaving knitting needles through a roll of wool at breakneck speed, she kept her eyes fixed on the task at hand and never looked up to acknowledge me.

On any other occasion I would walk in and dad would be sitting on his favourite armchair catching the latest Indian drama on one of the many Asian channels that we had subscribed to, usually surrounded by the odd crushed and empty can of Skol lager strewn incriminatingly on the coffee table, along with packets of scrunched up Hajmola Nuts. These nuts were his favourite and there would always be a packet of them nearby wherever he was in the house. The downside to him eating them was that they would give him the most outrageous camel breath this side of town which was disconcerting. Still he liked them and they kept him off the streets. Mum would usually be happily ensconced in the kitchen beavering away and making the roti for us with the pungent aroma of a hearty curry wafting its way through the room. The succulent mixture of spices and herbs always seducing my senses and setting my taste buds on fire.

But today was different; it was a watershed moment for our relationship. The day their only son was to shatter their hopes and discard any ambitions they had of me aspiring to be a success like a discarded toilet tissue, the moment they had secretly feared all their lives. 'Mum, dad what's going on?' I said, trying to disguise the trepidation in my voice. No sooner had I said this I found myself glancing over at the coffee table, my eyes widened, almost popping out of my head. There were no Skol cans to be seen, but there it was, the evidence that was to secure my imminent demise, my fall from grace with my previously doting parents. I cringed. All of a sudden I felt my hands becoming clammy, beads of sweat appearing on my forehead as my drugs stash laid there exposing me, their quasi son, as a druggie. There they were in all their merciless glory. The evidence; packets of white powder, a fiery combination of Colombian and Mexican charlie (cocaine) in four small wraps, laying there as a signed expose, my very own death warrant. I felt the hackles on my neck standing erect, it felt itchy, uncomfortable and the moment was far from roseate.

I later discovered that mum had moved the cupboard in my bedroom forward to put a rolled up bit of newspaper underneath to prevent it from rocking. This was an old and trusted Asian secret passed down from the days of yore. She had then stumbled across the packets containing the drugs stash that I had been secretly hiding and hording for months. Despite the fact that my goose was cooked, I momentarily pondered why in gods name we bought wonky furniture in the first place? Whilst growing up I remembered that nearly every cupboard, chest of draws or table had a folded piece of newspaper underneath it, why? I knew the inevitable; the prognosis was bleaker than a winters day, the writing was not so much written on the wall as spray painted in font two hundred. I was soon to be toast as the accusing finger of incrimination pointed suspiciously at me.

'What the hell have you become, my son...a bastard junkie?' dad roared, still looking out of the window, attacking me with the voracity of a school of piranhas, his face twisted and scrunched up as he turned to look me straight in the eyes. 'You have shamed me, is this what I spent all my years working for, to bring up a drug dealer?' His voice booming loudly around the room. I stood there shell shocked, grim faced and unable to move, my stomach rolling over as the seconds ticked by. All that was missing was the twenty three rapid zooming face shots by the camera as depicted in the myriad of Asian soap operas on the Sky channels, zoom, zoom, zoom to emphasise the tension and drama of the moment. The cameras would have had a field day, my eyes swept across the floor, I felt ashamed, anxious and so alone. He continued to raise his voice as the outpouring of hate, the venomous onslaught continued. 'Why are you not speaking to me, tell me what you have to say about all the drugs you are taking?' I could not fathom what he was saying to me, he was actually calling me a junkie, a heroin addict. Did he not know that heroin was for parasites, for gutless, crazy druggies who steal and assault to feed their soul destroying and filthy habit? He was categorizing me as one of those low life, scumbags. Did he not know me? I stared at him in total disbelief. The cocaine and combination of adrenaline was sweeping through me and began to distort my thoughts. My temporary paralysis was fleeting as I plucked up the courage to offer a plausible defence. 'Dad I have only tried it once or twice' I said clinging to my life long respect that my dad had earned from me, his only child. I was hoping for a shred of sympathy, a little leniency as the light of reality on the situation I had found myself in, continued to burn fiercely.

'You liar, I have seen your behaviour change.' Dad trembled with rage, his tension lined face offering no reprieve, no remorse. 'Where did you get the drugs from?' He continued to rant. 'Where?' the air remained poisonous and very deadly. His venomous and scowling tone, cutting straight through me. 'Dad please let me explain, I have only tried it a few times just to see what it is like, everyone at work, all my other mates have tried, it is not heroin, I am not a junkie…no-one I know is addicted to it, they just do it every now and…' dad, had heard enough and lurched forward grabbing me by the collar of my shirt and shaking me violently. This moment of clarity clearly assured me that my parents had made their minds up about me; to them I was nothing more than a low life druggie, a desperate and diseased soul…a lost cause!

In my panicked and confused state I thought of throwing in the line about me wanting to get married, hoping in my warped and demented mind that this would assuage dad's desire to cut my innards out and wear them as a garland around his neck, or to skin me and wear my skin as a fur coat. Luckily my subconscious mind talked me out of making such a schoolboy error, this clearly was not the time to talk of a joyous happy occasion where soft fluffy bunnies would be bounding around the living room without a care in the world upon me breaking this news to them. I had to deal with dad's imminent desire to shake the living shit out of my body as he continued to shake me violently. His face sweating, his grip steely and nostrils flaring like a bull, every second that went by. He wagged a condemning finger and shrieked 'don't lie to me, tell me the truth, how long have you been taking us for fools, when did you become a dealer?' A dealer are you kidding me or what, I could just about shuffle a pack of cards let alone run a multi national drug dealing business. He had clearly thought I was more talented and clued up about business than my usual goofy and witless expression let on. I was certainly no Columbian drug dealing cartel overlord, well not with four measly packets with a street value of sixty pounds tops. He continued to shake me like the proverbial rag doll, up, down, back and forth, my tongue rattling in my mouth, he was a man possessed.

'Dad please listen to me, I am not a dealer, I have only tried it a few times and that is it, I will stop…you have to believe me, I will stop from today, I will ne…..' Without giving me a chance to finish my sentence, dad threw me against the living room door, I connected with a blood curdling thud, bruising my back in the process and sliding down the door like a cartoon illustration. I looked anxiously at mum for a slim glimmer of hope, but she sat there sobbing disconsolately, wiping her tears with her chunni. The sewing needles lay resting on her lap and she never looked at me once during the entire incident, her disappointment in me was tangible. How would she face the community now? In Asian families this was the most crucial aspect and the core of everything, *'izaat' (respect)* what others, relatives, friends, the Punjabi community would think about you and your actions. Not losing your *izaat* was the name of the game. Mum looked demoralized and down beaten as the community wolves snarled back at me with satisfying glee, any shred of *izaat* went hurtling out of the window along with my credibility. I looked up at dad for mercy and slowly staggered back to my feet. When out of nowhere, I felt an enormously crushing blow to my face. Man he could hit hard....It felt as though I had taken the brunt of a twelve bore shotgun full on and from close range. I had been hit by a speeding train, a fucking juggernaut. I fell onto the floor again, clutching the side of my face, the pain searing through my body. The response was terrifying, decisive and deadly as I found myself in the heart of this maelstrom of violent chastisement. Dad was standing over me 'bhanchod, haramzada, haraami.' He picked me up and slapped me again, on the same side, he had hands like spades. I mean those bad boys were mean, a couple of anvils attached to his arms, the side of my face continued to throb, my brain pumped hard to make sense of this soul destroying incident, my eyes laced with fear. 'Dad don't hit me, you have to believe me, I am not a drug dealer.' I pleaded again. Bang – he hit me again – I careered over the standing globe containing a copious amount of alcohol from whiskies, rums and other bottles, as I toppled over the globe, the bottles came crashing down and smashed onto the floor. My luck was slowly evaporating on this day and I managed to sustain a horrendous cut across my hand from the Bacardi bottle as the glass tore through my hand. I picked myself up clutching my hand, infuriated, angry and frustrated that my pleas were falling on deaf ears and that my dad in particular was writing me off. The cocaine stampeding through my body, flowing freely in my system gave me false courage and fortitude, and the more my blood boiled the angrier I became...the more the blood trickled down my hand from my cut the more miffed and desperate I found myself. Dad went for me again swinging his spade like hand towards the direction of my face, if it had connected he would have taken my head clean off, I have no doubt, I would have been decapitated, the bugger was that strong. I ducked my head quickly, cranking it downwards, so quickly I heard several cracks in my neck, I thought I had broken my neck such was the ferocity of the head swerving jerk. I missed his powerful swing by a whisker and lost my balance, reeling backwards, stumbling into the door again and half on the floor, my injured hand scraping along another shard of the broken Bacardi bottle on the floor and making me yelp in agony. That was the straw that broke the camels back as I shouted with pent up frustration and unrelenting *fury 'just fuck off then......FUCK.....OFFFFFF......... if that's what you think I am.'* My nuts had grown the size of melons, the cocaine had turned me into the Incredible Hulk. I stood there with my chest puffed out; I gave him a piece of my mind I thought. The room fell silent as mum held her heart, and looked at me in stunned disbelief, the first time she had laid eyes on me throughout the entire episode. The saucer sized tears wetting her cheeks and dripping onto her lap. Her eyes, wounded, remained wide with shock, swimming with tears, so watery you could drown in them. Dad stood there glaring at me, firm jawed, steely resolve coupled with heart rendering disappointment. He was not moved by my outburst, after all having served to such a rank in the Indian army and defending his family throughout the sixties when racism was rife he had heard a lot worse....but not ever from his son. What now? Who makes the next move in this game of physical chess?

The Mexican stand off continued...what was I doing? – this was my dad, was I about to have fisticuffs with him? My head was spinning, so I seized the opportunity to escape this tormented situation. I clutched my hand, stemming the flow of blood with my other hand, squeezing it tightly. I stormed out of the house, slamming the front door behind me. I left mum sobbing in her hands and dad disgusted in my insolence, although a little surprised by the kahoonas I had displayed in standing up to him. I ran down the path taking my car keys out from my trouser pocket. I glanced at the lounge window over my shoulder and could see dad shaking his head through the blinds. I got in the car and carefully started it, trying not to spill blood over the seats. I wasn't sure where I was going, but it had to be sufficiently far away from them. My world was collapsing around me and fast. I needed to seek solace from someone. The one guy I could rely on in these circumstances was my trusted brethren – Dev.

CHAPTER 2

—ᴍ—

Dependable friends

Dev works as an accountant for a company in Hayes; and has been there a number of years. He was sick to death of being stuck in the daily grind of it all. At the same age as me, twenty four years old he was currently single, with no girlfriend to speak off, well for the last few years really, preferring to indulge in his hobby of tinkering about with cars. A guy of unimpeachable loyalty, an exemplary companion and a friend who has been through all the turbulent times with me, not to mention many rib rattling incidents. There would be a list of long elicited superlatives used to describe what this guy meant to me. Look up good, trustworthy and loyal mate in the dictionary and you will see his name written next to it. We grew up together, side by side, blow for blow and tear for tear, no matter what else; he was always there for me, always.

Our friendship has been tightly bound ever since those salad days when we were room mates at Derby University. Although he has always had a gullible nature, his heart is in the right place. His tendency to believe what is said in the first instance, and to say and do naïve things, stuff that made your toes curl has been his hall-mark since I first got to know him. Despite this foible and others he has stood the test of time and is a true salt of the earth and bon de ver to me.

I screeched to a halt outside Dev's house, honked the horn a couple of times and sat back tightly clutching my injured hand. I closed my eyes and relived those fatal, jaundiced words that had disgraced me. What had I become I pondered? My mind raced uncontrollably, this was not me. I loved my parents!

They say hindsight is twenty-twenty and if I could have turned the clock back this would be the ideal time, but I had to take responsibility for my actions, for my disgraceful outburst. I felt alone in my thoughts with the debilitating aftermath that follows on from a physical confrontation, I felt jumpy and very lonely. They say that fighting a battle already lost can weaken the spirit, and right now I felt like a lily livered pansy, a gutless wonder, a shamed and exposed druggie. How would they, why should they ever forgive me for my denigrating outburst? My life was worthless. The foundations were crumbling around me in emphatic fashion; I had crashed and burned, all for what? A few packets of poorly cut Mexican charlie.

Dev sat in the car, appearing as if from nowhere 'what's happening bro, what the fuck, how did you cut your hand?' He said worryingly. His mere presence edifying and lifting my weary, down trodden soul in an instant. This guy was the veritable mutts nuts, a man of true unimpeachable substance. And so I began to explain the whole sorry mess to him, a complete unedited warts and all representation of my insolence, my break down of communication and fall from grace. He sat there listening intently; his soothing, sympathetic tones reassured me. 'Okay, what's happened has happened – what we need to do now is sort this mess out, damage limitation is the name of the game.' What a star, I thought. He had used the collective word *'we'*, when referring to sorting the mess out. His problem was my problem, mi casa su casa. A rare diamond. This was always a good indicator that someone was firmly ensconced on your side.

'Thanks, man, but how do we sort this out? I have just told my dad to fuck off, he has probably disowned me...you understand me.' I responded in a deflated fashion. I have always been paranoid, sometimes too disturbingly paranoid and notions of me never speaking to mum and dad again were flashing into my head. 'I would next see them at their funerals – how harsh would that be...?' Dev put his hand on my shoulder and squeezed it firmly 'Don't worry bruv, I will call your uncle Sharm, he will patch this up, you will see, let's sort your hand out first.' With that, we went into his house.

He lived with his parents who were currently at a wedding in India and were not due back for a few weeks. Dev sorted me out with a bandage and some dettol as I nursed my wound, it looked nasty but I would live. Once bandaged, I sat down and necked a few aspirins. This would help the ease the throbbing pain in my hand I thought. I picked up a bottle of Cobra beer from the side table, my favourite, and took a well deserved sip. The drink instantly soothing the uneasy storm brewing in my stomach.

'Well at least it will stop you sitting at home 'mutting' over copies of Basanto Does Dallas with your hand cut up.' I simply couldn't muster up the strength to laugh with him, I was just not in the mood. I remained pensive, thoughtful as I replayed the incident over and over in my head, my skin prickly every time I recalled the expletive I had used, the fall from grace. My gaze wandered up to Dev. He cast me a sympathetic look. This was bad karma, kismet call it what you want. My chest continued to feel as though it was bursting with pain through my clothes.

'Bruv, I am scared that my puffed up pride has cost me my relationship with my parents?' I took another swig of beer. This and other such chains of thought were disturbingly shuttling back and forth in my mind as I felt the stab of guilt for letting my creators down, the drooping feeling of fatigue and worthlessness.

'Don't worry; your dad is a sympathetic, kind and damn straight chap. I am sure he will have calmed down when you see him, trust me it will be cool.' Dev then picked up his mobile and called Sharm. He was my dad's younger brother, a decent guy and was very well connected in Southall. Everyone knew him or knew of him, partially down to the fact that he ran a semi successful car repair shop near Southall BR Station. The shop was earning him a small fortune and he wasn't complaining, but in saying that he was a true goodfella, what you saw was what you got. He also had a penchant for a good drink, and would drum up any excuse just to get squiffy. You would always found him lurking somewhere with nefarious intent at every family occasion, and usually inebriated. Having a keen eye for the ladies and drinking copious amounts of booze were above and beyond his two achilles heels, and he was worth the entrance fee at any event when both vices were in full flow. He would be immediately transmogrified into a walking, talking, and drinking sex machine.

The qualities and sexual charisma of a Punjabi Tom Jones sublimely entwined with the drinking prowess of a Desi George Best. He was known in the circles as '*B.S.P...bahut sharab pinder*'– a pun on his name Sharminder. He never found out about his endearing nickname: thank god, as this crazy dude would invariably end up having a dust up with anyone and everyone after a few glassies.

There had been some infamous occasions where he would get physical with family members, especially the youngsters when he had been as pissed as a parrot on Chivas all evening. He would just throw his portly frame about on the dance floor, do the classic Bacardi on the head bottle dance and not to mention the curtain raising '*hoi, hoi* dance when he would grab the nearest unsuspecting hapless soul with his sweat stenched armpit draped around their shoulders. He would then jump around in a circle with them with a hokey cokey type type movement with his leg going in and out in front of him, all the while flicking his sweat over his victim. He also loved goofing around and was the kind of pestiferous and irritating uncle who would tease my cousins and me as we were growing up. He would love a good practical joke and where there was a giggle to be had, he would not be languishing too far behind. His wife Satwinder (my auntie) was sound as a pound and just let him carry on, any more laid back and she would have been horizontal. A lovely couple in every way. Although I was unable to see the woods from the trees at this time, this incident with my parents was the singular and most important watershed of my life. At this time my judgment was just enshrouded with anger and hostility, not to mention pain as my hand continued to throb cartoon style from my wound. I hated arguing with my parents. Don't get me wrong I am older and wiser now and I have learnt valuable lessons in life. I am a firm believer that arguments, experiences and incidents like this, shape you as an individual. Some times rowing is healthy, it get's rid of the bad blood, allowing both parties to listen and respond to one another's respective opinions, although in this case I did most of the listening.

Dev set up a meeting for the next day with mum, dad, Sharm, himself and me. It was at high noon, my house. I looked at Dev as he told me about the meet, the show-down at the Ok Coral; this was it, the time for redemption. All I could do was wait and pray for leniency. The clock ticked ominously towards my witching hour. How would they react, how? I remained pensive and very scared. My eyes, red with distress, roamed restlessly around the guest bedroom where Dev had allowed me to sleep. What was waiting for me when I saw them the next day?

CHAPTER 3

—⁓—

Murky world

My first encounter with cocaine/charlie started a year or so before the swearing incident with my parents. It all started one evening, my first ever hit was in my local pub in Southall – The Dhol and Duck. I was in the wrong place, wrong pub at the wrong time!

I had popped in for some well deserved snifters with Dev a few hours after we had both finished work, so that we could do the usual, and discuss the trials and tribulations of our mundane lives. I wanted to sink a few drinks, seeking to vanquish the misery of the working day. It was therapeutic and a good way to catch up with the days events. Inside the pub that evening, the usual plethora of uncles and dads lined the cushioned sofa style seats propped up against the inner walls, the red cloth worn and tattered from years of abuse, the foam popping through in certain areas. Excited voices peppered the air, frenzied gossiping, incessant chattering and clinking of glasses. Everyone was in their cups as the pervading atmosphere of merriment encapsulated the atmosphere perfectly.

'What was your day like?' I said to Dev who was perched up against the bar in his regular timely manner.

He looked rough, stubbly and unkempt. His shoulder length curtain hairstyle mopped over his dusky appearance, he had the kind of nose most boxers would have been proud to own and accompanying bug like eyes. He had always looked a tad rough, but today he looked his disheveled best. At five feet ten inches and with an average physique his personality was his warmest attribute, but hey looks to one side, he was a great mate, it was not as though I wanted to bed the fucker.

'Usual, staring at the screen and getting blinded by numbers, it done my head in' he responded.

'Why don't you leave and do something else, more interesting?' I said helpfully.

'Funny that I was just thinking the other day of being a consultant or something.' He took a hearty swig from his pint of Budweiser.

'Oh yeh a consultant hey....you have a BA Degree right?'

'Yeh.'

'What's the BA stand for, bullshit artist...come on bruv what can you be a consultant in, you have got the life experience of a foetus, what do you know about consultancy?' I said jokingly.

We both laughed as Dev playfully pushed my chest with his hand. 'Piss off, I reckon I can do something in consultancy. I don't know what, but that's where the money is, know what I mean.'

'Yeh course it is sweetheart – you are about as intelligent and consulting as fishing bait, sometimes you do talk bull crap. You actually need to be an expert in a particular field to be able to advise others, so really what your saying is baseless buffoonery.' Dev smirked and drank some more. 'stuff it let's get patti (drunk)' I put my pint glass down and shook my head 'bruv, I feel the need to do something outrageous, something different to escape my humdrum existence. I need some spice in my life, so that I can look back in years and say, hey been there and done that with a sense of pride or experience, know what I am saying?'

'Yeh I do, try being a consultant in how to avoid getting the beers in the pub, you fucking tight wad.' The booze lending a sharpness to Dev's retorts. Again we laughed out aloud as we inadvertently snorted beer out of our noses. The conversation flowed, we drank, and drank some more. The bhangra jukebox in the background was being abused with time held classics, as track after track rattled out from the speakers. The drink was flowing well, the mood was good, the punters poured in, and the complimentary piss soaked peanuts on the bar were being suitably devoured without a care as we settled firmly into the swerve of the evening. I wish all days could be like this?

Throughout the session I caught Dev looking over my shoulder and could see a worried expression on his face. Whilst I was trying to decipher what was going on, he sidled closer to me, shuffling his face next to mine so that I could feel his breath burning on my cheek. 'I am not being funny but this guy behind you keeps looking over here' he slurred worryingly. 'he is a big dude around Southall, what's his name...oh yeh...Spanish...' His whispering continued. 'He is connected and I have heard he is one fierce fucker, not to be messed with...we best get moving.' He looked serious and scared. 'So what, is he here?' I asked without making it obvious that our conversation revolved around him. 'Yeah trust me he is clocking us...I have heard he sorts you out with stuff if you catch my drift, be careful what you say.' Dev shifted uneasily on the bar stool. 'What do you mean is he look- ing at us right now?' I inquired. 'Yeah bruv, this guy is the devil. I have heard too much about him, lets go.' I was vicariously feeling Dev's anguish and reluctance in staying in the bar a second longer. 'Serious?' I asked. 'As a fucking heart attack, yeh.' Dev was lucid with his riposte. A picture was forming in my head. I did not want to look around and duly attract attention to ourselves and give him the cue to approach us, so I tried to play it cool and sipped from my pint glass whilst squirming uncomfortably on my stool. Dev rambled on reaching a feverish crescendo and seemingly one step away from signing up on his fan club website...'He is a fierce and uncompromising individual: The sort who will eat someone's sister for lunch and then come back for seconds.' No sooner had he said this, I turned my head, I needed to see what the fuss was about. As I was turning to look at him, I caught him sauntering up to us, right into our comfort zone, holding a half empty pint of Guinness 'What do you boys need?' He said menacingly. He spoke with a deep, gruff London accent. Spanish was six feet tall, had a shaven head and a face like a pit-bull chewing a wasp, and with his Popeye like frame cut an imposing figure, not to mention the multitude of scars and war wounds emblazoned across the battlefield his face was. He was a breeding, brooding beast of a guy, a fighting virtuoso and the heavy weight champion of drug dealing. He had swooped on his prey like a majestic eagle catching us with alcohol distorting our thoughts and mentally disarmed. (I had subsequently discovered that he had a Hispanic dad and Punjabi mum – hence the name Spanish or '*Spanjabi*' as he was sometimes known

– rather than his real name of Sebastian, that just didn't sound hard enough for the street.)

Without skipping a heartbeat I found myself drawn to him, like a moth to a flame, in fear if nothing else. 'What you got?' Here I was, entertaining him with my attempted street lingo, although I was not aware at this stage exactly what was about to unfold or how this moment was to change my life. He looked at Dev and fixed his eyes back on me, the corner of his mouth lifting into a wry smile 'Take this, do some in there (he pointed to the toilets) and let me know if you like it, I will be waiting here, there is plenty more if you do.' He leant against the bar and rummaged around in his underpants. He had his back to the patrons in the bar, the music was blaring and people were seeking solace from the troubles of the world in their cups, and so no one was any the wiser. He continued to fumble around in his nether regions and then produced a small packet containing a white powder. I was kind of relieved that it was only the packet that came out judging by the amount of time he spent with his hand down his pants and the disturbing look he had on his mug. He grabbed my hand and placed the packet in my palm. 'Now take that, hurry up.' I had a moment of paralysis, do I take the packet, do I give it back? Just too many god damn forks in the road. Still, I took hold of the packet and put it in my pocket quickly looking around incase anyone had witnessed the drug deal going down. The coast was clear. The murky, pit filled road to Scumsville had presented itself and this was my own way of facing up to my own nihilistic delusions about drugs. It was okay; after all I was just too strong minded to get addicted to anything. A combination of being curious about the effects that drugs can have on your life and doing something different were the prompts steering me towards the dark side, oh and not to mention avoiding the breath sapping fight that was invariably on the cards if I rebuffed this coyote's offer. Wealth of knowledge equates to wealth of power, and I wanted to know what all the fuss was about, why did so many people take drugs? What was the allure? I was about to find the answers, the sickly truth was all but knocking on my door. 'What is it?' I asked tentatively, still trying to maintain an ounce of street cred. His eyes squinted as he looked me up and down in disgust. 'It's fucking charlie innit - what about you pretty boy, want some?' He prodded Dev in the chest, whilst scrunching his face. Dev, always had an answer for everything and as cool as you like replied 'I would do but I have got a medical for the army tomorrow and if they piss test me, I am screwed, so I'll leave it, thanks.' Spanish then fixed his gaze back on me 'You will like this shit, trust me' He reassured me. 'I will wait here for you.' His scarred, pock marked face growing keener as he spluttered the words out. He sat on a bar stool and motioned with his finger for me to go into the toilet. The fiendish glint in his eyes carefully focused on me. He had been lining me up that evening, waiting for his moment to pounce on me as I let my guard down: It seemed that he had read the *'How To Be A Coyote book'* several times. The pressure was tangible and deadly real. 'How much?' I asked. 'Nah, don't worry, it's gratis…this one is on me.' He pounded his chest with his hand. I had never even had a proper spliff before, only a quick lug from my mates back at University when they would session. I needed to try it to see what the furore was all about. The party drug as it is called, one sniff from nirvana…I was looking to inject some verve into an otherwise hum drum lifestyle. I was about to try my first hit in the grubby toilets of my local boozer, classy I thought as a laid the packet down on the toilet seat. I never really knew what the hell I was doing – I knew I had to inhale it somehow, but wasn't sure – I couldn't find the instructions on the small see through plastic bag. I opened the bag and tipped a generous amount on the area between my forefinger and thumb. I placed the plastic bag back on the toilet seat. I felt dangerous and arrogant.

I had learnt that life is a game for warriors; it chews you up, spits you out and even shits on you for good measure. It is survival of the fittest. You need that jungle mentality, a dog eat dog upbringing to negotiate the snares, obstacles and pitfalls that we all face dressed up in a variety of imaginative events. This was now my time to do a bit of spitting and chewing of my own. You see we all start at the bottom of the food chain and try our best to climb up to the top. I was naïve and always have been, I was a proper goody two shoes home boy, back then anyway, you know the sort in bed by ten, eating coco pops for breakfast and owning a pair of furry slippers. I wanted a change, to be dangerous just once, to see what was on the other side of the fence – all that stood before me, the fence and all the heavenly glory was this illicit affair with this evil powder. I was just sick and tired of peering through the bars of life seeing only glimpses of the person I could become – more confident, alive and successful. Money, cars, power, respect, all I needed to do was get the confidence that I knew was nestling in powdered form on my hand and all that would be mine. I was amped up as I tried in vain to regulate my breathing. My hands were shaking as the adrenaline threatened to burst out of my body. This was my shitting life I thought as I took a last deep breath to steady myself and then with the single mindedness of an avalanche I pushed my hand towards my nose. One, two...three................. I inhaled deeply up my nostril – too deeply, as the surge of powder shot straight up my nose and directly to my brain. It was like a triple shot of espresso. I felt frazzled as I turned around and sat on the toilet squashing the plastic bag containing the remaining coke. Fucking hell, this shit was unreal.... I felt the endorphins doing the bossa nova around my body. I could feel the hackles on the back of my neck rising as my eyes widened and tried to focus on my surroundings. I took a few moments and steadied myself. This was the advent of my perilous plunge into the murky depths and drug obsessed abyss my life was to become for the next year. At that time I did not realize how deplorably bad things were going to get as I walked out of the toilet and back into the bar. I felt alive, like a man on fire, my balls were the size of coconuts as I strutted up to Spanish and Dev. Dev stared incredulously at me, I felt good, but also like an exhibit in the zoo as they both studied every twitch I made. Spanish stood up; he looked relaxed and pleased with himself. He gave me a piece of paper with a mobile number scrawled on it 'don't lose that, bell me up when you want me to hook you up, laters.' And with that he parted, disappearing out of the pub leaving me very much in the eye of the drug fuelled storm that my world had now become.

Dev began to interrogate me about the sensation I felt after my hit and I told him in graphic detail. At this time I did not realize what had actually just occurred, mainly because was I was still metaphorically doing bhangra with the white angels of death on the bar. I could feel the power and energy exuding from every orifice. I felt like Superman! However, unbeknown to me at the time, I had been the victim of the sting. It was one of the classic drug manoeuvres, the cout de gras of selling techniques. Spanish knew full well that after my first hit I would be back for some more, maybe not emotionally or through my own free will, but physically my body would silently crave for the same buzz, the endorphin rush that had engulfed me. He knew I would call him, and right to plan I did, a few days later, as all those before me did. He knew I would be a pushover. Unbeknown to me he had been observing me like a hawk that evening in the pub, my laughter, my mannerisms, my slight idiosyncrasies identifying me as a weak willed pansy ideally suited as bait for a cunning predator like Spanish, and at that moment, this was the point of no return. I was snared as his quarry. He knew I would be back for more no matter what, and a few days later, he was dead right…

A couple of months of following the same pattern of meeting him in the Dhol and Duck, mostly alone as Dev had made it clear to me that he did not approve of anyone taking drugs, let alone his best friend and that he would not want to be involved in that side of it. I thought to myself, what the fuck, of course I can handle the situation. Doing a bit of blow on a Friday and Saturday evening was my way of facing up to my demons, confronting the anguish and torturous nightmare that my life had become. I was the man, king of the world, as I took hit after hit, a little too frequently. Then, I would buy a couple of bags, just to replicate the same buzz I had felt earlier, sometimes, even midweek. Spanish was very accommodating and always available at the drop of a hat providing unsurpassed customer service, funny that. He would often just turn up in the Dhol and Duck and give me a bag, and when I went to pay he told me not to worry. He knew that the game was not so much short term satisfaction but long term gratification. He needed to get me adequately dependant and gripped on his gear, groom me so that in the future I may as well set up a direct debit to his account such would be my urge and craving for the stuff. He had done this to many before me, I was sure. He knew that all too well, and the 'freebies' were not quite so free in the grander scheme of things. I would start doing it in the toilets at work before I came home, any excuse, my body needed it.

Why did I crave so much? Spanish had planned my addiction and dependency meticulously, and his business acumen was savagely commendable. Now I knew that cocaine is very addictive, and was aware that once you start taking it, then it can be difficult to resist the craving and strong psychological dependence due to changes in the brain. Always being strong minded I had calculated that I would not become dependant on any drug let alone the odd bit of charlie. My psychological dependence became more of a problem than the actual physical withdrawal symptoms. I would hit my nadir, become moody when I missed a couple of weeks. The more I took of the drug, the more I felt my mind, my emotions and sense of direction spiraling out of control as my daily dose of charlie increased. Something did not sit right, but I was incognizant, unaware of why? The days weren't long enough especially in those early days. I would dream about my next shot always telling myself that I was not an addict and that I had too many balls to be addicted to anything. I was shooting four grams a day up my nose and always with a used twenty pound note, mainly in the toilets after work. Drugs have become an inextricable part of modern society, in the same way that cancer affects one in three, it is true to say that in some shape or form at least ninety per cent of the general hoi polloi are taking some sort of substance to eke out their existence, coffee, nicotine etc. Everyone starts off with a small amount but herein lays the problem. I will use the analogy of coffee: you start by taking one cup of coffee a day and hey for the first few weeks you feel alert, stimulated and your physical and mental performance has increased by at least twenty five per cent – no problem. Ah but this is exactly the problem, when that buzz and the effects of the caffeine dissipate several hours later your body crashes and you are left feeling depressed and low. You therefore need to regain that supremacy and verve that you had and sink another coffee or two, BANG! – You are back in the zone, just when they thought you were washed up. After a week or so that single cup of coffee doesn't quite cut the mustard as your brain (serotonin levels) have become accustomed to the one cup of coffee and it fails to produce any enhanced performance, it basically does nada, so in order to get the change of serotonin levels and the twenty five per cent performance enhancement you need another cup of coffee on top of that one and this cycle continues, and before long you are on four or five cups of coffee a day just to get the same buzz that only a few months before you got with one cup of coffee. This is why and how punters get hooked on drugs such as alcohol, coffee, chocolate etc. This is not an exact science but it is what generally happens. Furthermore caffeine and heroin are also derivatives from the same family and scientists suggest that consuming twenty two cups approximately of coffee in one sitting would be akin to having a decent shot of heroin, as both drugs rely heavily on changing the levels of serotonin and release of dopamine which affect the neurotransmitters in the brain. Neurotransmitters are the chemicals which account for the transmission of signals from one neuron to the next and they stimulate the muscle fibers to contract, along with playing a role in pituitary and adrenal glandular functioning.

So basically all drugs become poisons in high enough doses and those of you who drink alcohol and bang on about your personal crusade against drug abuse, never acknowledging that you yourselves are involved with a powerful drug should button it. In the same way, many cigarette addicts have no idea that tobacco is a very strong drug. We are all addicts to something, some people just don't realize what their addiction is, think about what you love doing, love eating and then try living without it – it is not easy. I am not justifying why I took drugs but what I am saying is before you judge me, take a closer inspection of your vices and then see what the score is.

Chapter 4

Naughty vices

Anyway, if things weren't bad enough, worse was still to come as my drug taking led to other vices that I would never have contemplated had I had any sensibility about what I was doing. Spanish had told me about a brothel being run on Southall Broadway – Dirty Sandhu's. It was where all the mini cab drivers went for a bit of how's your father when they were in-between jobs, or when the night was dragging. It was a perennial magnet for perverts, fetish mongers, businessman and guys like me who just wanted a bit of physical and emotional (well not a lot of that) support. Some guys just wanted a taste of the honey pot to see what it was like, others one last chance of glory before being strapped down and ceremoniously cut down with the shackles of matrimonial incarceration. It was the insider's ticket to heaven, the ladder to total immersion and sinful indulgence.

The mission statement was to leave the punters completely content, with lasting fond memories and essentially gagging for a repeat performance as this was all important. The lasses within were very accommodating and would serve you up like nobility in every way, they were consummate experts in their trade. Three Asian chicks, and one token gori (white girl) for those who fancied something different on the menu.

I know you are probably judging me, (that is my paranoia kicking in again) and saying what a kunjar (pimp), you started doing drugs, you then started shagging filthy prostitutes – what sort of man are you? you disgust me blah blah. Listen to me, I know how you feel but whenever I went to the brothel I was coked up out of my head, out of it, I know that is a weak excuse but hear me out. I just went there for a bit of companionship, physical support, emotional support call it what you want, that was it, someone to snuggle up to, to hold and yeh other stuff did happen, but shit always happens in Dirty Sandhu's – that's just the way it was. When I was doing it, getting my swerve on, then any social wisdom I had went careering out of the window, my life had become very messy.

My favourite moment by far was when I was being serviced by Pam, my regular Indian girlfriend at Sandhu's. They say that life is not about how many breaths you take but about how many moments take your breath away. Well that phrase aptly personified this sexual encounter when I was on the receiving end of the mother of all blow jobs from this seductively clad vixen, totally immersed in the breathless grip of passion as she sucked, licked and devoured me to ecstasy. She was the only one I would use and she remained my regular bit of crumpet. She was twenty two years old, had fair skin, lovely toned legs, and a sexy bum but was as dumb as a truck, not that we discussed quantum physics in our clandestine liaisons of course. All said and done she was still my regular, gundi, ice queen. She had bucket loads of talent, oodles of it seeping through every god forsaken orifice. I got to know every meandering curve on her delightful body. Sometimes all I had to do was close my eyes and I could see her groaning with unadulterated delight in the darkest depths of my dreams such was the effect that we had on each other during the tenure of our strong, powerful and totally immersing 'relationship'

I had continued to visit Sandhu's many times, and had even received many freebies from Pam, sometimes she would just treat me as her boyfriend such was my allure to her, it was insane, a true girlfriend experience with kissing, touching and all sorts allowed. She really doted on me unlike any prostitute I had ever heard of doing, and to be honest I was not complaining, as the visits increased and the price dropped to virtually next to nothing, saving me a cool fifty pounds a time that I had first started paying. What a cracker! The drug taking continued as did the visits to Pam for some time until a month or so before the swearing incident with my parents.

Eventually as my drug dependency was waning dramatically, I stopped and reviewed the shagging situation in perspective as well. I was visiting a flaming kushty (hooker) in a seedy apartment in Southall acting like a total deadbeat, a total disgrace. What happened to all the dreams I had when I left University, you know, be a millionaire by the time I am thirty, get a flash car, go on loads of holidays, have the two point four kids, the rabid mutt, the house, the beautiful wife? Is this what my life had amounted to? I thought disconcertingly, many a time. I was determined to leave behind the car crash that my life had become. Turn my back and escape the teeming carnival of street life, the drugs, the prostitute, the feeling of worthlessness: It had to change and fast!

My first mission then was to get rid of Spanish the drug dealer. Pam would come later (not literally).

I had been talking to other cronies and drinkers in the Dhol and Duck over a period of time and through these conversations had discovered that Spanish had actually mixed some of my cocaine bags with white heroin as well. Bastard, low life fucker I thought as I gritted my teeth upon being told this in the bar from a reliable fellow drug addict. My anger would have been convincing if I was able to shake off the imminent urge to get my next bag. I was now realizing why my body craved the next fix of drugs so much more physically. It was in essence down to the microscopic amount of heroin crushed amongst the cocaine. I knew it, cocaine is just not meant to be that addictive. It is called snowballing, a favourite for some of the veteran drug users in the metropolis. On its own cocaine has not got the same addictiveness and dependency that heroin has got. If he had tried to get me to take a hit of heroin that night in the Dhol and Duck; I would have grown a set of gonads and told him to kiss my arse or words to that effect. I know the score with people who become junkies even after an innocent hit of heroin from a cigarette, better known as tooting, one toot and you are perpetually doomed. Someone gives you a cigarette with a bit of heroin crushed or just rolled in with the nicotine and you merrily smoke it as you do, thinking that it is nothing but a normal roll up i.e. Old Holborn etc. It is only a day or so later you are hit with that desperate urge to have another roll up. No that's not any roll up, but that same one, the one with the *special stuff* inside it that some kind hearted stranger / drug dealer had offered you that fateful evening. Bang – that's you goosed, they have inherited another victim, another drip feeding cash machine, and the weaker willed the better, any business is good business. You had better say good night to the judge. You will soon be stealing from your mum's purse, selling stuff from your house, breaking into cars to feed your burgeoning habit, you will become a slave to heroin for life, cluck all you like, try and close the door to this filthy habit and it has seen it all before. It will consume your very being, gnaw away at your soul and core, ripping out your heart and force feeding it back to you for fun, and when it's finished with your pathetic carcass it will spit you back out in the gutter of life. Trust me I have seen it all before, there is no escape, it will come back and haunt you for the rest of your pitiful existence. Then one night I had arranged to meet Spanish in the Dhol and Duck to confront him about mixing the bags. I was a customer, albeit a suicidal one and I had a complaint about the service. I knew full well that he had no scruples about fairness whatsoever and was more than capable of putting me flat out on the cold pavement surface in a pile of my own teeth and blood without a bat of the eyelid. These thoughts were hanging over me, lingering there ominously. I had just heard the duplicity, the cheeky chicanery he had used to entangle me in his depraved web and it was time for retribution. I would punch him on the nose as he walked in, and then stomp on his head or glass him, but even all that seemed a bit excessive and far too nasty for a good desi boy like me, but the evil thoughts continued to circulate with sickening pleasure. My mind conjured up a variety of possibilities and demises for my prey.

I continued to scheme, when he suddenly appeared in all his glory. Before I could compose myself he swooped up on me like a blood thirsty bat going for the jugular.

I was taken aback by his swiftness and stood there exposed, helpless and like the Lone Ranger. I quickly regained my composure and my bravado returned albeit tentatively. I was trying to pump myself up, getting ready to plaster him across the four walls of the pub. I stood there and looked into the whites of his eyes, reciting an old samurai saying in my mind – *'na musho mawo dero'* - *'he is dead and he doesn't even know it'*.

This was my inner war cry, my starting pistol, the Punjabi haka. I sadistically cackled inwardly. This was it, his time was up and there was going to be a situation, a balls out fight was on the cards. Did he not realize that he was one blow, one strike away from being a fully fledged corpse? The adrenaline skipped around my body. I had no fear, no trepidation, my tail was curled up and I wanted some.

'What do you want geezer, usual shit or what?' He said calmly, his hand turned downward mimicking a hand shake and crucially concealing the bag of gear, a trick that would make any aspiring magician proud. I knew his games, I thought to myself, I could handle them, or did I? My thoughts ebbed and flowed, what do I do? He was a trail blazing guy with an unbreakable and nasty character, but today was my day in the sun; this was going to be my most profound moment of my life to date. The day I faced up to my demons and turned my life around. 'What is it?' I said confidently, lulling him into a false sense of security, the calm before the storm.

'What, it's the same shit bruv, what are YOU saying?' His retort was menacing, he had clearly smelt a rat, a dirty stinking one. The air hummed with the imminent sound of my bones breaking, blood trickling down the side of the bar, and the deathly lament of my funeral procession parading through the street outside. The more we talked, the more we just stood there and done nothing, the more scared shitless I was becoming. I could literally feel the energy seeping out of my body. The anticipation was slowly draining me; it was sapping my energy more than the potential physical encounter itself. I stood there in focused silence, what now I thought? He was looking more and more vexed, and the more vexed he was looking, the more I was transforming into a pink fluffy bunny before his very eyes. I was one breath away from clucking like a fucking chicken such was the ball busting intensity in this cauldron. I looked at him some more, not quite sure how to respond, but although god loves a trier, Spanish didn't seem to be so forgiving as the unearthly silence was quickly followed and punctuated by an angry and erratic burst 'Are you getting fucking fresh with me, are you?' I gulped. 'If you are I will cut your bollocks off and feed you them.' That was it, he had sucked the juice out of my hostility, my knees knocked and I felt my heart trying to jump out of my shirt as I squeaked with my newly found helium voice. They say never break eye contact with a coyote or they will smell the fear. This advice was dead in the water as I broke that rule averting my eyes to the floor sheepishly as I spoke.

Now what Sherlock I thought? I tried desperately to disguise my fear and retorted with the stealth an elephant, trying desperately not to dribble a verbal diatribe of inarticulate bollocks, which I was certain was coming.

'It's just that someone said that you mixed up some...err..h...heroin...with some of the packets you gave me before.' I was desperately trying not to sound too challenging and pushy, that was a good move, at least the words had come out, I nailed it, my confidence was returning slowly. Spanish looked me up and down in disgust, his brow furrowed and lips tightly closed. He wasn't stupid, he could clearly see my jangling nervous frame, my jittery and neurotic mind, my trembling legs dancing the bhangra rain dance underneath me. I tried in vain to get the beasts back under some semblance of control and order. They continued to dance their dance with uncontrolled and reckless abandonment, and no such loyalty or devotion to their master, the little 'dancing bastards.' The threat of them buckling underneath me all too alarmingly real and petrifying as I sucked in some much needed air through my mouth to steady myself, my knees continued to knock. I was now realizing why he was so feared, bracing myself for the inevitable weeks of eating through a straw and pissing through a tube as he snarled - 'Whoever told you that is fucking lying, understand.' He pointed and threatened me with his finger as he waved it under my nose. You could cut the testosterone in the air, it was that tangible. His features turned hard again, I saw him clench his fists as he moved a step closer. I immediately sensed that an out of place twitch, a wrong look would have brought on a merciless battering as my chosen prize, a senseless head kicking in frenzy for having the temerity to tango with the Devil himself.

I could now actually smell and taste the testosterone snorting out of his nostrils as I stayed on course to achieve my next objective of not pissing my pants or soiling my jeans, in public at least. 'No problem.' I said, as I stepped back and handed him a score, with all the steadiness of a plate of jelly, my hand shaking like a leaf. I was hoping he didn't notice. He did! 'No, no, have this one on me. He insisted, as he looked down at my unsteady hand 'one day you can sort me out for all the favours I have done for you.' I felt repulsed, I was very much sitting snugly in his pocket and he was loving every second of it, watching me squirm and cower down to him. Don't get me wrong I would rather have slept on a bed of killer rats, drank a cup of cold sick than be stuck in the cross hairs of this devil, but what could I have done? Bullies like this are motivated by fear, weakness and other such manifestations, and I had signed up to this treatment, the day I let him permeate my existence. This was my biggest faux pas. He looked at my hand, and playfully slapped me around the face a couple of times as he handed me the plastic bag. I could see that he was now beginning to foam and salivate as little dribbles appeared on his lips. His pressure cooker had been turned up on full gas as he said sarcastically 'Don't listen to everything you hear, it will fuck you up.' His voice sounding as though he enjoyed toying with his victims, like a cat with a mouse, gently pawing away, prodding and scratching the surface waiting for a wrong twitch, an accidental look, and then WHAM - seizing the moment with a cornucopia of mayhem and limb busting violence. No sooner had he offered me that advice and chilling words, he was gone, like a puff of smoke, vanished. He left the pub to meet up with his gun toting gangster and skag head friends leaving me in shreds. I had left my ability to stand up for myself firmly at the entrance and egress of the pub. It was all over, I was in his pocket. I was a lifer, an on remand prisoner in the warped and demented world of drug taking. There would never be an escape, NEVER! How could he do this to me? Who did he think I was? Some fluff ball, pee in the straw rat, mindlessly spinning on a wheel in a cage, if he did - then the reality was, he was on the money. This was me, a snared and petrified drug taking rat!

Despite this incident, I knew that the way forward was not to confront him, this would be an exercise in futility, brutal and smattered with spilling blood. The name of the game I mused, was all about avoidance. The reality was that I had taken my last bag from him, that was for sure. When I snuck into my bedroom at home that night, I put the drug stash behind my cupboard along with the other few bags that I had accumulated over the preceding weeks as my drug dependency waned. I put this down to a combination of strong will power, determination and necessity to change my life around. I would simply put the stash of drugs behind the cupboard in my room hoping to one day dispose of the lot. That was before mum had unearthed my dark secret and the packets of drugs a mere month later revealing '*her find*' to the household.

So I moved on with my life making a pact with myself, no more drug buys, no more visiting the Dhol and Duck, no more bumping into Spanish or his henchmen. Although, I had moments of weakness on the odd occasion, like the day at work when I had taken the hit before coming home to face the music with mum and dad, my dependency decreased ten fold and I was on the winning furlong of eradicating and expunging the powder from my life altogether. This was the tremendous will power that mum had instilled in me through her uplifting chats with me as I was growing up. She would say 'putt (son) if you put your mind to anything then have the conviction to carry it through, do it one hundred per cent or don't bother in the first place.' I was one hundred per cent committed to get married and needed to tell mum and dad, nothing else mattered to me, simply nothing.

CHAPTER 5

—⁓—

El conquistador

On sparrow's fart on the morning after the beating I had taken from dad, I woke in my pit at Dev's house after an uncomfortable nights slumber. I could hardly move my hand and I thought my jaw was broken. The effect of the aspirins I had taken before bedtime had worn off and I was in even more pain. The adrenaline and dosage of cocaine from the day before had subtly masked the real extent of the pain that I was in. I looked at my watch and was pleased that I still had a few hours of freedom before I was kippered by dad and probably Sharm too. I was sure that he would not be finding the funny side of me having half of Colombia's drug stash in his brother's house and running some kind of drugs cartel from the leafy suburb our street was.

I knew mum would be thinking what 'lokhi' (people) would say if they found out? All these questions and fears continued to race through my mind as I got ready. In the midst of the chaos of that incident last night, one thing was abundantly clear to me now, very lucid; I would never be taking another drugs fix for as long as I had a hole in my arse, that was definitely the wake up call that I had needed, the timely kick up the derriere. I had insulted my dad and it was definitely the last time, even if Spanish held a gun to my head, or whatever. I had shamed myself by swearing to my parents, that has never happened before and I never thought those words would be coming out of my mouth in such a way. I had stooped to gutter level, outside the realms of parental respect that every Asian lad should have for their peers, when those scornful words had poured out of my cake hole. I felt like crying, what an absolute loser. I would treat them like a raja and rani, anything they wanted me to do. I would walk on nails for them, I loved them after all. They are my life, and I would make it up to them. It was clear, my decision today would be no more drugs, no more visiting prostitutes, ever, not that I would share that particular pledge with them of course. I sat there licking my paws, wallowing in my own self pity but very determined to carry through with my convictions.

In life you meet lots of bad people, loser's and players, arrogant imbeciles, lots of guys like Spanish – the world is full of them. The great characters out there rise above it all, and look down at them from great majestic heights laughing at their debilitated frames eking out their sad existences, as they try to outdo, scam, and deceive each other in every possible way. This was not the wretched and pathetic existence that I wanted to be associated with anymore, the state of pitiable vacillation. I was not like Spanish or whoever, I was me, a decent bloke from good stock, with family values, good ethics and a sound and solidified upbringing by two genuinely good parents. I would never let them down again. I sought solace in the conviction and determination of my words. I had been a big time loser, an arse and I believe everyone should get to be one just to realize that it is better to live a fulfilling and righteous life, than one of lies and debauchery. I now realized that it takes fortitude and self belief to seek out a fulfilling and virtuous life. It is good for your soul and essentially your karma, you know what goes around comes around, that sort of thing.

Today was to be my destiny and new chapter in my life, I prayed some more. I would be changing once and for all today. I would also be telling my parents that I would be willing to meet Punjabi girls with a view to marrying them, whenever and wherever, even within the next few months if that would make them happy. Surely they would be ready to forgive me then, I silently prayed.

Dev parked his car outside my house, the Temple of Doom as I sat nervously in the passenger seat. The time: five to twelve. As sure as eggs were eggs, I could see Sharm's car parked up on the roadside. He was punctual and I knew that he had got there earlier to discuss my '*case*' with dad: a kind of family crisis meeting. I looked at Dev; he looked relaxed as he got out of the car. I soon joined him on the pavement at the edge of my drive. I felt his reassuring pat on my back soothing as he gently eased me forwards towards the house, the lions den. 'Come on lets get it over with.' he said alleviating my fear and anxiety. I stood there for a moment trying to regulate my breathing, in, out, in, out, nice and easy. I placed my hand on my chest and felt the rhythm of my heart as it beat ferociously, relax, deep breaths, relax. It was working, albeit very slowly, my breathing was steadying...I realized I had left my car keys at Dev's house and would have to ring the doorbell. What a bad start, it would have been better to utilise the element of surprise and sneak up on them like a stealth ninja.

As I pondered this thought, the door opened and a steely faced Sharm stood there, he gave nothing away with his calculated poker expression. He was good, a master of guile. He had been expecting us, they had been expecting us. uncle Sharm had struck with unerring and laudable efficiency, opening the door and greeting his victims, cutting us off at the pass 'get inside we have been waiting for you.' he muttered.

I walked in with Dev in tow and through to the living room, the scene of yesterdays carnage. I was keen to see if the globe had been fixed and if my blood had been mopped up? I don't know why, I guess I was just morbidly curious. The globe was patched up and tucked away in the corner of the room still looking incriminating and taunting me as I walked in. Dad was sat there in his armchair slowly drumming his fingers on the arm rest, and pensive in his thoughts. He looked me up and down with a look of bitter condemnation on his face, a look deserving of contempt and scorn. Mum hovered close by, standing with her hand resting on the top of the armchair also immersed in her cocktail of thoughts. Over on the three seater sofa sat Dev and Sharm with Sharm's paisley shirt almost camouflaging him with the floral design of the sofa he sat on. On the table lay a mug of tea, I could see the brown residue frothing at the top of it. Sharm picked up the mug and took several loud slurps in quick succession, each one getting progressively louder, the first of the slurps scooping up the frothy brown skin from the top or *'malai'* as it is known in the circles. I watched in horror as it passed his lips and down into his mouth, it looked like the dead skin of an animal, gross.

I shifted my eyes back to dad's feet. He was wearing green coloured chappals and I could see the serrated gripped sole stretching out to the sides. This invoked painful memories as I remembered how mum who had a similar pair many years ago, would sometimes slap the gripped chappal sole on my arm when I was naughty as a young child back in those days of green, with the stinging sensation lasting for weeks and making me a good candidate for the NSPCC. I breathed a sigh of relief. At least both mum and dad were there in my sights and I wasn't at the end of an ambush by snipers entrenched in a machine gun nest, armed to the teeth with AK47 machine guns and ready to gun me down like the rat I was: resembling a scene from Saving Private Makhan: or similarly walking in on a firing line primed and ready to fill me with lead, executing me in histrionic fashion like a cheesy Bollywood movie. I sat down and my eyes never left the carpeted floor and those chappals. I was too ashamed and downright bricking it.

The situation was a fickle land mine waiting to erupt at any given moment, all it needed was one false slip up, one wrong word, one Freudian and skittish remark and the bell would be ringing for round two. The wise money would have been on dad and Sharm creaming me, pretty easily, without much of a retaliatory fight back. It would have been the most one sided fight ever, trust me. I was feeling like a tranquilised mouse.

Sharm started the proceedings in the makeshift kangaroo courtroom 'right Kam, I know what has happened…and you should be ashamed of yourself talking to your parents like that, in my day if I swore at my dad I would be getting juttia (a beating with chappals) for ever. It is disgraceful and it would be a good start if you said sorry.' Without a seconds thought I looked up 'mum, dad I am so sorry, please forgive me, I should never have swore at you...it will never happen again, I promise.'

Dad looked up unconvincingly at mum who reciprocated the look back at him, whilst Sharm looked on, his face breaking into an uncontrolled smile, I had softened him up, that was the easy part out of the way. 'I want to make some lifetime promises to you right now if you will just give me five minutes.' Dev nodded his head encouragingly and gave me the impetus to continue despite the pervading atmosphere of hostility surrounding me. 'I will never touch drugs again - I promise.' I continued. 'What you found is not stuff that I was planning to take but...well...I had given up some time ago.' I looked at mum, at Sharm, Dev and back to dad. 'But this guy keeps hassling me and giving me stuff, he is not the sort of person I want to mess with, but that's for me to sort out.' I had a captive audience, everyone in the room sat and listened. I saw dad looking down at my bandaged hand and then back up at me. There still remained an underbelly of furious silence distinguishable to me, as he continued to gawk straight at my scrawny apologetic face. To be honest I could not blame him for remaining apathetic with my explanation. 'I will flush those drugs down the toilet right now, once and for all and I will be clean.' I spoke with relief, my voice cracking slightly as the words gushed out. 'I admit I took some last night before I came home, but even then that was going to be my last time. I am going to turn my life around.' I scanned the room for a reaction. There were sighs of reprieve, of ease all around.

Dad then nodded his head in approval, mum smiled comfortingly, Sharm sat in front of me scrutinizing my humble explanation, while Dev looked on 'I have also decided that I want to get married and am prepared to visit and talk to any girls that you put in front of me. I will get married within the next few months if you want.' I sat back and waited for the reaction. I was met by stunned silence. I scanned mum's eyes and they were swimming with sympathy and comprehension to my predicament, she was on my side. Sharm rubbed his hands down his thighs and nodded his head in approval. Dev, well he just sat there staring. Most importantly I had to win dad's vote, he was the head honcho, el queso grande, and the true heartbeat of the household as is the case in most Asian houses. If he were to rebuff my pledge, my heartfelt declaration to transmogrify my existence, then it was all but futile.

The seconds ticked and ticked some more, when. Dad stood up and produced the stash of drugs from behind where he was sitting, why was he hiding it?, did he actually think that I was going to rob him and escape into the sun with the loot, how much of a depraved drug dealer did he think I was?

'Come with me.' he beckoned me to follow him. He walked out of the lounge door and through the kitchen to the adjacent toilet downstairs. He then began to open the bags one at a time and poured the contents down the toilet. He was stood there for five minutes flushing Mexico's finest down the toilet without flinching. Did he expect a reaction with this charade? He didn't get one. It was what I wanted in any case. I watched the last remnants as they were tipped unceremoniously into the watery moat. I stood firm, my eyes forming a blurry mist 'thanks dad.' I whimpered. 'That is the best way to end this, sorry for swearing at you. I really didn't know what I was saying, I didn't mean it, I love you guys.' He pulled the handle down and we watched the water whisking the powder away and out of our lives. He turned to face me, he looked stern, my breathing started to fluctuate erratically. Was he still angry? He did not smile. Was he going to clock me again, should I brace myself?

My mind was in emotional turmoil. He was going to kick me out, my inherent paranoia gripping me like a vice. It was planned. I was the next episode he would be flushing out of his life, once and for all. Why dad, why? He reached out, his spade like hands inched ever closer to my face, it was round two, I heard the bell, I saw the referee. His hands gripped my head as he pulled me tightly into his chest. It was all I had yearned for. He hugged me tightly 'No more son, that is the end, you stop taking drugs from this day and we will forget this ever happened.' He continued to squeeze me tighter to himself. His strength was phenomenal, his herculean hugging grip oozing the *'tutti' (shit)* out of my pants as I fervently wrapped my arms around his body and felt the purity and devotion of his words moving me. I shed tears of happiness as we buried the nightmare we had all found ourselves in, firmly behind us. This was the time to start afresh, with newfound hopes and aspirations for my future. A daughter in law would be the icing on the cake for my parents right now. It would make their hearts sing and bring contentment and self satisfaction to their lives along with mine. A divine intervention was the tonic and what was much needed to mark this life changing moment in our lives.

I had now had enough with sitting at the crossroads of my life, procrastinating. It was time to develop myself, bring some character to my existence and become the person that I wanted to be - a decent and moralistic

Punjabi guy. I looked up at dad and said through tear soaked eyes 'No more dad I promise, I won't ever let you or mum down again.' Mum was standing in the kitchen observing all along with Sharm and Dev. She walked in and I hugged her tightly, kissing her forehead. She was so cuddly and warm. We were once again a family unit. I was so happy. We sat back in the living room and mum put some pakorai on the cooker and brought in some famed Asian teas with lechi's and a few other secret colonel type recipes. We drank and laughed and carried on for a few hours after that. I could sense the pleasurable satisfaction on everyone's faces as my parents could finally hold their heads up in the community again with self worth.

They could now poke two fingers up at *'lokhi and his mates'* They could have a sense of pride again, that their only son had declared himself fit for marriage and especially as no-one outside the inner circle other than Dev would unearth my dirty, dark secret. The day was joyous and the secret was safe. I went to bed that night with the knowledge that the only thing that mattered in my life was making my parents happy. The future was exciting and mum assured me that she had four or five suitable beaus lined up for viewing within the next few weeks. That was quick, had she foreseen this day or was she that well connected? It was the latter, everyone knew and loved her and I didn't blame them, not one iota.

CHAPTER 6

Gorgeous girls

I was true to my word and from that watershed day in October when I had promised my parents that I would quit the life of debauchery, I did not even look at drugs let alone take any and I felt alive again, truly euphoric. I just avoided Spanish at all costs and no matter what the temptation I would never slip down that slope again. Throughout the following months I had heard on the grapevine that he was baying for my blood, my money and for some nonsensical reason wanted to make an example of me for insulting him and not returning his calls and avoiding him. He would text me, call me and even wait an entire evening in the Dhol and Duck for me or so I was told, but I was out foxing him. What was his innate problem with me? I didn't care, I had moved on and it was time he found another gullible victim.

I was also receiving text messages from Pam where she would desperately try and entice me back to Dirty Sandhu's with offers of freebies and happy hour specials. I was simply not interested as I knew that even one last fling would be a slippery fall from grace and back down the alley of depravity. I just simply avoided any phone calls from Pam. I wanted a break from the bad influences in my life. Pam's texts and voicemails on the other hand became more and more chilling with threats that she would find out where I lived and tell my parents, a humiliation and fate worse than death. They could just about handle the drugs but the discovery of visits to prostitutes may have been a waiting land mine, and the death knell of our relationship. I had become a regular cash cow for Pam with my bi weekly visits and she was determined to get me back into her evil clutches, at any cost such was her sedulous perseverance. I even received a message from Sandhu himself, who was owner, slash, pimp, slash henchman for his thriving house of ill repute.

'*Pay up one thousand in debts owed and you won't receive a visit - bhanchod - I will find you.*'

Debts owed, what was this imbecile talking about I said to myself? I always paid for Pam's services upfront, well most of the time anyway. His next message shed some more light on the situation.

'*You got special treatment bhanchod, the debt of a thousand pounds is outstanding as that is what you should have paid in the first place, drop the money off, or you will see.*'

I decided the best bet was to simply ignore the fools that were hounding me. I know I have been an idiot, a fool, doing drugs, seeing prostitutes but I lost my way with life, I took a wrong turn on the highway, but at least I have got back on the right track again that is the main thing. It was all an experience, whether good or bad, it was still an experience.

Right now though I just wanted to get married and move away somewhere with my wife whoever she was and wherever she was, to start afresh, a new start and new beginnings in an area far away from the trials and tribulations of Southall. There had to be more to life…I hoped and prayed.

I went through the usual ritual of meeting up with a variety of dusky Punjabi women with a view to marrying them.

The search for miss right was long, arduous, and very keenly contested; with each would be suitor keen to make a good and effective first impression. My search took me to the lush and verdant jungles of the Amazon, the cascading and thunderous waterfalls of the Angel Falls to the arid plains of the Sahara Desert. I searched with great fervency for my beau, leaving no stone unturned in my quest. Oh okay I exaggerate, it boiled down to a few houses in Birmingham, Leeds, Ilford, Slough and Luton to be precise. The quest for love and prosperity started around mid October and a few weeks after I had declared that I was ready to take the perilous plunge into marriage. The visits took me all the way through the New Year and into January, February, and then March when I finally found my 'sapno ki rani' (lady of my dreams).

Most of the encounters were initially set up by Sharm and mum combining forces, and on some occasions, we relied on the trusty Des Pardes to deliver the goods. Sharm knew everyone in Southall through his work as a mechanic; his garage repair work shop was earning him a small fortune. Mum on the other hand knew many biddies from the gurdwara, and this was like a veritable match making set up and the first stop for matrimonial connections. Sharm, in his adapted role as a middleman or bacchola as we say in Punjabi set up my first meeting with Ravdeep. Oh yes delightful little creature she was, with creature being the operative word. I am sure Sharm had been sozzled when he set this encounter up, that or snorting my former drugs supply from behind my cupboard, it just did not make logical sense.

Every meeting was always memorable for many differing reasons, but Ravdeep from Leeds, with her pre prepared questionnaire was a hoot, described to me by Sharm on the telephone as a very beautiful Sikh kurri, degree educated blah blah. When I walked into her terraced house in a run down part of Chapel Town I had to do a double take, I mean I had this mental image of this phat and sexy princesses floating alluringly down the stairs, with silky smooth skin, a size eight figure, and a cute smile. Instead I was confronted with the beast from twenty thousand fathoms. I mean any more hideous and she would have been wrapped around with yellow hazard tape and condemned. The pig tusks protruding through her nose gave me my first indications that she was a Frankenstein experiment gone hideously wrong. Throughout our *'meeting, examination, grilling.'* I kept staring at her mouth for fangs, or a lizard like tongue to flick out and hiss venom in my eye. At one stage she scratched the side of her face with her fingers and fixed her snake eyes back on me 'So where would you take me then, for our honeymoon?'(no doubt sizing up the size of my wallet).

'Back home to Loch Ness or the squalid depths of hell for you my dear.' The temptation to say this was consuming me.

Needless to say, we never darkened one another's hallways again. Thank god for small mercies.

The next girl I saw in my mum and dad's arranged marriage process was Maninder from Birmingham. A sublime write up in the Des Pardes set the atmosphere nicely. On paper she certainly whetted my appetite and seemed divine. I was excited. When I met her I was on the money with my pre conceptions, she was nice, pleasant and above all attractive. However, the air of serenity began to alter as soon the Wicked Witch of the East appeared on the scene, her pestiferous and truculent mum. I immediately sensed that there was something rotten when her mum insisted on sitting in on our '*private meeting*' with us. I mean what did she think I was going to do, jump on her daughter and roger her senseless to consummate our meeting and check out whether she was any good in the sack?

Her mother answered every question I asked Maninder. She asked me questions on her behalf, and she was practically inviting herself on honeymoon with us, if it got to that stage. Now I must admit I did have a fetish of having a threesome, but mother and daughter from an arranged marriage meeting just didn't capture my imagination or float my boat, it was just, well, bloody sick. On one occasion during the interrogation I checked under the table for a foot pump to see if her mum was using it to operate Maninder's lips, she may as well have been.

I was by now becoming increasingly disheartened as we left the celestial Maninder's des res and made our way across town to Ilford to see another suitor. Amarjit. She wasn't quite as bizarre as the first two but there was no chemistry, I just couldn't imagine sleeping with her and that was that, plain and simple. I don't know what it was, she looked redundant, and as if she had been hibernating all her life, there simply was no verve, no spark emitting from her doleful frame.

The next couple of girls followed the same routine of a quick bite of a few samosas, a sip of tea and down to business with the meeting in the next room while the families entertained each other in the adjacent room. We trudged back, visit after weary visit. Mum and dad began cursing me after each refusal, in the car, at home, after work, by carrier pigeon, even on the phone at work. They seemed to think I was being far too fussy and insisting that I would never find anybody suitable, as my standards were so high. I fought my corner valiantly and assured them that when the right girl came along, and if we both clicked, I would unequivocally say yes. Several weeks passed, a month passed, a few visits here and there, the list of girls and visits continued, the samosa's continued to be consumed, the conversations got drearier by the day. The bottom line was it was generally me turning the girls down then vice versa. I could not help it, and despite the efforts from mum, dad, Sharm and of course Des Pardes Newspaper, I did not want to live the whole of my life with any old buck toothed wonder that fancied me.

This next victim on the hit list was an exceptionally stunning local lass - Rita, someone I had known from back in school. Mum had set this meeting up without me even having a look at her photo or even known her name as both mum's were pals at the gurdwara and set up the meeting after talking about it the night before. Rita was good looking, I mean this girl was fit, a real fire cracker of a lass and had a string of guys pursuing her like deranged and frothing lap dogs back in the day. She was every guys dream and trust me anyone with a pulse, every red blooded male wanted a piece of her. The trouble being, I knew that she had no qualms about gratefully accommodating every bloke with a pulse, opening her sexy legs in a whim for anyone within a certain radius from her house, including me, more than once. Anyone in search of long lost innocence would need to do some serious rethinking as she boasted more notches on her headboard than you would care to imagine.

She had long held the covetous title of being the '*local slagstitute, a kunjari, an imperial round the block tart* and *local bike*.' She was never backwards in going forwards and did not know how to say no, no matter who asked. They say never say never, but in this situation, it was as sure as it comes: She could never be my future wife, I just knew too much about her sordid past and there was no escaping that. It was ingrained in my head and the damage was done. During the meeting she kept giving me the sort of long lingering look that some kind of slag would give...the sort saying that I will let you eat my chocolate knickers tonight if you play your cards right. I will let you cover me in cream and then lie back with my eyes closed whilst you pretend you are a hell bent hungry pussy cat. As we sat and talked privately in the garden of her house, I shook my head as we both reminisced about our school days. She told me that she was willing to settle down with her future husband and forget the past, start afresh and that is why she had agreed with her parents to go through the arranged marriage process. We exchanged numbers as friends and I had promised that I would stay in touch in the future, and perhaps invite her to my wedding and she agreed vice versa. I wished her good luck in her adventure to seek out her beau and with that, my search continued.

The following weekend around the beginning of March, mum showed me a picture of a girl from Luton – Kiran Sidhu. She was from a respectable family and looked smart, pretty and well educated I thought, beginning to sound like a Des Pardes advert myself. I was however becoming desensitised at this stage having seen so many girls and my cynicism prevented me from fully immersing myself in the what if's. I agreed that she looked nice and so mum set up the meeting the following day.

We arrived at Kiran's house, a nice detached house in Luton. A golden statue eagle welcomed us onto the long cobbled driveway as we all got out of the family's car, my dad's cherished Honda CRV. Mum was excited and dad was his usual relaxed self while Sharm raced up the path and knocked on the door. His child like ebullience and effervescence galvanising all of us as he always did. The door was opened by Kiran's mum – Preeto, small and round were the best two words to describe her, oh and acid tongued would be another two, but I only discovered this much later. She welcomed us into her humble abode and guided us into one of her three downstairs living rooms. The house was well maintained, and it was clear that the family were not short of a bob or two as I continued to admire the décor. Inside was Manjit – Kiran's dad, a true gem, and exceedingly nice chap.

He ran a newsagents shop with his wife Preeto on the High Street in Luton. They had been doing that for over fifteen years. This explained their obvious financial security as I looked around nosily at the objet d arts meticulously placed throughout the house. He shook dad's hand and hugged him, the same with Sharm and then with me, all with fervent humility.

His warm welcome in particular made me feel at home right away. Preeto similarly hugged mum and placed her hands together *'sasrikaal.'* to the rest of us as we all sat down in our respective seats. Friendly faces, warm smiles and welcoming arms, things were going swimmingly. After the usual conversational pleasantries were exchanged between the two parties, Preeto brought in plate after plate of samosas, pakoras, jaleebis, onion bhajjis and a plethora of *'mattia' (asian sweets)* The sugary smell wafting teasingly around us, enticing and seducing the senses without a care for subsequent dentistry fees.

As I chomped away, I scanned the room and saw photo's of Kiran up on the wall, wearing her gown and hat when she received her degree, with her mum and dad on a beach on some sun kissed island and plenty of other photos of her as a child. She looked nice and my excitement began to mount, where were they hiding this beauty, my lady of the lake, I mused.

The lounge walls painted light brown, with pictures of the guru's hung up, Guru Nanak, Guru Gobind on his horse and picture after picture of the Golden Temple and the Taj Mahal casting imposing figures as central and focal points of the room. The plethora of holiday souvenirs, trinkets and baubles adorning the large wooden cupboard set against the wall in the dining area of the lounge, sidling furtively next to a well stacked book case nestling with a variety of weird and wonderful books. On the mantelpiece there were more framed and incriminating photographs of the family, plenty of people with bad haircuts and outrageous moustaches hanging off their upper lips – and that was just the women. It appeared at this early stage that the family consisted of mum, dad and daughter, the photo's led me to believe that this was the case.

The place was well maintained and I was already impressed.

A few moments later as I took a swig of my tea and nestled comfortably into my seat, in she walked: BANG! It was Kiran – like a mystic wind. I had been hit by the sexy as fuck truck as I desperately resisted the temptation to drool down my chin.

Here she was like a welcoming mirage in the desert, dressed in a blue Asian suit expertly showing off her curvaceous and amazing body. Her perfectly manicured feet, her nails teasingly painted in red nail polish, snugly sitting in silver Gucci shoes, her silky black hair gently caressing her shoulders, her big brown eyes and fair skin, the list was endless.

She walked in and flashed me a smile as she greeted my parents. Just the mere sight of this ray of beauty was like an aphrodisiac cocktail, the very embodiment of grace, refined elegance, and intoxicating beauty – I was drunk on it, and I wanted seconds, thirds...

There was a certain '*jena se qua*' about her. A mystery, waiting to be explored. She sat down opposite me. 'Hi.' I played it cool. We exchanged nervous looks.

'Hello.' her soft dulcet tones enchanting me. I was struck by a thunderbolt, she was fit and I wanted to talk to her more but I waited patiently until the parents agreed that we could go into the garden and chat to each other.

'*Mugambo*' *(evil Bollywood villain)* was not so much '*kush*' *(happy)* as having a fucking, screaming orgasm.

I licked my lips several times trying not to look like the desperate and possessed wannabe that my tongue on the floor was depicting me as.

Then without further ado, I saw the green light and I launched myself towards Kiran (not in that sense you sick pervert) and made my way to the garden door. We went outside for some privacy to get to know one another. I was like a possessed rat up a drainpipe as I stepped towards virtue and abundant hope in the figure of this eye candy: Like '*Golam*' had once said – she was '*precious*'… I was very interested.

We sat on her patio chairs and chatted away like a couple of old mates. Music interests, hobbies, culinary taste's, you name it we discussed it. The conversation ebbed and flowed and I felt myself instantly attracted to her. My pheromones were in hyperactive mode. Her fresh faced, unblemished and fair complexion immediately melting my bosom. She had intimated that her parents had been putting a lot of pressure on her over the last year to settle down. She mentioned this fact to me three times, not that I was counting. Kiran was twenty two years old and had just secured a contract as a solicitor in a practice in London and her mum and dad were keen to get her settled down now that she fulfilled all the pre requisites of being ready for wedlock, namely education, job and now ready to rear kids. We talked and talked, I felt at ease as the conversation flowed nicely. Towards the end of our allotted one hour slot, I turned to her, the ray of intoxicating beauty sat in front of me, the lady of everyone's dreams - 'Kiran, I really like you.' Her smile accommodating, reassuring and uplifting. 'I am going to tell my parents that from my side it is a yes, a resounding yes, what about you?'

She paused, looked me in the eyes 'It is going to be a... yes from me.' The girl from Del Monte did not let me down.

I wanted to scream. I was elated. We surreptitiously exchanged phone numbers, just as an insurance policy, in case there were any objections from our respective parents to us being able to date pre wedding. What would the community think after all?

Now that we had said yes to one another, in most circumstances and especially back in the motherland there would be talk of dowry, the goods, money, treasures, artefacts and estate and in some cases livestock that the woman brings her husband prior to wedlock. This is also known as '*trousseau or dahej*.' The groom in return would give what is called '*dower or mahr*' gifts etc. This would be normal practice and both parties would be completely acquiescent with this arrangement. However, thankfully, both of our families had discussed this and did not want to get embroiled in the politics of it all, especially as for one, it would have been difficult smuggling in a herd of cows through customs to offer the bride's family if it went ahead. Dowries, originated from the upper class families and were outlawed in nineteen sixty one in India. They have resulted in over twenty thousand reported murders over the years as parties reneged on the initial promises and arrangements. It still goes on despite its prohibition and dowry abuse is on the increase despite the government warnings and threats, this is where the dowry is considered insufficient or paltry. The woman is then subjected to brutal treatment, burnt alive on occasions and finding themselves the '*victim of accidental trips and falls, causing permanent injuries.*'

Luckily, this was not of concern to us as we marched triumphantly back in the lounge from the garden.

We made our announcement together. It felt good. Everyone hugged and cheered. My mum, the fluffy bunny, started crying, the emotions were flowing. Manjit cracked open a bottle of Black Label and the dad's had a well deserved skinfull in celebration. The long pot filled journey had come to its end. The Holy Grail had been unearthed. Kiran laughed, she looked pleased for her parents, and after all, they had had their wish granted. Their daughter was going to be settled into a good family and I was about to become the luckiest guy alive, marrying a dream of a wife. We drove back to our house and my heart was full of glee. Finally my troubled past was behind me and I was on the crest of the worlds biggest wave. It was my turn to live la dolce vita – the sweet life...

CHAPTER 7

—⁓—

Teething problems

The date for the wedding was set – twenty sixth of April, only six weeks away and I felt so ebullient and deliriously excited.

Finally, I had a spring in my step, a fire raging in my heart and a burning desire in the very pit of my stomach. I was thrilled. Things were happening and developing at break neck speed. Within the next few weeks, we visited each others houses just to have some food and drink and good conversation. We loosely referred to this 'ceremony' as the '*rokha*' and it was just our way of cementing our relationship and promise not to enter into any other matrimonial proposals.

Furthermore, the wedding invite cards were sent out to all our relatives, over three hundred to be precise and muggings here copped the arduous task of writing them all out with the odd bout of carpal tunnel syndrome or wankers wrist as it is known in the circles adding to my woes. Mum and I visited our nearest and dearest to dish out some of the invites and personally invite our close family. They were all definite attendees, but we also paid visits to those relatives clinging on by their fingernails on the peripheries of our inner circle. It was our sadistic way of looking into the whites of their eyes and seeing if they were going to attend, or whether they would try to smokescreen us with some weak hearted excuse. The old classics, like already having booked a holiday at that time or having to stay home and watch a documentary on deciduous trees, walk the goldfish or something equally slippery and duplicitous. All these excuses and more were easier to decipher when they were sat in front of us facing the music.

We had decided on not having an official *'kurmai'* *(engagement)* due to the lack of time and decided to just go straight for the registry and Indian marriage cere-mony along with the reception all on the same day. This would also essentially cut down on costs. I could not fathom my luck. I was on the Orient Express of gravy trains and there was not a buffer in sight.

It was surreal and it was what we both wanted, well it seemed at times me more than Kiran, but I talked her around in our many conversations on the phone. She was not so keen to rush things as her parents were. I could not place my finger on her reasons and why this was the case? Nevertheless, in the grand scheme of things, my In laws decisions about the date prevailed and won over any resistance that Kiran had put up about postponing the wedding date to June or July. I punched the air with delight when the date was ratified over the phone with my dad and my father in law, this was my dream, and I just wanted Kiran in my arms forever. Although we had only got to know one another for a few weeks, it was one of those situations when I just knew that she was the ONE. She was everything to me. I even had her name down as *'jaan'* *(my life)* in my mobile phone. Sick and corny

I know, but hey, it was true, she was my life companion, the engine in my clapped out shell of an existence.

We chatted regularly on the phone and things were great, especially the getting to know each other bit, or honeymoon period as it is called. The period when your partner can do nothing wrong, when you are loved up to the hilt and blinded by the cloak of passion. Wow - I love the way the pus just trickles out of your zits when you squeeze them, the way your farts slowly travel up and grab you by the throat, or the way you snort like a pig when you laugh. They can do no wrong and this honeymoon period affects everyone no matter who you are. However, despite the rose coloured spectacles being worn by me, I was slowly beginning to see a negative side to her permeating through the beautiful exterior, the kind of knuckles dragging on the pavement apathy that was slowly rocking my foundations.

The more we talked on the phone, the more it seeped through like a bad smell, the more she displayed the qualities and traits of someone who was a sure fire candidate to stand someone up at the '*altar*' in a manner of speaking. What the hell was wrong with her? To say that it did not play on my mind would be an understatement. She was the best thing that had ever happened to me and had I met her a year or so ago then I would never have sunken to the depraved depths of drug taking and sleeping with hookers. I needed to establish the root cause of her impassiveness, to establish her apprehension about the wedding being so soon. Was it because she was unable to get time off work? Was she getting cold feet? Did she really love me?

I needed answers and some reassurance. This time I decided that I was not going to be euphemistic about my approach to the question. I would be upfront and direct. It was the only way to resolve, and remove the spectre of doubt hanging over our relationship. So, one day I asked her a couple of weeks before the wedding, whilst I was twiddling my thumbs at work. We had been chatting away on the phone as we did so often putting the world to right when I decided to go for the bulls eye 'Kiran I wanted to ask you why are you so hesitant about the wedding date being so soon, are you scared or something?'

On one hand I was trying to maintain a careful approach to the question, as I did not want to back her in a corner so close to the wedding or make her feel uncomfortable, and on the other hand I thought it was a perfectly reasonable question.

I needed to give her the confidence to be able to converse with me about anything throughout our lives together. She tutted, not the response I was expecting 'Why do you keep asking me the same question Kam, you asked me when the date was set a few weeks ago and every time we seem to speak you keep wanting reassurance, what is your problem?'

'Come on darling, you have hardly been overly enthusiastic have you?' My heart festering the feeling of someone not really being met half way. 'It is though someone is forcing you to go through with it, you know, I am not seeing or feeling you are there one hundred per cent or anything.'

She snapped back 'Well the answer is the same as the last four times you have asked me. I told you it is just a big step for a girl leaving her parents and everything, you will never understand what it feels like, so will you stop asking me and let me sort my own head out, I am just a little nervous is that okay with you. Don't worry I am not about to stand you up in the gurdwara or run away with your best mate?' I hated it when she joshed with me in such a way and I felt the blood go to my head as her words pierced my heart like a serrated dagger. However, despite my inner turmoil, I remained cool; the last thing we both wanted was to have a full blown argument two weeks before the wedding, that would have been disastrous.

I composed my response in my head and replied soothingly 'hey chill girl, you know I only ask you cos I care about you and stuff, no sweat I wont ask you again.' With that the subject was dropped immediately, no questions, just dropped like a hot potato, for now. 'Okay, that's cool.' she seemed a little more relaxed.

'Well maybe once more when you are in my arms lying on the sun kissed beach lapping up the Caribbean waves, I will then ask your naughty arse if you have made the right choice.' I could not resist the temptation to push the envelope a little further. Luckily, she laughed, and the anxiety and paranoia on my part was assuaged. I have always been a bit of worrier. I had learned to cope with it, slowly. Overall, it is not a bad thing as it kept the fire in my body burning and kept me on my toes, most of the time.

Throughout our engagement and weeks of courtship, we both met up and introduced one another to our circle of friends. She met Dev one day after work. I had picked her up from her house and told Dev to meet us in Slough – there was a lovely Indian restaurant with delightfully succulent culinary treats, all the poppadums you could eat, smothered with mango chutney, dish after dish of exotic curries and an array of other balti recipes to intoxicate the senses of the staunchest gastronome. Similarly, she had arranged for her best friend Tina to meet us there. This had all the makings of a superb date. Kiran and I as the two love birds, accompanied by both of our best friends who incidentally were both young free and single and to top it all we were all about to indulge in mouth watering Indian food in a salubrious part of Slough (yes there is one somewhere) What could have gone wrong? I thought, as I picked up my sassy lass from Luton in my blue Vauxhall Astra. We negotiated our way across the car park that is the M25 with *'Juggy D's'* many classic tunes blaring out of my speakers at volume ten *'Sohniye and Meri Jaan'* along with old time classics from *'Apna Sangeet and Alaap'* – they just don't make them like that anymore. Kiran looked gorgeous, but then again what was new? She sung along to the tracks as we made our way West. We were like any ordinary, courting couple.

We arrived at the restaurant like a pair of hungry hippo's and upon entering I immediately noticed the ever punctual and reliable Dev propped up at the bar area sitting comfortably in his work attire supping a pint of Elephant Beer. 'Kiddhan Dev.'

'Hey bruv, you finally made it, I had better cancel the bloodhounds I sent in to sniff you out then, ha ha.'

We hugged as we always did when we greeted. 'Let me introduce you to the lovely Kiran.' I said excitedly showing off my sexy missus to Dev. It was the first time he had met her in the flesh after having seen her on a multitude of photos over the preceding few weeks. Kiran stretched out her hand anticipating a reciprocal hand-shake but Dev stood there gob smacked and displaying all the reflexes of a dying slug. All that was missing was his tongue rolling across the carpet and drool dripping down his chin. After an uncomfortable second had passed I piped up 'err, earth to Dev are you still with us?' I said jokingly understanding full well Dev's reaction to Kiran's natural beauty. I playfully punched him in the chest as he snapped out of his hypnotic state. 'Oh sorry, I was just lost…err…in your beauty…he told me you were gorgeous… but I did not expect this.'

We all laughed and they shook hands, eventually. I beckoned the waiter over with my hand and requested a table near the window. I always wanted to see what was going on in the street when I ate, people gazing I called it. It was therapeutic to me. As we sat down in our seats by the window, Kiran and Dev exchanged the usual conversational platitudes about work and families. I looked up and noticed a young, smart Indian girl walk into the restaurant wearing a sharp black business suit – very soigné I thought to myself. She looked over at us and caught Kiran's eye. She was tall, slim and had long black silky hair, with a fair complexion. She looked pretty. Kiran saw me looking and peered over her shoulder as she was sitting with her back to the door. 'Here she is, how are you sweetie?' Kiran said as she leapt up and tightly hugged her best friend Tina. 'You made it then?'

They both walked over to us and stood across the table, 'any probs getting here darling?' Kiran enquired. 'No just the crappy Bath Road was slow but it was cool, I made it in one piece.' She spoke with eloquence and on first impressions gave a professional and intelligent account of herself. She pointed to me 'so you must be Kam, I saw your photo, how are you?'

I stood up and was about to make my way around the table to shake her hand or hug her. I wasn't sure quite which one but stopped in my tracks as she curtly moved her gaze on to Dev with ice like impoliteness. She was oblivious to the friendly manner in which I had been preparing to welcome her, and had been accustomed to greeting friends and family without quibble over the years. I quickly sat back down, feeling a little disgusted by her uncouth and unmannerly behaviour.

'And you are?' She had locked her steely gaze on Dev's wiry frame. Dev smiled and replied in his usual non confrontational and friendly manner. 'Kiddhan, I'm Dev.'

He thrust his hand out and she smiled before shaking it.

'So, how do you two know each other?' she asked Dev.

'We have been buddies for a long time,' he smirked, 'get me a few drinks and I can tell you all the horror stories about him later if you like.' His cheeky impudence went down well as Tina flashed a smile and sat down next to Kiran. *'Hmmm, frosty little thing isn't she,'* my negative devil had popped up next to me, *'she hates you, she hates you cos you are a big time, former cocaine sniffing tosser.'* The devils, unwelcoming and excoriating comments, cutting me to the quick as he had form for doing so. My negative devil had the tendency to kick me in the ghoulies every now and then with jaundiced and scathing comments especially in unfolding situations where my body felt an air of unease and discomfort. The trouble was that whenever he appeared and got to work, he was invariably always right, the little bastard. On this occasion, I ignored him and attempted to ease myself into the flow of the excited conversation between Tina and Kiran. Man these two could talk for Britain as their conversation ebbed and flowed.

I had heard enough and cheekily interjected with the subtlety of a Sherman Tank 'so Tina, tell me about yourself then.' This was my ice breaking, tried and tested move, hey I already knew lots of stuff about her anyway, lots of intimate stuff, I had extracted the information previously from Kiran through general conversation.

She works as a solicitor in West Drayton, is currently single. She has known Kiran for about ten years and they have always been best mates. They went travelling to various countries around the world together, and she has an OCD (obsessive compulsive disorder) for red, ranging from lipstick, to shoes, handbags and apparently owns many sets of red lingerie according to Kiran, a point that made both Kiran and I laugh when she told me about her in the car before.

Tina looked at me with disdain, rolling her eyes, and then back at Kiran peeved at the discursiveness of my question. She answered back irritatingly 'hold on, Kiran told me that you know all about me, so it looks like I have caught you out lying already.' The poison ivy then shrilled like a Macbethian witch as she accusingly wagged her withered hag hand in my direction. We all laughed with her, albeit on my part, nervously. Was she playing with me? I could not put my finger on it; she was a complex bunny and not really my cup of tea as she continued in her strange line of questioning.

'What sort of stuff will YOU do to make Kiran happy when she marries you?'

Both of them smirked as the spotlight fell squarely on my head. The cartoon type perspiration flicked off my brow but I kept cool, not showing her any signs of being too nice. I knew she would mistake it for weakness and naivety.

'I have got lots of things planned, exciting, adventur-ous plans and I can't wait to be with her so that we can both have the time of our lives.' There have that you truculent BITCH I thought smugly. I was satisfied with my lucid and concise response to the surprising air of malevolence that began to creep into the dinner date, in particular from a some what hostile Tina.

The waiter who must have sensed the atmosphere denigrating and who had been patiently waiting in the shadows assessing the optimum moment to pounce, stepped up to the table with menu's. He swiftly handed them out and stood perched with his notebook and pen primed and ready to take down our drinks orders, a timely intervention I thought, almost like the bell sounding in WWE. After a whirlwind of suggestions and deliberations, we finally ordered our drinks and starters. This was a good break and gave us time to metaphorically take our gum shields out and have a breather from the inane tangent the conversation had taken. As the waiter walked off, the mood settled and the initial fencing and testing had been replaced with a more relaxed and tranquil dinner date. I was then miraculously getting on better with Tina, and all reservations we had initially formed had dissipated dramatically. I put it down to the initial reign for supremacy, the jostling to be chief out of the group. Now that we all settled down, everything was more serene.

After a couple more drinks each and once the main dishes had been devoured by all of us I left the table and walked off to the rear of the restaurant where the toilets were located to answer a call of nature. I went in and done the business content that the date had now progressed nicely after the bizarre start as tensions and chemistries seemed to be present between us. I opened the door to come out of the single unisex toilet, putting one foot back in the hall when I bumped into Tina who was next in line to use the toilet. I smiled 'don't worry love I have left the toilet seat down, and the lid is on the toothpaste.' I joked with her, or so I thought. Tina did not laugh; she had been waiting all right, but not for the toilet, but it seemed for me. She leaned into me closer, her body naturally blocking out any feeble ideas I had sought of burrowing my way out of the situation 'all I want to say is don't you dare mess her about. I know about guys like you, and I know what you have been up to.' She squinted her eyes and peered through the narrow slits that had formed. Her face scrunched up and contorted like a caricature, she went on 'she is one in a million to me, and has been hurt before. If you ever hurt her, I will personally sort you out. I mean that. She is special and means the world to me, the WORLD.' She hissed menacingly and with authoritative malice, emphasising the word world by poking me with force in the chest with her index finger and sharp nail.

I stood there gob smacked and unsure of how to respond to a big brother speech from Kiran's best friend. Tina stood waiting for a response, her hands on her hips and with a dark hue over her face. She looked serious. I cleared my throat 'Okay, I hear you.' I mumbled uncomfortably as I turned my body sideward's and squeezed past her and back into the restaurant.

My thoughts spinning with the fear that she had unearthed my dark drug using secret during that tumultuous period in my life. How had she found out? My hands shook, she would tell Kiran and that would be it – divorced in a whim. I returned to the table and sat down attempting to be as cool as *'Fonzi.'* I surreptitiously snuck back into the conversation with Dev and

Kiran without any awkward questions being asked about why I looked like I had lost a pound and found ten pence. Tina returned and chatted to me as though nothing had happened which confused me even more. She was all smiles and full of chat. Damn, she could act well.

After settling the bill we parted company and I dropped Kiran off at home after a kiss and a cuddle in the back of my car in a remote country lane around the corner from where she lived. She had been reluctant to do this but I managed to persuade her with a few tried and trusted one liners, not to mention the three cocktails she had consumed, she was putty in my paws.

My thoughts however were elsewhere and I was unable to immerse myself in the moment. I drove off on the journey home with my feelings twisted from the events that had unfolded. I was elated that the evening had gone well with all of us getting along, apart from the bitter taste in my mouth from the sinister intervention with Tina outside the toilets. This was baffling and was a potential ticking time bomb. I really could not fathom why she detested me so much? Was she just being overly protective of her friend? The thoughts percolated in my dizzy head as I drove onwards.

Tina looked the pestiferous and meddling type of 'chica' who would derive sadistic pleasure in breaking up a happy home. Why did she dislike me so much? What had I ever done to her for her to treat me with such contempt?

As I continued to lick my wounds and make my way home I consolidated my thoughts and sought solace in the fact that I would deny everything if Kiran ever asked me about my past. Secondly, after I married Kiran,

I would ensure that we got the hell away from people like Tina, who just seemed bad news to me. That would expunge the problem and keep the skeletons well and truly hidden in my closet. I felt satiated with myself and clung on to those comforting, analytical thoughts as I lay on my pillow that night.

CHAPTER 8

—⁓—

Duplicity

This one time, Kiran and I, had arranged to meet up for a spot of lunch in Desi's Chicken World, precisely nine days before the big day. It was also the time when I had decided to start to grow my quasi beard in preparation for the wedding day when I would be able to look impressive with my traditional Indian kurta pyjama outfit and turban. It normally took me about a week to start to resemble Worzel Gummidge as my hair grew at an alarming rate. I was therefore confident that I would have an unkempt and fluffed up forest hanging off of my face by the time the day came around. Already my face was a stubbly mess, but the name of the game was perseverance and I was up for the follicular challenge.

We ordered our drinks, a Malibu and coke for the lady and a double Jack Daniels and coke for me along with some succulently coated chicken wings with barbecue sauce to wash it down. We chatted about our busy days at work, the forthcoming wedding and caught up on the latest intel in the community. The lunch date was going sublimely.

A short while into the date as the chicken wings were served by the waiter she answered her phone, it was Tina. She chatted away to her best friend for a few minutes whilst I sought the opportunity to devour another handful of chicken wings. What is a man supposed to do? The wings were heavenly and I guzzled away in sheer delightful indulgence. In my excitement and with greasy barbecue fingers, one of the wings flew out of my fingers and onto the floor next to our table. Damn! I looked around quickly, there were a handful of customers in the restaurant, but luckily, no-one had seen my accident. Even the waiter was unaware. Kiran had her body turned from me sideward's facing the door and had not seen me acting like the nipple I was. There was a *'black wing down, a broken arrow, a gladiatorial wing on the loose.'* I sought my moment to look under the table and rescue and retrieve the lone wing. I searched around and could not see it. Don't you just hate it when you drop something directly under your feet and it ends up on another continent or somewhere much further away then where it should have landed? I searched everywhere, but it had disappeared, but wait, Kiran's black leather shoulder bag lay there, open mouthed, gaping, and welcoming. The ideal sanctuary for a solo, crusading, and determined wing. You are joking? This was disastrous! I looked back up at Kiran. She was busy chatting away and I was out of her line of vision, so I ducked back under the table and sunk to my knees rummaging rapaciously in her bag. I had to find the wily winged fox before the alarm sounded.

A few seconds after I had found the beast, nestling all too comfortably on a piece of folded A4 paper. The white sheet now charcoal stained with barbecue sauce smeared accusingly over it. Shit, was this work related paper-work? I was in extremis. If she found out then I would be worm food. I looked up at her, she still did not have a clue what was unfolding behind her, the turmoil I was going through. I opened the A4 paper to scrutinise its importance as I stealthily slipped the wing back onto the table top. I opened the paper carefully with the tips of my fingers, being especially careful not to spread the barbe-cue disease anywhere else. My eyes opened wide as I saw the heart wrenching salutation *'to the girl I love.'* at the top of the letter. My heart stopped momentarily as Kirans voice began to fade out into the background. I sat back down on my seat, quickly stuffing the paper back into her bag so as not to arouse suspicion, incredulous as what I had seen. This was not happening. My fiancée was cheating on me. I would be a laughing stock in the community, what would *'lokhi'* think?

Kiran continued to chat along with Tina without a care in the world; she looked so happy and content. Unbeknown to her a volcano was erupting a mere two feet across from where she was sitting. She was two timing me and that was why she wasn't keen to get married, because it didn't fit in with her fancy man's plans. I gritted my teeth and struggled to stop myself from wailing like a banshee and throwing the table over. Kiran finished the call 'okay...bye, bye my love, see ya soon.' and focussed her attention back on me 'Kam what's the matter, are the wings off?' She picked one up, the one lying incriminatingly on it's side on the table top, to inspect it. *'Play it cool Kam, play it cool'* My inner voice pleaded with me to box clever, practically implored me on its knees with both hands clasped tightly together for a subtle way to assess what the situation was, before wading in with my size tens flailing. Okay, my inner voice done its job well, I listened to it, a warrior of unimpeachable honour; it was out boxing me on this occasion. I sat back in the chair and laughed 'nah I just remembered I was meant to phone this client back at work, but I forgot. I might have cost the company a few thousand pounds, fuck.'

I was convincing. So much so that I actually made a mental note to phone my boss after I had dropped off Kiran later that evening just to make sure. More importantly, I had to find out what was really happening here, slowly, catchy monkey. I cogitated further as the hamster in my brain raced around its wheel at Olympic speed, offering me suggestive ways to seize the letter for my personal forensication.

Bang, I got it, the hamster had screeched to a halt on the wheel. 'do me a favour can you grab me the wine list behind you.' I said slyly, knowing full well that if my devious calculations had been correct then she would have to get up for a few seconds and get it from the other table as it was just out of harms way. Dutifully she was up, her back turned for a nano second as she picked up the menu. It was too late, I fucking got it, and it was by now nestling furtively in the back pocket of my Levi's. She did not have a clue, she might have been good at two timing me, but not smart enough to outwit me in situations like this. I gratefully took the wine list from her and placed it on the table. 'I am just gonna pop to the loo, I think I have got *'tuttia' (the shits)* back in a minute.' I stood up, pretending to hold my bum with my hand and all the time acting, lying through my teeth, just as she had been doing to me all along. Kiran looked disgusted 'charming, a bit too much information though, are you feeling okay, you are acting weird you sure you are alright, do you want me to get a bottle of wine while you're gone?' I was focussed on the task at hand and walked past her, ignoring her and treating her with the necessary contempt. I needed to read the note, letter or whatever it was. He was a dead man, whoever that cockroach was, that much was a certainty. I walked past the toilets and out into the car park via the rear entrance and fumbled around for the note. I read it with furious anticipation;

'To the girl I love, Kiran, you will always be my true love, ever since you came into my life there has been no one else. Your smile, your laugh and your wicked sense of humour, as I have said many times there is only one Kiran, and that is a compliment to you. I just hope that one day you will find your way back into my arms and stay there forever! - XXXXXXXX your lover XXXXXXXXXXXX'

I screwed the letter up in my hand. My head was dizzy. I felt my body shaking as the inevitable adrenalin zipped through like an express train on a one way trip to nowhere. Why would she do this to me? Who was he? How long had she been seeing him? Why? So many questions, so many expletives were springing to mind…My world had collapsed in a whim; I saw visions of myself sitting in a gutter in cardboard city, inhaling opium from a community heroin pipe along with holding and burning silver foil with my lighter trying in vain to chase the dragon. All roads were leading me back to this murky nadir, my mind searched for the answers, not one. I took a breath, let's get this over with. I wiped away the tears that were streaming down my face. They returned with vengeance, streaming uncontrollably down my cheeks into little reservoirs on the floor beside my feet. Get a grip you jadool, go in there and find out why if nothing else, why and who he is? How long has she been seeing him? I straightened the letter out, ironing out the creases, my hands shaking and barely being able to hold onto it. I felt like a big girls blouse as I blubbed once again, after everything I had been through, just when my life was on an even keel, this had to happen. Why me? Why me? I shook my head and walked back into the restaurant. I walked towards the table. I saw her talking on the mobile once again. It had to be her lover, her head flicking from side to side, playing with her hair with her fingers, as she cackled away at his jokes. All the signs were there with bells on.

What a callous and cold hearted bitch she had turned out to be. She was rubbing my nose in my own vomit, pissing on me when I was being burnt alive in the fire of bigamy. She was unbelievable, a witch. I felt like grabbing the phone and throwing it across the room letting it smash into a thousand pieces and then going over to it and stomping on it just for good measure. The treachery ran deep into her pores, even infesting her clothes, she simply smacked of subversiveness as the wound ran deep into the bowels of my heart.

I could resist no more 'so I suppose you want to tell me how long you have been CHEATING on me hey?'

She looked stunned, her face screwed up, the shock of discovering her deep rooted secret had scooped the rug from under her feet as she visibly tried to regain her composure. My eyes boring holes into her...I continued without remorse for her feelings 'come on who was that on the phone… Is that HIM – give me the phone?' My panic and anger threatened to boil over. Kiran did not utter a word in defence, not a squeak. I had caught her '*in flagrante delecto' (red handed)* – practically with the smoking gun in her hand. I could see her literally buckling, her legs crumbling under the weight of guilt as I continued with my questioning. Her silence, her being caught out was galvanising me more as my rant continued more vociferously 'It's a fucking disgrace – why have you done this to me, answer me?'

Kiran put the mobile phone carefully on the table without terminating the call and piped up 'have you finished… firstly, this is Tina.' In the background, I could hear Tina shouting '*hello, hello, Kiran – you okay?*'

Kiran picking the phone up continued in her relaxed manner 'It is okay I will call you later, I am okay really I will just sort this situation out.' Kiran put the phone back down on the table and fixed her gaze back on me. Situation I thought, she was mocking me…my blood pressure continued to rise, as did my disappointment.

'Now seriously Kam, what the hell are you talking about, I am really upset and confused?'

Her temerity and nonchalant attitude continued to baffle and provoke me in increasing measures. There is one thing I despise more than anything and that is if you are in the wrong, then just god damn admit it, face the music and lets thrash it out…But just don't deny it. I reached into my jean pocket. I took out the damning and implicating document, slamming it unceremoniously onto the table and said angrily. 'Don't play innocent with me Kiran I know exactly what's going on…' (I paused to read the rubric at the top of the letter) '*to the girl I love.*' My words choking me slowly. 'Who is he, tell me?'

Kiran staring down the barrel of the gun, averted her eyes from me, her confidence eroded before my very eyes. She sat there caught out, in the jaws of certain defeat. She replied, her voice full of trepidation and regret 'oh no, you weren't meant to find out like this.' The knot in my stomach tightened and my wounded body remained powerless. I took a swig of Jack Daniels desperately looking for the answer at the bottom of the glass as I sat back bracing myself for the inevitable and irrevocable sob story of how she had been two timing me for some deadbeat and shit for brains.

The headlines sickeningly churned around in my head as the knife twisted without remorse, first boy meets girl, girl has affair with second boy, first boy, and girl's engagement falls through as second boy and girl run off into the sunset. First boy scours the earth looking for them so that he can nail second boys arms and legs to a wall and beat his marriage breaking sorry arse all day long with a metal pipe. I snapped out of my down trodden and warped thinking and croaked 'so you're not even denying it are you?' I sobbed quietly. 'I love you, how could you do this to me?

She sat there silently, looking at me, studying my reactions; she looked petrified, truly afraid. I could take no more and raised my voice in anger 'you are one cold hearted...bitc...'

'Just STOP!' - Kiran interjected angrily. 'You don't understand, you have got this all wrong.'

I wiped the tears from my cheeks and sat back in resignation on the chair. I could see the handful of guests in the restaurant listening in, positioning their ears in our direction as the cabaret show played on for those ghouls.

'Kam before I tell you.' (She leaned across the table and tried to take hold of both my hands – I pulled them back in disgust at her patent audacity) 'I need to know if you trust me, do you trust me?' She probed at my defences like terriers in a badgers set. Not being able to resist the temptation I retorted 'well it's not looking fucking clever from where I am sitting let me tell you, I find a love letter from your lover and you ask me if I trust you, you really are something else.'

My sarcasm suitably cutting and apt for the moment I thought smugly. She looked me straight in the eyes...

She then dropped the bombshell, the low blow, straight in the knackers ...'he's my ex boyfriend Jags Dhillon...'

She looked me right in the eyes. A sign that someone is telling the truth, besides she had no reason to lie in this situation as I practically had all the facts sitting in front of me. 'we broke up two years ago, he used to be violent...he got sent down for a few years back then on some charge, I don't know too much about it, but he was out of my life, or so I thought...'

A painful look widened her eyes, as she drew from her frame of reference; her hands shook as she steadied them on the table top, clasped together, fingers overlapping each other. I kicked myself for jumping to the wrong conclusion. I remained tight lipped and kept my mouth firmly closed, after all one foot in there was bad enough let alone finding room for the pair. She continued 'he has been writing to me ever since, this letter, his latest one only came this morning. He is insatiable, and he tells me in his letters that it helps him while away his time inside.' Kiran then continued to give me a warts and all insight into their stormy relationship from a few years ago.

Un – fucking – believable. This was not what I was expecting. I was flabbergasted by this news as I listened intently taking another swig of Jack Daniels, my emotions churned up and kicked around like a football. I studied her face for clues, for an insight into the truth of what I was confronted with, there was no doubt she was telling the truth. She handed me her mobile phone 'if you don't believe me then call Tina right now and she will confirm what I have just said as she is the only person who knows about what happened and his letters.' I waved my hand, saying no, it was okay.

'I would never cheat on you.' She snapped 'all those times you kept asking me about whether I was getting cold feet about the marriage, it was not you, but it was the worry of what he would do if he found out. He is crazy, I have even heard he has got access to guys with firearms…he is capable of anything.' and she went on in meticulous detail of how Jags letters often depicted the sinister and seedy world that he inhabited both within and outside the four walls of prison. Just my luck I mused painfully. Just my frigging luck! I tried to disguise my cartoon type gulps as she outlined occasions where she saw his violence first hand within their short lived relationship years before. Times when he would snap over trivial matters with his violent mood swings and hair trigger temper. She insisted that he never laid a finger on her but would take it out randomly on passers by including some poor guy on a bike who he beat so badly after an argument about the amount of time she was spending talking to and going out with her friend Tina amongst other friends.

'I am sorry I had no idea...' I shrugged my shoulders and lifted my hands up, open palmed and saying 'I didn't have a clue.

'But why have you got the letter in your bag now and why didn't you tell me?'. I asked curiously.

'I received it this morning and I snuck it out of the house and managed to read it at work. I was going to destroy it in the shredder at work as I do with the other ones he sends me, but today I forgot, you know time of the month and stuff, my heads not right. Look I was going to tell you in the next few days as it was bugging me...do you understand?' She asked inquisitively.

I took a final swig of my drink as I felt an overwhelming sense of relief racing around my body, I got up walked around the table and gave her a big warm hug and kissed her forehead. 'It will be alright, I do understand. When we get married, we will look for a house far away and start our lives afresh where people like him will never find us. It will be just you and me.' I said comforting her and squeezing her tight to me. She stood up and hugged me, her head resting on my shoulder, our hearts beating furiously against one another. Something was bugging me, I had to ask, and the temptation was just too great;

'Did you love him...did you go all the way with him?'

I seized the moment to ask the questions that would otherwise gnaw away and eventually engulf me like a cancerous tumour. These two questions were the most important in any blossoming relationship, and many a prospective courtship has fallen by the wayside when the Asian girl answered yes to both questions to her future fiancé.

Certain character traits are inbuilt in all of us trussed up in different guises, anger, lust, greed, and jealousy to name a few. In this particular moment I had become the standard bearer for the green eyed monster club. An Asian guy wants the knowledge and the confidence to say that he was the first one inside his girl's knickers, it's as simple as that – no ifs, or buts' and I was no different. I knew I had slept around but this was rather accepted in the Asian circles. I had to do that because I was a bloke, a caveman with animal instincts, spreading my seed, sowing my oats, call it what you want, it boiled down to the bottom line, a bloke could get away with it but the girl – HELL NO!

I held my breath, watching her reaction with the attentiveness of a meer cat as she composed her response,

'No, I never loved him…we did sleep together…. but I never had sex with him, if that's what you want to hear.'

Little magical fairies descended from the ceiling playing harps, little dhol players appeared in the corner of the restaurant and the world was full of joy, she didn't give it to him, she was saving herself for me. Thoughts of her kneeling on the bed on all fours with another guy forever eradicated from my mind. I felt like the luckiest guy alive, she was mine, all mine. Oh joy oh joy. Kiran smiled and squeezed my hand. The constant babble of recrimination was beginning to give me a headache and I was grateful that I had managed to get to the bottom of it. 'It will be okay.' She purred.

It was all the reassurance I needed and my heart was singing once again as I held her close to me walking out of the restaurant. I found myself subconsciously looking over my shoulder as we made our way back to the car no doubt as a direct result of the camp fire horror stories I had just been regaled with. I was not sure why I was doing this especially as I had the safe knowledge and satisfaction that Jags was rotting away in a jail cell some-where. Far from getting his grubby little paws back on my baby girl again, and when he was released, she would be but a distant, faded memory as we got on with our lives somewhere far away.

CHAPTER 9

Illicit liaisons

On the Sunday before the wedding whilst mum and dad were out doing essential shopping for the wedding I called Kiran at home, as I was unable to get hold of her on the mobile, Preeto answered. I warmed her up as per normal with the usual conversational pleasantries but immediately noticed the old dear was a tad frosty for some reason.

'Hello mum, I can't get hold of Kiran, I was just wondering if she was at home.'

Preeto paused and then snapped back indignantly 'she not wants to speak to you!'

She never quite spoke the Queen's English but that just sounded funnier when she said it in such a belliger-ent manner.

I could definitely sense animosity, hostility and could almost hear the snorting of her nostrils through the receiver rather like a bull before the charge. 'Mum is anything wrong, you sound upset?' I had to call her mum as a term of endearment. It is what Asian boys did to show both parents equal respect, the cheesy classics like 'I have not only inherited a wife but also another mum and dad were all too common in groom speeches at wedding and engagement receptions. It made me want to hurl to be frank as this old hag wasn't fit to fill one of my mum's boots let alone both.

Don't get me wrong I had nothing against the old crow but she was now beginning to get on my nerves as every question, remark I made she cut me to the quick with snappy retorts. The flaming kushty I thought, as I asked her what time Kiran would be back home. She then fired the sixty four million dollar question at me, the ball breaker 'You have been eating drugs.' Upon hearing this I cringed, the accusation hit me like a sledge-hammer, this was bad news – how the hell did she know. I pressed the receiver closer to my left ear, maybe I had misheard her, surely she hadn't rumbled my dark secret, unearthed the jangling skeletons from my closet. I had to be sure, this could potentially ruin everything and with a week to go before the big day, this was fatal. Anyway what did she mean by eating drugs, it was not as though I would sit there in my dinner suit wearing a bib and tucking into a hearty plate of chips, magic mushrooms and some cannabis sprinkled with a smattering of cocaine for that true gastronome and culinary experience. I tried to remain calm, being careful not to disturb the hornets nest in this delicate situation. I knew I had to come out of this encounter with my reputation intact or else I would be like an apocryphal Lemming hoisting himself off a cliff, doomed and dead meat.

'Mum what drugs, what are you talking about?' I muttered unconvincingly, hoping to enshroud her with my smokescreen. She wasn't deterred from her investigation 'I know you have drugs, someone told me. You should be ashamed of yourself trying to marry my daughter when you are a disgrace to the community. I will tell her that we will cancel the wedding...she will NEVER marry someone like you, you kuta bastarda.' Her jaundiced and scathing verbal onslaught slaying me like the dog I was, as I desperately held back the tears. I listened intently, whilst completely befuddled as to how she had discovered my drug abuse. The death of a thousand cuts continued 'Don't phone here again, you not talk to Kiran, you drug boy.' I was stumped. She called me a drug boy, she made me sound like some kind of circus act...and next on stage ladies and gentleman, please put your hands together for the world famous drug boy, who will impress you with his ability to snort twenty eight lines of smack whilst blindfolded and hanging upside down by his *'tuttay.'*

With that, she slammed the receiver down emphatically. I stood there for a few moments trying to take in her excoriating comments and fathom what this meant. My kettle was boiling and it was over before the fat lady even got to sing a note.

I was devastated. My pity soon turned to anger as I walked in the living room and sat on the sofa licking my wounds. What could I possibly do to salvage any credibility with Kiran or her fire breathing mum? The future was very far from being orange, it looked, more crimson with someone's blood splattering across the sidewalk as I thought up ways of exacting revenge on the fool who had sung like a canary to my mother in law about my past drug taking.

I disconsolately walked into the kitchen and cracked open my special occasion bottle of Bacardi Black. I poured a very generous desi home shot into a tumbler and necked it neat, no dilution, no rocks, and no shit.

What the fuck is wrong with these people I thought. I just seem to be getting negative vibes from everyone, god damn, as I sunk the next Bacardi…and then another.

It was Monday morning - I awoke from my crib with breath like rotting cow dung. My itchy, scraggy beard irritating me. I felt exhausted as I tossed and turned for the invariable twenty minutes as my duel against the snooze facility on my alarm clock raged on. I reached out for the mobile just to check if Kiran had got my twenty five stalking messages that I had left her the day before and whether she had called back. I had even set the ring tone to the highest possible volume so that someone in a coma lying on the roof would have got up if it had rang. Nothing, zilch, not even a god darn offal laced sausage. I got myself changed, groomed and readied myself for work. My beard was now beginning to itch. I had been growing it for the last week now in preparation for the wedding day when I would be kitted out with the traditional Asian ensemble and the beard was a symbolic part of the chosen outfit set aside for that day. I still had thirty minutes or so. I tried her number once more, my desperation exacerbating as every second ticked ominously by, when after a few moments of ringing, she answered. YES! I jumped up from the breakfast table, spewing bits of cereal down my chin in my excitement.

'Kiran I have been going insane, are you Ok, why have you not been calling me back, I don't know what's happened, are you still there?' Too many questions Kam, calm down, my brain was in overdrive as I mumbled and stumbled my opening gambit with my beau.

'Listen don't worry, it's cool.' This was not the kind of reaction I had been expecting, was she lulling me into a false sense of security for some reason? I couldn't be sure as my paranoia crept up on me furtively. 'Have you spoken to your mum recently?' I probed nervously. 'yeah yeah, she told me that you run some kind of West London drugs team and that your empire stretches around the country and that you are bad news, oh and not to get married to you.' Kiran replied nonchalantly.

'What, you kidding me or what?' I was stunned.

'Look I think she heard it from some old lady at the gurdwara, you know how people get jealous and stuff, and how gossip spreads. Anyhow I have put her right and told her that you have never touched drugs in your life and that whoever began spreading the rumours is malicious, so she took my word for it and that's that.'

The sudden anguish of the remarks bound my thoughts as I asked 'Kiran, are you sure it was someone from the gurdwara?'

'Yeah I think so, anyway what does it matter, it is all rubbish. I remember last year some of the mums were saying that I was sleeping around after they saw me with some old college mates in town, so sticks and stones. As I said I have put mum straight and told her not to listen to idle gossip. She is cool now but expect her to be a bit frosty with you for the first couple of times she sees you, that's just her way with people who she has any doubts about, you know she wears her heart on her sleeve type of thing.' I felt the release of endorphins race throughout my body as the relief of not being excoriated and exposed as a druggie had been squashed like a bug splat on a windscreen. I could have reached through the phone and smooched Kiran passionately for her unrelenting support and faith in me, the true stables of any successful relationship. We said our goodbyes and I went to work edified by the thought of Kiran stoutly defending me as she had done today throughout the rest of our lives together. I was very much in lurve…

I looked at my watch, seven forty five in the evening on a Tuesday night, a few days until the wedding, and approximately one hundred and twelve hours and twenty five minutes of freedom standing between me and the shackles of matrimonial imprisonment.

I sat on my bed chilling and listening to mushy and moving tracks such as Challa by Gurdas Maan on my mp3. He certainly knows how to tug at your heart strings as his majestical lyrics and haunting beats takes your heart and soul on a tantalizing journey through nirvana and back. Here I was, a young stud about to get his wings clipped with my pending marriage to Kiran on Sunday, and all I could think about was how to get all my affairs in tip top order before I settled down and became a 'banda' (man), and before this wild cat was tamed. The clock was ticking and I knew that there would be a stampede and influx of hell raising relatives coming around to stay days before the wedding, so the loose ends needed tying up.

I had been getting calls from Pam from Dirty Sandhu's brothel hassling me every now and then over the last six months to go and see her and rekindle the loosely termed 'relationship' that we had. What she did not realize was that I was simply not interested anymore and had moved on in my life. On top of this I would also still receive the token threatening text and voicemail message from Spanish or one of his cronies telling me to meet him at the Dhol and Duck for a quick friendly pint. I was well aware that this would invariably end up with me being bound and gagged with piano wire, shoved in the boot of his car before being tipped over a bridge.

I was not about to let the lure of a cheeky pint in my favourite haunt trigger my demise. Again that life was behind me. My past was my past but these thoughts and others were a few things lingering that needed sorting out. I also needed to change my mobile number at some stage, needed to sort out our honeymoon to name but a few. The Caribbean looked lush and appealing and was what Kiran wanted.

I flicked the computer on and double clicked on Barbados on the favourites folder. All that was needed was a few credit card details and paradise beckoned in less than a week. Two weeks of being pampered like a rajah, five star luxury and mouth watering treats to savour, fulfilling our every divine whim. I punched the credit card details in and histrionically hit the send button. This dream escape was setting me back four thousand big ones, but it was worth every penny just to wake up in bed next to my sexy goddess with her silky tanned legs fervently wrapped around me. Done...holiday booked, one thing less to worry about.

My mobile number would be changed after the wedding, so that I could erase Spanish and Pam from my memory once and for all. I would rent out an apartment in Maidenhead, Berks and use that as a platform to find a house for us after the honeymoon. Well that was the plan and what we had discussed.

The only thing that was still bugging me was to actually get Pam to stop calling me, stop annoying me with her stalking text messages in the early hours of the morning. She had been one of my confidants in times when I was low. She provided me with a true girlfriend experience whenever I saw her and although I did not owe her anything so to speak, I just wanted to let her know that

I was about to embark upon a new chapter in my life and that she needed to understand that, allow me to breath, to live and just back the fuck off. I picked the phone up and dialed her number, it rang and it went to voicemail. I paused after I had heard the tone deliberating about whether I should or shouldn't leave a message. I waited for a few more seconds and then decided to be impulsive and go for it;

'Pam, it is you know who….erm, I will try call you later but it has been six or so months and you keep calling and texting me. It has to stop, please understand it is not you….It is just that I won't be visiting you again, it is nothing personal but, well, because things have changed now and I am getting married and stuff you know…..ahh fuck it I will come and see you in a minute, I can't do this over the phone…'

I felt like the village idiot as I put the phone down. I was the worlds worst at leaving voicemail messages and was getting hot and stuffy under the collar. I would need to go and see her, the personal touch and tell her to her face that all this nonsense would have to stop once and for all.

I called Dev 'hey deputy dog - what you up to, you fancy hooking up for a pint bro?'

Dev was always mister reliable 'yeah no probs, do you want me to pick you up in twenty?' He said enthusiastically.

'Yeah that would be good, but let's go to Ealing or somewhere other than the Dhol and Duck, that prick Spanish has been hounding me again, so I just want to stay out of his way so close to the wedding and all that, if you catch my drift.'

'Yeah cool bruv.'

'Oh, just one more thing. I just need to make a quick detour and tie up a loose end with Pam at Sandhu's, I will only be five minutes max, you okay with that?'

There was a long and uncomfortable pause before Dev eventually piped up disappointingly 'what, I don't believe this, you still shagging her bro, what's the matter with you, you have a fucking good looking girl like Kiran who most guys would die to be with and you are visiting a hooker, you are out of order man, big time?'

'Dev take it easy mucker, don't be such a spanner, I told you I haven't been seeing her, I haven't seen her for ages. I would never cheat on Kiran you know me better than that, I have moved on trust me, all I need to do is to tell her face to face as she keeps ringing me up every ten seconds demanding that we get it on together, she is deluded bruv. Today will be the end of her harassing me once and for all, you believe me right, I have not been shagging her anymore, trust me on that?'

Dev listened intently and then accepted my explanation after the initial resistance and discord. He said he would be over shortly as I pinned a picture of me and Kiran up on the mirror, she looked scrumptiously gorgeous and soon she would be mine...

CHAPTER 10

Countdown

Dev text me telling me he was outside my house in his car. I got in and we drove off heading towards Dirty Sandhu's for the last time. As Dev parked up a few streets away, I told him that I would be out in a few minutes depending on whether she had a client in with her; I knew she would make time to see me even if her client was in mid stroke with her. I mean I had that kind of mesmerizing hold over her. I don't know why this was? – Hell, I could even have been her pimp, a future career maybe I laughed to myself as I walked up the narrow staircase in the service road at the rear of the shops on the Broadway. I rang the bell and the door was opened by Shalina, a buxom South Indian goddess as she described herself in the adverts that I had seen in the local papers. 'Kiddhan is Pam about?' I muttered sheepishly, just wanting to get the whole sorry ordeal out of the way. She looked at me inquisitively at first, the half forest on my face throwing her for a split second. She had seen me many times before but the lift was not quite reaching the top floor, and then we had it, her face beamed at me effusively as she finally managed to piece together the jigsaw. She invited me in.

Pam was in her room and was preparing for a client who was due to arrive imminently. I had ten minutes to carry out my mission with military precision before closing the door on this clandestine relationship for the rest of my days. I mean why would I opt for a hamburger like this when in due course there was a juicy and sizzling steak waiting for me between the bed sheets at home? Although in all fairness she was a mouth watering burger when we got it on, but that was then and this was now – Kiran was in my life now and for forever more.

I walked into Pam's boudoir. She, as always looked very soigné. She dangled in front of me like a ripe and juicy carrot as she reached out to grab my hand, her mere touch sent waves of ecstasy through my body, her fresh perfume stirred the juices in my body, and my heart was beating rapidly. She was a consummate expert when it came to raising a guys blood pressure, after all she was well versed in her chosen occupation. She crossed and uncrossed her legs patently trying to entice me into one final and dangerous liaison with her. I remained staunch and did not deviate from my mission as I continually overcame the burgeoning and tangible sexual chemistry between us.

She squeezed my hand 'I knew you would come back to me, couldn't resist hey?'

'No, no Pam that is not why I am here, look I left a...'

'I heard your voicemail message, and am upset, you can't stop seeing me just like that, it has been over six months since you last came here, you know I have always liked you the best and I always look forward to seeing you, please don't leave it so long again.' I took a deep breath and cut in 'this is getting more difficult, It is over, it was good while it lasted, but seriously, no more stalking me, no more calls, no more nothing. I am getting married in a few days, so this has all got to stop NOW...you hear me?' Despite the warning I had given her, she continued to tilt her head from one side to the other, as though she did nor really grasp what I was saying, her eyes closed narrower, her brow furrowed, like she didn't care what I was saying. It was as though my words had not registered through her dense skull. I had always known that there was no danger of her cutting a career in brain surgery or pharmaceutical medicine, but now I was a little perplexed by her casual and nonchalant approach. What was she up to? What was this previously hell bent stalking hooker plotting? Then the penny dropped as did my knackers...

'I have called Sandhu to come over to see if we can negotiate something for you. He should be here in a couple of minutes and said he will make you a serious offer to stay, an offer you won't want to turn down.' She snarled this news to me, with a look of satisfaction spreading like a bad rash across her face.

I was suspicious. Why had she called Sandhu when he had been threatening me in text messages for months? I was being set up. I quickly began to make excuses to leave. My heart, beating faster, my nerves jangling and my life span nearing expiry. Unnervingly I went to pull my hand away, gently and without arousing too much suspicion, but she clung onto it, clasping her other hand on top for added security. I felt vulnerable and looked over at the adjoining door directly in front of us, next to the bed and leading to another room. The place where I was sure the pimp or his henchman would sit to ensure the security of the girls. Any moment now I thought, any moment now that door was going to burst open emphatically with a gun toting and demonic Sandhu running out towards me like a demented Zulu warrior baying for my blood as I remained gripped and snared by Pam's grasping talons. Almost like a scene out of the Godfather when Luca Brasi was butchered at the bar when on a mission for Don Corleone. I tried to pull my hand away subtly but she held on.

'Okay, that's cool. I need to go now, like I said to you, things have changed and this is my final visit no matter what.'

I looked over my shoulder once or twice just to ensure that nobody was sneaking up on me and then back at the adjoining door. It stared back at me, smouldering, dark and mysteriously. What was lurking behind it with sinister intent? What secrets had it held over the years? How many skulls had been cracked within this stronghold, this underground chamber of horror? The coast was clear, for now.

'You will have to stop calling me – okay?' I was getting ready to leave, Dev had been waiting for me patiently in the car and I needed a well deserved thirst quencher in the form of a frothing Cobra beer. Upon hearing this she looked devastated and her entire demeanor dramatically changed. She then pulled her hand away violently 'so you think you can just use me and then leave you prick, you have got another thing coming, I have always given you discounts because I thought we had a connection, I thought you actually cared for me' she said angrily, her true colours being displayed resplendently. I reeled back from the shock of her venomous and scathing outpouring.

'But I do care for you otherwise I wouldn't have bothered coming today.' She cut over me 'don't say that, you are lying to me, I thought we could maybe start a relationship and you could help me get away from this life, that is what you would say to me isn't it you lying toe rag, if you think you can just walk in here and fuck my life up then you haven't seen nothing yet. Sandhu will be here any moment now and I will tell him that you used to play a bit too rough if you know what I mean. He is going to fuck you up.' I studied her face and tried to make sense of her censorious words when she suddenly stood up off the bed and lurched forward with her right hand slapping me as hard as she could muster across the face, leaving the imprint of her hand tattooed on my left bearded cheek. I staggered back, the ever growing bristles of my beard digging decisively into my face. I was not expecting her to take the news so badly, after all it had been six months, and I thought she would have got over it. More alarmingly I was curious why the hell everyone I seemed to piss of recently had an over whelming desire to slap me across the face. I mean can everyone just stop flipping slapping me for a frickin minute or two.' I quickly ditched this thought as I readied myself for a hasty retreat, a tactical withdrawal before the situation exacerbated anymore than it had.

I stepped back, I was confident that these were mere empty threats used to point score and cause as much damage to me as possible whilst enabling her to save a bit of face from this encounter. I turned to leave, she jumped in front of me 'so this is it then, you walking out on me, did you really ever love me then, tell me if you have a backbone?'

I pushed her out of the way and stormed out of the room, I was glad to see the back of her as I raced through the hall and out onto the metal staircase 'you will be sorry I promise, you haven't heard the end of this you haramzada.' She continued to scream from her room.

I began walking down the stairs, desperate to get away from this stalking, possessed lunatic. Suddenly, I saw a bright flash coming from down the alleyway, right in my direction. It lasted a second at most. I quickly looked but could see nothing. What was it I thought nervously? It was very bright and illuminated the service road and staircase which I was on. There was a distinct lack of street lighting here and it was impossible to see the exact spot from where the flash had come from.

I knew that Sandhu was coming, or had arrived already and I did not fancy sticking around to see how much of his reputation of being a fearsome, unpitying and ruthless tyrant was accurate. On top of this I did not fancy having a fist fight with his henchmen either, especially days before the wedding, as a black eye or piano teeth from them being knocked out may have slightly spoiled the wedding photographs.

I even ran to the spot where it had come from and waited for a minute to see if I could see anyone lurking in the shadow of the night, but the alleyway was empty, soulless. I then ran out of the alleyway and approached Dev, he was sat in the driver's seat of his car, his trusty black coloured Ford Focus. He was enthusiastically engrossed in conversation talking into his mobile.

I tapped on the window and he opened the door and let me in. He talked for a few more moments as I sat there cogitating and nursing the left side of my face where Pam had caught me with that ferocious slap, she possessed a lot of power for a small lass I thought as my face continued to sting. She was not quite in the same league as dad's slaps but she had the potential to inflict some damage, she was like the heavyweight champion of hookers - (right hookers).

Dev looked at me anxiously, his voice was jittery as he surveyed my rattled reaction and saw me clutching my face. He quickly terminated his call and turned to me inquisitively 'what the fuck happened?' He looked concerned for me.

We made our way for a quiet pint in one of the boozers in Ealing. I entertained Dev with the finer details of my final encounter with Pam. I asked him if he had seen a bright flash or anyone coming out of the service road.

But it was pointless as he was positioned in the opposite direction, he did not anyway. As we got to the pub and propped ourselves up at the bar I soon forgot about this and celebrated my remaining days of freedom with my best friend. I knew deep down that Pam's threats had been nothing but desperate efforts to get me to continue to see her. I knew the score and it was the usual reaction invoked in girls who I had dumped before. We both laughed it off, the dirty deed had been executed near perfectly and that was the end of that particular problem, of that I was confident.

My mobile rung several times that evening as I sat drowning my sorrows with Dev. Pam left a string of abusive and bile filled messages, which I suitably screened and ignored – caller ID was great wasn't it?

Dev dropped me off back at my house a little later. Naturally, I continued to screen all the calls and a little later amused myself listening to the messages as

I indulged in a hot chocolate in my kitchen. A few more days and my number would change anyway and that would be that as I trotted off to sleep, exhausted and drained from the day's events. The side of my face settling down, and pain gradually assuaging.

Wednesday morning at work and I looked around the office and could see the usual gathering of monkey's tapping away furiously into their computers and batting off the incessant stream of dimwits who kept phoning the customer service line honestly thinking that any one of us give a flying tutti about their little dilemmas. I am so bored but know that all I have to do is eke out my existence for one more day tomorrow and then I would be as free as a bird. No more work for weeks, YES!

The working day went quickly and I managed to escape with my insanity intact and without getting fired for abusing someone over the phone. I made my way home through the traffic, my Apna Panjab ring tone blared out from my suit jacket pocket. The jacket was draped across the back seat as I tried to reach over for it. I left it and would check who called when I got home as I was only ten minutes away. It rang again, I ignored it…remembering the old adage that if it was important then they would call back. Whoever it was had obviously heard that adage before as it rang again and again. The persistent little bugger, surely it wasn't that daft tart Pam hassling me again, I suspected as much so turned my music up drowning Apna Punjab out with my CD with, well err Apna Punjab. At one stage I had this weird dolby surround sound acoustical concert going in my car, all that was missing was the reems of bhangra dancers and dhol players skipping and snaking away to the chorus on the bonnet of my car.

I tapped my fingers on the wheel and continued my journey homeward. I parked up outside my house and noticed that there were several cars on the road which I recognized as belonging to my uncles and aunties from all over the country. The preparations were well under way including making the vats of daal, saag and other Asian food. I retrieved my jacket from the back and took out my phone, I was surprised, seven missed calls but no messages. I checked the missed call list expecting them all to be Pam's mobile or Dirty Sandhu's reception number, but I was wrong, they were all from Kiran's mobile. Shit, had something happened I thought as I pressed the return call function. Kiran must have answered in a nano second screaming down the phone 'how could you do this to me, why would you embarrass me a few days before the wedding, I trusted you!' She was crying uncontrollably, hysterically.

Before I had a chance to speak, Tina came on the line 'all men are bastards, I knew you were wrong for her and I am glad she has found out about you before she done something stupid and married you. How do you feel now you have lost her you fucking loser?' I could still hear Kiran crying in the background as Tina consoled her 'don't waste your tears on him he is not worth it, it is good you found out now, trust me it is for the best.' I could hear her in the background. I needed to know what the charge was that I was being accused of as I asked Tina repeatedly to pass the phone over to Kiran so I could get an explanation. Tina refused point blank continually shouting 'it's over, it's over, now leave her alone and move on, jog on you mug, you have hurt her enough.' I shouted back 'Just give the phone to her now, NOW!' I was desperate and it worked as she handed the phone to a sobbing Kiran.

'My darling, please tell me what's happened, I told you that I don't touch drugs, I promise I never will, I love you, why are you crying, what's happened?' Kiran angrily said she would call me back in ten minutes once she has composed herself as she could not speak at the moment. I asked her to promise me that she would and it wasn't some classic fob off.

She snapped 'I said I will call you and I will, I want some answers.' With that she cut the call short. What did she deserve to know, I was truly baffled. It must have been something she had heard.

It seemed to me that no matter what happened, this bloody wedding had someone's nazar or jadu on it – nazar means to look at someone with evil eyes. It is said that if you are going through a purple patch, i.e. a run of good luck, then be circumspect as someone out there might put their nazar on you. This means that they may look at you with bad intentions, a bit like Damien from the Omen and your gravy train will most certainly hit the buffers in grandiose style.

Jadu on the other hand is a more sinister way of saying nazar and is another old wives tale. The word is synonymous with the words evil, bad luck and misfortune and actually means spell, i.e. casting a spell. It is feared within the community and the mere mention of the word will have punters looking at you suspiciously watching what they say. Jadu strikes fear into the hearts of the most superstitious Asians out there. It is supposedly a way of bringing someone heaps of bad luck and resembles the old African voodoo curse that was often cast on people back in the days of yore, and to a certain degree it still goes on now. It is said that every human possesses spirits and has one in particular that looks over them at all times. Like a guardian angel spirit. Therefore voodoo is traditionally a spiritual system of faith and ritual practices and its power is believed to strongly influence the forces of the universe and that of human behaviour through casting a spell on the person's spirit. In some cases there is a myth about dolls having pins stuck into them to replicate the area on the victim where pain will be inflicted. You would not find anyone in the Asian circles who is a believer in Jadu going to the extent of buying an effigy of someone else just to perform this ritual, mainly because it would cost them too much to make it and it simply because it is not the preferred choice of attack. However there was more than one way to skin a pussy and other ingenious ways to carry out their ill deeds without too much quibble. If you were going to be on the wrong end of the '*curse of jadu*' then you would probably not even be aware as the stealth tactics deployed by these hard nosed criminals were hard to detect even for those ghost busting anti jadu aficionado's out there.

The suspect would be innocently invited into your home and then whilst engaged in a tayt y tayt with you or your family would surreptitiously leave something within the address in a hidden location.

An object that would not be discovered, that was discreetly ensconced in between the sofa, behind the fridge, in the cistern in the toilet, anywhere, somewhere: Where you the hapless victim would not think to look on your routine jadu patrols.

The object would contain evil curses and all the jadu you could shake a stick at, performed in some far away ritual in a dark and musty cave, probably by some voodoo doctor/witch with a long wispy beard, curled up at the bottom, dressed in mystical eastern robes and smelling like the armpit of a dead skunk.

The sneaky jadu goer would then distract you whilst they planted the killer object right under your snout in their chosen spot whilst stifling their nefarious snigger. Once the deed was done they would skulk away into the shadow of the night like a silent assassin. The other more sadistic and sinister methods deployed by the gold members and subscribers of *www.jadu.com*, would be to bring in a dead animals / persons ashes into your home and then leave the ashen residue on your carpet or sprinkle some into your cup of *chaa* when you were suitably distracted.

This strategy was only for the purely evil and demented buggers out there and was considered a step up in the higher echelons of the Jadu world. You would kind of be a black belt in the ancient art of Tae Kwon Jadu – the way of the spell. Oh and before you sit too comfortably in your seat, you can rest assure that everyone has got at least one or two in their family tree, and we all know who she is don't we?

As you can see this paranoia was overwhelming at times. It made you look over your shoulder at all times, as well as searching for bits of cadaver floating in the froth of your tea when your suspect was in the same room.

I remained sitting in the car waiting patiently for Kiran's return phone call. Exactly fifteen minutes had elapsed since our previous exchange and I was becoming more and more anxious as I wiped the sweat from my brow. Then, the dulcet sounds of Gurdaas Maan edified my heart as my ring tone played Apna Punjab again. I braced myself. I didn't want to seem too desperate so I played it cool and after the third ring I answered 'Kiran, can we please talk about this. If it is the drugs then you have to believe me, I don't do drugs anymore, you believe me right?' I got in first with a bit of damage limitation and got my bit out of the way.

'Look, I just want some straight answers from you, no lies, no trying to pull the wool over my eyes ok, this is important to me?' Kiran's voice cracked as she spoke. 'I don't like anyone making a fool of me and that is the bottom line, just be straight. It will help me make my decision right now.' This was going to be a watershed moment in both our lives, one wrong answer, one slip up and the wedding plans were going up in smoke that was for sure.

She continued 'I want to know what YOU are doing visiting a brothel on the Broadway?' How the hell did she know about that? My brain ticked over quickly. This was a knee shaking jolt, although I was feeling a sense of relief that she was not going to be asking me any probing questions in relation to my drugs misuse, so that was edifying. As for being straight with her about the brothel visit, no way, I wasn't about to fall for the time old chestnut of honesty being the best policy.

On this occasion it would have been suicidal. Honesty being the best policy was for suckers, and I wasn't anyone's sucker (well apart from Spanish).

I may as well have pulled out my samurai sword and plunged it into my intestines and committed hari kari on the footsteps leading up to my house rather than cough that I was also guilty of that charge as well.

So I done what any bloke would have in the same situation and told a white lie and denied everything. I felt valiant and wanted to test the mettle of her source. Let's see if she could prove it and pick me out in the line up with the smoking gun in my hand. 'Look I don't know what you are talking about, this is absurd and you are making me out to be some kind of pervert or something, who told you that I went to a brothel?' My calming tone and nonchalance adding to the ruse. Hey I told you I could act. My defiance took Kiran by surprise and I could sense that she was beginning to crack under my bluffing and smokescreen of lies. Her retort was caked in doubt, in second guessing uncertainty 'well, someone posted a photo of you standing outside this address with this prostitute girl standing in a doorway behind you, and on the back of the photo it just says Kam visits brothel.' I was flabbergasted, the steam continued to bellow out of my ears and I demanded to know who had sent the photo, who was trying to jeopardize my wedding, and when she had received it. She said that she had found the single photo with the inscription on the back in an envelope on her doormat when she awoke this morning and was so upset when she saw it that she immediately called Tina to come over to comfort her. She said that she wasn't sure if it was me although Tina was one hundred percent adamant that it was. I must admit, I expected nothing less from the half snake, half woman Tina so shrugged off her claims immediately. Kiran told me that she had phoned me to ask me if it was me standing on the staircase outside the brothel and why someone would do this if it wasn't me.

I asked her if she could make the person out in the photo properly and she stated that the image was too distorted and the lighting was poor. I was officially off the hook, but would make some enquiries to find out exactly who was trying to jeopardize my wedding with tales of my drugs background and now the brothel visits.

The low life scum would get their punishment, their life expectancy was decreasing as the days marched on, that much was certain.

All fingers were pointing towards Spanish, who else? He had taken my escaping his clutches as personal. He was also well connected in the area and was incidentally the one who had told me all about Sandhu's brothel. That was it, he had set me up, fitted me up like a kipper. He was working with Sandhu, it was obvious. They were a nefarious double act. It all made sense to me. We said our goodbyes. She was reassured and we departed on good terms.

Thursday was a manic day where I was whizzing around town like a blue bottle fly getting last minute stuff for mum and dad for the wedding. I must have made a dozen or so trips to various places often herding the odd gaggle of biddies from one place to another, picking them up from home, dropping them off again. Most of them were soft and cuddly and you couldn't do enough for them, but then there were the others. The ones that more often than not I would be fighting off the waft of halitosis and skunk like body odour, not to mention the invariable wet pensioners fart that would be squeezed out as they wriggled around in the back seats commenting on the world as it careered by.

My Punjabi was sketchy to say the least and I would often be nodding in agreement to absolutely everything they were saying. They must have thought I was some kind of psychopath as all they could see was me grinning and nodding saying '*hanji*' *(yes)* to everything they said. Still this was my duty and I fulfilled it impeccably. As the day progressed more and more guests started to pour in to visit and to set up temporary home for the next few days. The decorations were also up and I was only maintaining brief phone contact with Kiran now, as we had decided that it would be bad luck if we were to see each other before the big day. Like I could get anymore bad luck I thought. Dev was always on hand to help pick things up and assist around the house. He had also taken time of from work as any decent friend would do.

My mobile phone started ringing a couple of times throughout the day and having checked the caller ID, it was PAM the luddi (prostitute) hassling me yet again, I mean this was becoming increasingly annoying now, had she not got the message the other night. I was beginning to suspect that she had set me up with the photograph that evening. After all, she had known that I was coming over before I did. The crafty bitch I thought angrily. I guess she was not overly impressed with my heart rendering break up with her on Tuesday night. My game plan of changing my phone number after the wedding and honeymoon was even more lucid now, especially as Pam was steadily honing her stalking ability since the *'break up!'*

The evening was fun filled with the elders drinking, eating, and laughing raucously as they reminisced about their carefree upbringings in the fertile soil of the Punjab, the motherland. I would sometimes love to listen to these conversations as they truly edified my heart and reminded me of my Punjabi roots. The state of Punjab and all five million hectares of land are located in North West India, and are divided into seventeen districts. It's main industry being the growing and supplying of agricultural produce such as fruits, vegetables, sugarcane, cotton, oils, seeds, dairy, poultry, spices and livestock. The hospitality and warmth of the Punjabi people is incomparable and they have an unrivalled exuberance for life.

After everyone had tucked into his or her roti with the accompanying saag, aloo matter and daal. We all turned in and called it a night. Mum and my auntie Satwinder however continued to beaver away until the early hours of the morning. They were a couple of roll up the sleeves work horses and sleep was a trivial issue when it came to putting on a show to bedazzle the community. They eventually turned in around four am. I tossed and turned on the bedroom floor as my grandma – Deesho slept like a log in my bed, occasionally letting out a satisfying groan and throat grabbing fart as she rested her weary bones.

It was only right that she slept comfortably at her tender age and was yet another common Asian tradition where you would generally give up your bed to your guests when they came to stay, especially if they were elderly and infirm as was the case here. Only a few days left and my life was complete, my excitement bubbling over.

Friday morning was like a cross between being stuck in the rush hour of Piccadilly Circus and the frenzy of a stock market traders floor as hordes of guests who had been staying over from virtually every corner of the globe including relatives from India, Germany and Canada were dashing around the house, eating breakfast, going in and out of the toilet, sitting on the stairs and just being in the way. The other twenty or so guests were still asleep, strewn across the living room floor resembling the Burma Railway covered in an array of 'chaddars' (blankets) and sleeping bags, generally making the place look like a squalor, a half way house for drunken oafs and the homeless.

All I wanted to do was to brush my gnashers, have a pee and maybe splash some aftershave lotion on, but even these minor tasks were looking treacherous as relative after relative kept popping up out of the woodwork. It was like a scene from a zombie film or a first person shooter computer game whereby no matter how many times you gunned them down; they kept spawning and walking towards you with outstretched arms.

Still, I had the stag do to look forward to tonight but couldn't help but worry about what my masochistic comrades had been plotting for me. I just prayed they would play nice.

CHAPTER 11

Boys will be boys

It was Friday evening and stag night. I left the preparations to my best man Dev and he had organized the stag jamboree in a newly opened pub in Greenford called Bhangra Haven. This was arranged and concocted much against the wishes of mum and dad, who insisted that I had it a couple of weeks before. I fully understood their reasons as to why I should but there was a method to my madness. I had spoken to Dev previous to this and had told him that I was unable to get any days off of work and any chance of going abroad were slim if not non existent. He bought this excuse, hook, line and sinker along with all of my mates. So the only alternative was to have the rather watered down stag on the Friday, a couple of days before the big day disabling any devious thoughts that had been prepared to serve up to me had we gone away somewhere for any length of time.

I called the local minicab firm to come and take me to the pub. I must admit my heart was beating a little faster than normal as I continued to burn up excess energy cogitating about what was waiting for me as an alternative to the lad's trip away. My mates were not that easily deterred and I knew full well, that they would have been concocting something menacing to send me off. However, my faith and trust in Dev edified me; he would not allow anyone to go to drastic lengths, shaving my eyebrows, waxing my crotch or whatever. He would have my back. The cab whistled off down my street.

Dev, as the best man had made all the relevant phone calls and assembled Southall's finest in Bhangra Haven, a newly opened bar slash pub, slash gentleman's club situated in the hub of Greenford. I was to meet them all there at seven in the evening.

I looked at my watch and it was seven on the nose as I stood outside the venue with the blue neon light flashing seductively and enticing me in. I could hear the faint sounds of laughter and Punjabi music coming from within the pub doors, soon to be my drinking cesspit I smirked nervously.

I walked in and over in the far corner of the pub was ten to fifteen of my best buddies, from work mates, old school friends and other acquaintances. In amongst the flock was Dev looking very dapper in all black. Others propped up at the bar were old brethrens like Surinder from Hounslow, another good bloke from the good old school days. Then there was Firoz, who had gone all the way through nursery, primary and finally secondary school with me. I mean at one stage it got so bad I was contemplating taking an injunction out against him for stalking me. He was like my shadow but then we lost touch. There were other goodfella's and I was impressed with the turn out. They were all totally immersed in their cups and chattering fervently to one another. I walked over to the group and shouted 'oi oi bhanchod.' Although this was an offensive word, it could be used in circumstances such as these as a term of endearment. Dev looked up, and walked over towards me, complete with Guinness in his hand hugging me voraciously.

'You made it then sunshine, thought you were gonna leave the country.' We laughed. 'I was just about to contact all the airports to be on standby, infact where's your passport I might have to seize it when you find out what I have in store for you.' We both laughed again, albeit on my part a little more jittery than Dev. Meanwhile Firoz, Surinder and the other guys all came over to us 'kiddha kuta, what brings you over to this neck of the woods then?' I said as I patted Surinder in the stomach. He laughed and we all greeted each other with hugs as we always did. Before I knew, a drink was thrust into my hand by Firoz 'here you go Kam, drink that and it will erase the sins of a lifetime, fuck it in that case you had better have three pints, ha ha.' and with that, the festivities were well and truly underway without further ado.

The evening progressed well and a few more friends turned up, the mood was sublime. I was truly living la dolce vita.

At some stage throughout the course of the evening through my drink fuelled haze, I saw a young wiry looking Asian guy approaching me. I could see Dev and Surinder whispering that he was selling cocaine. We told him to push off, and said emphatically that we did not take drugs. He scuttled away. I was proud of myself for snubbing him and it was a sure fire reminder that I had definitely learnt to live without taking illegal drugs. I continued sinking pint after pint of Cobra as I had a strong hankering to get plastered tonight. I also indulged in various alcoholic delights such as Chivas, Jack Daniels et al. Through my alcoholic haze I could see everyone chatting away and generally having a great time. Dev was in fine fettle as he continually chatted away often into his mobile. There were wind ups, silly games and the token let's see who can pull the one Asian girl standing on the other side of the bar who in a clear suicide attempt had ventured unbeknown into the lions den that evening. I stood at the bar laughing as a few of the braver souls amongst us including the hapless Surinder sauntered over to their prey who was enticingly perched on a stool. One by one they went licking their eyebrows with a wet saliva stained finger and flicking their collars up as they cruised over. After patently feeble attempts to pull her they were sent packing complete with tail between legs to raucous laughter and consoling pats on the back from the gang.

The bar was by now filling up and the whisper amongst the boys was that there was a strip bar room set aside upstairs for the connoisseurs amongst us. Dev had booked it and motioned for all of us to take our drinks upstairs. I passed my tumbler of Chivas to Firoz to hold as I quickly made a pit stop in the little boy's room on the ground floor. The others started to walk up the stairs to this newfound nirvana.

I went to the toilet and stood firm by the urinals steadying myself with one hand against the wall as I opened the floodgates. In my drunken stupor I amused myself (not that way you darn pervert) as I counted in my head how many seconds I could pee, knowing that my personal best was an outstanding three minutes in one sitting. I started impressively and this was going to be a photo finish as my thick, frothy stream gushed majestically into the ceramic urinal. As I stood there with a look of intense satisfaction emblazoned across my face

I was aware that another reveller from the bar was now standing at the urinal next to me and happily going to work. As I was coming to the end and nearing the ceremonial shake, I could disturbingly feel the guy looking at me, staring at me having a slash. What the fuck? I did not want to look. I mean this was awkward. I felt uncomfortable and uneasy, but I glanced sideward's. The fella, an older Asian chap, stockily built and standing at an impressive six feet at the very least, quickly looked away. They say that every time you are drunk you have a moment of clarity where you snap out of your drunken state and are able to lucidly see what is happening. This had now become my moment of clarity as I quickly zipped up, swivelled on a two pence, and made my way hastily to the wash basins. I knew that Dev and his fellow cronies had been planning something sinister and naughty for this evening's Stag party, but I was praying that it did not include being buggered to within an inch of my life by a musky smelling and perverted stranger in the dingy toilets of Bhangra Haven, because that was just not cricket.

I kept my head down as the water ran over my hands and I then heard the door open and shut. I paused for a moment then looked up in the mirror. The weirdo had left, thank god. I staggered back to my mates upstairs who were sitting around a crescent shaped stage. The centre piece being a young English rose wrapping herself around a pole on the stage and gyrating her hips to the Latino music.

'Where have you been geezer?' Dev quipped as he handed me a pint of something.

'I had to go for a piss, what's this?' I said pointing to the pint as the metaphorical smoke bellowed out from the head of the pint. Dev smirked 'this will put hairs on your chest...hey boys he is here.' He shouted to the others and before I knew it, the boys had surrounded me like locusts on a feeding frenzy. In the commotion and gathering we all stopped and stared open jawed at the '*sapno ki rani*' who was now writhing on the floor having removed her bra displaying her weapons of mass destruction. I took one sip of the pint and almost keeled over backwards as the back of my throat disintegrated from the surge of heat this alcoholic punch was generating. As I came back from unconsciousness I asked Dev desperately as though I was giving him my dying declaration, 'what, err, what...the fuck is in this, you trying to kill me you krazy kat?'

I could hear the guys whispering excitedly, the devious cogs of my impending doom were spinning in the hurly burly of what was rapidly becoming my very own '*Battle of Little Bighorn*' – yes this was '*Colonel Custer-jits last stand*' and there was no way I was slipping off the hook with this mob, no way.

Dev and the guys all laughed and a voice from the back started the ten to one countdown. The pint glass was lifted up to my mouth, ten, nine, eight; the voices getting progressively louder, coming to a crescendo, seven, six...I started to gulp the pint down, little trickles seeped out of my mouth, down my chin and onto my shirt, five, four...I was almost there. I did not pause for a breath as I continued to wolf it down, my head was already spinning, I felt sick, three, two, one...I slammed the empty pint glass on the bar top to a rousing cheer and punches of '*Yessss!*'

Almost immediately, my stomach churned and tried to identify the noxious substance that had been force fed into it, I went to retch, but nothing came out as the onlookers laughed, I went to retch again but again nothing came out. I felt nauseous, I felt like I was about to slip into a long coma, about to die a painful death. The laughter continued. The Grim Reaper was on standby in the car outside, revving the engine, twiddling his black cloak, bracing himself to escort his next victim to the subliminal level, such was the peril. After a few moments, I managed to snap out of my state of despair and endangerment. I settled down and wiped my chin with my sleeve. I turned to Dev and slurringly asked 'mate, seriously that was vile, what did you put in it?' He quickly rattled off a disturbing list that included Bacardi, Jack Daniels, Smirnoff Vodka, Southern Comfort, Pimms and others that I cannot recall. It was a suicide shot mixed together with lemonade used to tranquilise horses or something. It worked; I was god damn hell for leather *'patti' (drunk)*.

I then remembered my shirt being taken off and being sat down in a chair bare chested. Someone then tied my hands behind my back and to the chair as the sounds of Shaktee kicked in from the speakers behind me. I saw a blindfold being placed next to me on the table as my ticker went into overdrive. As I sat there queasily looking up, a few sheets to the wind, I saw the most gorgeous *'gori'* wearing black fishnet stockings a lacy bra and knicker set snaking her away across the floor towards me. Her big rose red lipstick glistening in the dimly lit lighting of the room. I metaphorically stood to attention in my seat as she placed a can of whipped cream on the table next to me. The boys were laughing, the music was alive and she gently stroked my thighs as she moved in closer. Dev looked at me and winked as she puckered up and kissed me full on the lips. I was in heaven as this angel flicked off the top of the whipped cream and without skipping a beat had removed her bra. The boys cheered enthusiastically much like watching a goal being scored at a football game. The gori seductively sprayed a generous amount of cream onto her breasts and then picked up the blindfold and placed it over my eyes tying it in a knot behind the back of my head. I was excited and silently pleased. This was after all a memorable and fantastic treat, thanks boys; OR so I thought. Unbeknown to me at that time, but the boys had by then cleverly switched the gorgeous gori with a leather clad moustached guy who crept in swiftly replacing the gori. He already had pre prepared whipped cream smeared over his nipples (which I later discovered were gyno boobs or moobs as they are known) and was subtly taking the gori's place in the proceedings much to my subsequent distaste and horror. It pains me to reveal that yes the inevitable happened. I ended up licking the whipped cream off his nipples as everyone laughed uncontrollably. I felt the salty taste of his man nipple, as he jiggled it about in my mouth, the bitter taste of a musty cologne now alarmingly registering in my brain, the recently shaved manly bristles pricking my mouth and lips as he pressed his moobs deeper and deeper into my mouth causing me to gag.

He removed his half bitten and sucked nipple from my mouth, whilst still hovering over me, the blindfold was then removed for me to see my prize standing over me, his boner protruding through his leather shorts and gently jabbing me. I screamed 'you fuckers, let me out.' The boys fell over tables laughing holding their sides, what side splitting entertainment. The moustached guy kissed me on the cheek and left. Thankfully, rather quickly before I could wrestle free and take a swipe at his knackers.

I remained in the chair. Dev then signalled for the next act to come on stage. They then brought in a roly poly strippogram who then performed for me. This beast was twenty stone plus, with the accompanying flies buzzing around her armpits and snatch. Her make up looked like it had been put on by Coco the Clown and with her knee drooping and sagging boobs she bounced rather than walked over to me. She straddled me, crushing my piece under her corpulent, juggernaut thighs. The boys clapped and performed bhangra moves around me, shouting, and hollowing in ecstasy at the sight of the roly poly gram wobbling her sagging jugs in my face. The stench from her snatch wafting up to my nose, gagging me, making me retch; flea bitten, vulture devoured and a rotting tutti smell overcoming me. The prickly, rotting pubes from her snatch prodding and pricking me down below as my 'old fella' ducked for cover and hid expertly behind a bunch of my pubes as the war raged on. After she had finished me off, literally, the boys felt charitable and bought the original gori back on for her final performance much to everyone's delight, none more than mine as I was trying to wiggle my toes, feeling for sure that my femurs in both thighs were crushed beyond repair.

Once the gori had finished prancing around me, she walked off to rapturous applause and wolf whistles. I was released from the chair. I immediately drank a pint of water as I told Dev that I was feeling a bit sick. Dev then turned to me, changing the mood 'I have heard that Kiran's ex is out of prison and he is back in with a nasty crowd who have got access to guns and the sort.'

I looked at him incredulously; trying to actually focus on his face, and not the adjacent pillar, as the drink jubilantly seeped through my system 'are you joking me?'

'Just thought I would tell you mate.' Dev chipped back.

'What?' I wiped my mouth with my arm and shook my head. I did hear him right. I focussed back on my friend as the commotion and festivities around me continued. He shook his head and said 'yeh some geezer told me before.'

'What geezer?'

'I just heard it somewhere, and I think he knows about the wedding too.'

'Fuck off, right, you kuta. This is part of your stag do wind up, ha, ha…yeah you got me for a minute.'

Dev's expression did not change. At least I think it didn't as my eyes blurred over, the drink concoction taking its grip on me.

He whispered 'you know he is bad news and I think' he might start something if he knows where the wedding is, why don't you call it off for a bit?'

I was drunk but this comment was downright stupid 'what do you mean call it off, I can't just call it off you idiot, this is a wedding not some fucking doctor's appointment you can just call off. Sometimes you talk shit bruv, you know what I mean.' Drink, or no drink. I heard that comment, that shred of advice clearly and made my feelings known.

Dev remained silent realising he had put his size nines well and truly in it. 'okay it's cool, you know what your doing don't you, It is going to be *'phat.'* With that Dev walked back to the group leaving me shaking my head in frustration. I sipped some more water to soak up the gallons of booze drifting in my body.

I had a call of nature and wanted to go and shake hands with the unemployed so I made my way slowly but surely down the stairs to the toilets downstairs. I walked down the stairs and saw Firoz coming up towards me. He said that a guy downstairs was asking about me. I asked who he was and he said that he didn't know, maybe someone who had turned up late for the stag night. We both shrugged our shoulders and I continued to the toilet. As I walked in there were several punters using the urinals so I walked into a cubicle shutting the door behind me. I was at bursting point. After a few moments and as I was gleefully peeing to my hearts content, I heard Dev's voice from within the confines of the toilet. It seemed that he was talking to someone else and they were waiting for the urinals to free up. He was in the throes of talking to James who worked with Dev and was also part of the stag party. They rambled on about this and that as I carried on my business. Suddenly my ears pricked up upon hearing Kiran's name being mentioned. Hello, I thought, what is he saying then?

I had always wanted to be a fly on the wall and hear what people really thought about things, you know get beneath the surface of the skin and all that. I listened intently as my grasshopper training from my Karate days as a youth kicked in. 'Yeh she is one of the nicest girls I have ever seen. I mean she is a diamond, a real salt of the earth, I would do anything to marry someone like her, you have got to see her mate, and then you will know what I mean.' I was relieved. It was a nice to have heard this comment by Dev and it helped me forgive him for his earlier comment about calling the wedding off. I smiled and then waited for them to leave before I flushed and came out of hiding.

The toilet was now empty apart from a cubicle a few down from me where the door was closed. I walked over to wash my hands when I heard the other toilet flushing. I took a few moments to style my hair and wipe off the red lipstick that was now smeared across my upper lip. I looked down and then back up at the mirror admiring myself and trying to remain on my feet. That was the main objective. The water I had previously gulped down assisting to stabilise me. It kept me from toppling over into a crumpled heap on the toilet floor. I stood there for a few more seconds when suddenly I noticed a stocky Asian guy standing behind me grooming himself in the mirror a few feet away. We both vied for mirror space from the only mirror in the toilets. I was about to look down at my hands in the wash basin again when, my eyes widened, as it dawned on me. It was the same man, I had seen earlier. The six foot, stockily built Asian guy who had been standing next to me at the urinals earlier, the toilet bugger merchant. Here he was again standing there a short distance behind me having just come out of the cubicle. I panicked, what were the chances of us both being in the toilet at the same time, no way?

I froze momentarily as I looked at him, still standing behind me. I had to get a grip of myself. Play it cool. It was not as though he really looked like the buggering type. I put it down to mere coincidence and moved out of the way as he obviously wanted to use the wash basin. I turned to walk out and past him when he piped up 'Kam isn't it?' He pointed his finger at me. I stopped dead in my tracks, scared and apprehensive 'nah, not me mate, I am....err, Gavinder.'

Of all the names I could have thought of I invented the most obviously made up one possible, even I wouldn't believe me.

He walked closer to me 'okay Gavinder, lets cut to the chase you *bhanchod*, I am Sandhu, I know you have heard of me because you have been a naughty boy shagging one of my girls, right?'

My knees buckled as I fought hard to stand up straight from this revelation and partially down to the booze running through my body.

'You owe me a thousand pounds and I want the money within the next few days or I am going to visit...let me see...Kiran is it...she might just find out all about your little affair with Pam, catch my drift *phudee (fanny)*'

This was blackmail. There was no way I could let him get away with this. What could I do? I was sobering up quickly as the reality of the situation was beginning to become vividly perspicuous. A few burning questions came into my head and fuelled by the drink I asked 'so it was you who sent the picture to Kiran's house wasn't it?

He looked at me without uttering a word; he was a handful, a mean fucker. 'And telling my mother in law about my drugs?'

He looked like a seasoned veteran in the school of hard knocks, greased back jet black hair and sharp unrelenting features on his oval shaped face. It was clear that he could handle himself and some.

He replied 'yeh that's right and if I don't get my money they will hear the graphic details.'

My anger boiled, but I knew better than to pick a fight with him: not before the wedding. He had nothing to lose and I had everything to lose, aside from which I really did not want to taste soup through a straw for the next few days lying in ward ten of my local '*horse and pistol.*' That would have been a school boy error. He then tapped my cheek with his hand a couple of times (at least he didn't feel the inclination to slap me) and walked out of the toilet leaving me to contemplate my fate. The consolation at this time, if there was one was that I had escaped without getting rogered by the phantom stranger hanging around the toilet, a small but welcome relief, and as mum always said look for the positives in a situation.

I returned to the stag group as the first signs of self doubt meandered into my mind. An hour or so later of sipping more water and collecting my jumbled up thoughts, I felt my jittery body beginning to show the first signs of relaxing as the boys were drinking up. What could he do to me? I would deny everything anyway. The dancing, singing and drinking was slowly drawing to an end, as we all started to make our way home in respective cabs. I staggered into my bedroom and collapsed on the bed, my weary and heavily intoxicated frame relaxed into the contours of my tempur bed. I shed a few tears as the vast magnitude of threats played on my mind, despite my earlier resistance and resolve in the aftermath.

I just had to get Sunday out of the way, then, after the honeymoon none of them could ever find me as I would be moving far away and starting a new life. I wiped the tears from my cheeks and rested my head on my pillow drifting off into a deep slumber with the consolation of this thought.

CHAPTER 12

—⚏—

Unwelcome guest

Saturday morning had finally arrived, and it was only a mere day before the big day. I woke up with a pounding headache very much cursing the amount of liquor I had consumed the night before. I was grateful that I actually woke up in my own bed and not strapped to a lamppost in the middle of the High Road in a French market town in my birthday suit. After freshening myself up and taking some paracetemols, I went downstairs and into the living room. There was a hive of activity as Sharm and Dad were busy moving all the furniture into the garage including the sofa and television. This was to make way for the evening party when the house would be brimming with even more relatives than there were at present.

I said my good mornings to everyone and after eating some left over samosas decided to get changed and helped out around the house, shuffling about half cut and smelling like a brewery. Dev then arrived a short while later and helped to decorate the living room with my other cousins, with balloons, banners and stuff. Meanwhile I helped dad arrange the drinks and beer barrels in the conservatory. This was where dad's bar was kept. It was basically a wooden shelf with some seats on the other side, but he would refer to it warmly as his bar. The place, where great family decisions were often made.

Today was of course the day for the dreaded yellow stuff to be smeared over me or *'vatna / maiyan ceremony'* where all the women would get their chance for redemption, to avenge the years of being victims of my bad jokes and teasing.

This was the day that every woman worth her salt would have penned in their diaries. The day just before the wedding which they would look forward to knowing full well the humiliation that was facing every groom in this most anticipated of traditions? A yellow, thick, gooey tumeric paste and staining cream would be applied to the groom's limbs and facial area in a bid to make him whiter for the wedding day whilst the women (in some cases the apostles of Satan) chanted and sang hymns and *boliyans (songs)* with delightful glee. This ceremony is also referred to as *ladies sangeet*, which basically means ladies singing. I sat there in the garden with my cheesy tootsies nestling comfortably on a small wooden plank that had been planted underneath me otherwise known as a *'patri'* whilst a large red cloth was held directly above my head by some of my aunties and younger female cousins. The ladies then began to sing a variety of Punjabi *boliyan* tracks, getting more and more carried away as they rattled on. Without a skip of the heartbeat there were handfuls of the yellow staining cream coming at me from every conceivable direction as I was prodded and smeared with the substance. This ritual is said to cleanse and balance the body for marriage; right now I wasn't feeling very clean and balanced especially as one of my scatterbrained aunties –

Gachwalpreet, wife of my mum's brother, both punters living in Canada, managed to poke a bit of the cream in my eye, causing me temporary blindness. As I cursed under my breath, I found the pain was short lived and managed to quickly recover with a splash and rub of water from the same ditsy auntie. She redeemed herself!

The yellow tumeric cream continued to be applied making sure every nook and cranny was covered. The songs were sung with great fervency and pride with everyone laughing and having a good time. Mum and grandma were especially happy, they were content because they were finally marrying off their boy and just the glow and enthusiasm coming from my mum's face made my heart swell with pride. After the yellow stuff had been suitably applied I stood up and had to walk to the end of the garden carrying a plate of rice, money and not forgetting the remnants of the yellow paste. After a few more rituals I was free to escape. Tradition states that I have to keep the yellow paste on until the morning but with the impending party this evening I had already squared it with my parents that after the ceremony I would be spending the token thirty or so minutes in the shower scraping the paste off with a hammer and chisel. They were okay with that. I later changed into my evening *garms* and was ready to have a memorable time.

Around six in the evening the guests started to arrive, well only a few to be frank, the remainder of them would naturally arrive at around seven or eight despite the invite card specifically saying that the event started at six, thus upholding the time held Asian ritual of turning up significantly later than the advertised time, a practice endearingly known in the circles as *'arriving at Indian time'*, passed down from generation to generation and fondly ridiculed. The remaining guests did in fact turn up later than advertised, much to mum's wrath, but nevertheless the party rolled on swimmingly. The ladies were wearing colourful Asian suits and the older men were looking dapper. Everyone looked relaxed and in the party mood. At around eight in the evening most of the guests who were invited to attend were here and were busy talking, eating and drinking. All the ladies were in the living room, whilst the older uncles and dads were in the conservatory propped up by the bar. Dad was the bartender for the evening and simply loved being the host. He looked happy and a million miles away from his disappointment on discovering my drugs secret months ago. How times had changed for the better as the swell of harmony and enjoyment shuttled majestically through the house and our lives.

My friends and I all stood on the patio in the garden each with a beer nestled refreshingly in our mitts, when I felt the vibration of a text message on my mobile phone in my jeans pocket. I reached in to retrieve it as we all continued to chat fervently about the wedding and the stag night. Here we go; I thought another death threat from Spanish, another expletive ridden message from Pam or Sandhu. As I read the message, my expression turned to shock as I reeled back in horror.

It was not what I had been expecting, far from it. You had to be kidding me! I thought in utter dismay, this was surreal.

I nodded my head for Dev to join me away from the pack 'Dev you will never guess who just text me and said they will be turning up to the wedding, I don't fucking believe this, go on who am I talking about?' My voice beginning to crack from the shock of the message.

'Go on…oh…not…..err…that bloke…. Spanish…oh shit, what does he want?' Dev's eyes full of shock. I shook my head 'No but that would be bad too. Who else would properly mess my day up – just think about our past?' I prompted Dev to recall our salad days as youngsters. Dev became distracted and dismissed my question momentarily looking over his shoulder instead. He was looking through the patio doors leading into the conservatory and into the kitchen at the commotion erupting between a couple of guests. As the rumpus progressively got louder he tapped me on the shoulder and we both walked towards the patio door entrance to inspect what was occurring. We looked on as two guests were in the throes of exchanging words with one another. The dad's were looking on nervously from their positions as we were.

I could sense the under currents of violence brimming menacingly. The guy dressed all in black seemed to be verbally getting the upper hand of the guy wearing his dad's blue chequered suit. The suit was overgrown as the sleeves draped down over his hands and the trousers were curled up several times at the bottom, so that the bottoms did not scrape along the floor. I mean firstly who wears his dad's suit to a night before party and secondly who was this freak of nature? I could not recall this pip squeak of a character ever gracing any family occasion in the past and here he was going a couple of rounds with black clothed Ninja guy, who similarly I did not recognise especially as he had his back to me throughout the rumpus. Who were these two clowns? Both of them it seemed desperately trying to upset the ambience of my party. We leaned in a little closer to hear the exchange of words as did the uncles and dads brigade as they looked on from their seats in the conservatory.

I could see the back of the hulking black vest guy in mid flow pointing down into the chest of the pip squeak guy. I could see the tattoo of a *'khanda'* bulging from his left bicep, the symbol, and emblem of the Sikh faith. The emblem represents the faith, divinity, and creative power of god. It basically consists of a solid circle (called a chakkar – which means a wheel and is a timeless circle, like yin and yang), tow crossed swords (called kirpans – the weapons of Guru Hargobind and individually called 'piri' and 'miri' - signifying balance amongst other things) and a double edged sword in the centre (signifying the creative power of God). The tattoo looked impressive but the question still remained who the hell was this guy? Black vested guy continued; 'bhanchod – you still taking your medication... you have to be one crazy kuta to wear a suit like that (he then looked at his watch) and anyway what you doing up so late on a school night, it's bedtime for you sunshine, now hop along like a good little boy with your mug of cocoa....bhanchod, kusra (transvestite).'

At this time, not one of us realised that this situation was a ticking time bomb and so like the ghouls we were, we just continued to watch in true rubber necker fashion. Pip squeak remained staunch and looked on, even from where I was standing this was false bravado, and surely he did not want to tango with the man mountain stood in front of him.

Black clothed guy stepped closer to him pointing his finger menacingly 'oi bhanchod - you still here? You are like a weird cartoon character, now go and find your fucking illustrator and do one.'

You would have thought that pip squeak would have backed down from the rumpus after being poked in the chest, being on the receiving end of the jaundiced attack by this darkly dressed assassin, but no he was not finished. In a tremendous display of fortitude, valour, and downright stupidity he quickly retorted 'at least I am related here - who are you anyway? Who invited you?'

On hearing this impudence from pip squeak, the black vested muscle man lunged for him whilst shouting 'oi meray tuttaya de baal noo kungi maar maachod.' (translated – comb the hair on my balls you motherfucker) as he was forcibly restrained by other guests and the dads who had leapt up at this point to join the melee. You could literally see the steam coming out of his ears as he continued in his attempts to free himself from the various arm locks and other limb holds they were administering on him. It was almost a trailer for WWE as they went from submission to submission grappling with his flailing arms and legs. All the time this muscular dude inched forward continuously, still snarling like a rabid mutt and trying to capture the brave rabbit stood cowering in front of him. I tried to assist as did Dev but we got momentarily pushed back in the stampede as friends from the garden rushed forward to break up the fight. They eventually prised the big guy off and his victim quickly disappeared into the background, hiding amongst the other revellers, pip squeak was worm food, dust, history for the rest of the evening. Never to be seen again. I was curious and needed to find out who this black vested guy was. I asked Dev and he shrugged his shoulders. No sooner had I asked the question when black vested guy turned around and walked towards the garden, through the conservatory and past looks of indignation from the uncles and dad's. He saw us and started laughing raucously from his altercation and the patent satisfaction that he derived from scaring pip squeak. He cackled heartily giving off a superb impersonation of *The Hooded Claw*.

'It's...Ranj...what the fuck?' I said in the most shocked and disheartened tone that I could muster.

Dev's eyes almost popped out of his head. I looked at the text message and then up at Ranj, oh my god, the panic had set in. I guess on the text when he meant '*I will be coming to the wedding*' he meant it, the whole kit and caboodle. Black Ninja guy was Ranj, an old school acquaintance. He was the ass kicking, eye gouging, village terrorising dragon of unsympathetic ugliness. A guy not to be messed with. Ranj pointed at us as he grinned cheekily, his body language and facial expression depicting '*I got you*'. He started to bowl over to us swinging his arms majestically, flashing his gold tooth and winking at random guests. At six foot tall, a crisp goatee beard and spiky hair, a long nose and small round eyes cased on his square face, he had always been an imposing man mountain. His muscles were abundantly evident, even through his clothing. Even his vest appeared to have a six pack. Today he was wearing a tight, black vest, black combat trousers, along with steel capped Doc Martins, coupled with his gold earring in his left ear. He was just as I had remembered him at school – a hard man. He was the very anthisis of serenity and placidity. A walking disaster movie with a destructive and belligerent temperament. It seemed from early impressions that he had not changed one iota. I was now afraid, very afraid. I mean he was the kind of guy who would give Michael Myers from Halloween nightmares.

'Oi kidaa Kam saab.' He pulled his chuddies out from the crack of his arse cheeks with his hand, yawned and massaged his crotch for a few seconds.

I looked on and nodded my head. 'Hello bruv.' My voice full of rejection and disappointment.

He turned to Dev and gave him a friendly but powerful punch in the chest as he focused back on me. He thrust his spade like hand out crushing my bones as his vice like grip squeezed my hand. 'Thought I wouldn't come to my mates wedding ey?' He squeezed my hand harder. especially since you didn't invite me, bhanchod.' His antagonism obviously fed viciously by erstwhile grievances ingrained in his memory bank from the years I set out to avoid his phone calls and duck any school reunions, knowing full well that he would be there. 'So, I haven't seen you in donkey's years Kamster where you been hibernating then son?' Ranj said looking at me quizzically and suddenly letting go of my crushed, limp hand.

I flexed my fingers to get the feeling back in them. I then took a few moments to brace myself and opted for the friendly and non confrontational approach to calm the fire crackling in this situation. 'I like your tattoo Ranj, when did you get it done?' I enquired. It worked as I threw him for a second 'Ahh, a few years back, it has come out well.' He slapped his Popeye like left arm with his right hand in self adulation of his bodily artwork. One of my smaller cousins Sundip walked past us towards the house when Ranj, distracted, turned to him grabbing him by the arm 'go and get me a beer and hurry!' His face twisted, and meeting little resistance from twelve year old Sundip who scurried off on his mission without quibble. I looked at Dev, what was this guy even doing here? I felt as sick as a parrot. In the background the dad's had been studying Ranj's every move assessing whether he was friend or foe, and were only now beginning to settle back into their seats as they could see me seemingly chatting to him without quibble. 'Kam saab - who is that bhanchod over there staring at me with the caterpillar eyebrows?' I looked at him incredulously, was he taking the royal piss out of me 'That's my dad man!'

'Nah way, kuta, he looks well different, flipping hell, his brows look fierce...no offence, damn, he's changed from when I remember him.' He laughed to himself and shook his head in incredulity. Everyone knows a Ranj, a mate who hangs around with them, someone who is always getting into trouble. A loose cannon who is waiting to land you in a big puddle of shit when you just don't have the shoes for it, and now he was attending my wedding. He was an unwelcome guest, a bad smell. Wherever he went, trouble was not far behind. I knew this from school. He was suspended no fewer than six times, all for fighting and swearing at goray in Punjabi. This was bad!

In a way, I was relieved that pip squeak had crawled back under his stone and wisely decided against doing the tango with Ranj. I remembered only too well some of the dust ups he used to have as we were growing up. The man was a pugilistic genius, indomitably fearless and even as a youngster would outfox local skinheads with his fast hands and fast feet. He relished violence, any kind, any type of blood spilling would satiate this beast. In the midst of battle, I recalled how he would actually enjoy the sickening crunches of bones breaking and ligaments tearing. He had never been a soldier of self control or restraint and with his inherited ox like and herculean strength; he wore his badge of terror with mischievous pride. My little cousin Sundip returned with a can of Fosters and dutifully handed it over to the bully.

Ranj cracked the can open and gulped down the entire contents within ten seconds squeezing the can in his hand and burping as the coup de gras. He burped again this time in my face covering me with the combined stench of cigarettes, halitosis and Fosters. He looked inside and saw one of my female cousins from the Midlands serving food to some of the mums, his eyes widened in perverted glee. 'Oi oi who is she then?' He tapped me in the stomach with his hand 'cor...I would play her like a Punjabi dholak, she would definitely, one hundred per cent get the three P's...'

'Hey, the three what?' Dev mumbled, his curiosity got the better of him for a split second.

'PURE – PUNJABI – PASSION!' Ranj's eyes lit up like a Christmas tree as his irritating cackle reverberated around the garden. Even at school, he had always had a sexual appetite like a raging hormonal forest fire and with the self confessed nickname of Whiskas: as he would put it so succinctly – because nine out of ten pussies preferred him. It seemed he was still very much the sex addict and with a keen eye for the ladies.

'Look mate that is my cousin, leave it out alright.' I put him straight. He was now crossing the line and my blood was boiling. 'No sweat Kamster saab, don't get your knickers in a twist, just playing mate that's all, this is just friendly fire.'

He picked some peanuts off the garden table and chomped on them as he muttered 'so anyhow who is the ugly, half blind, sado masochistic weirdo who has decided to marry you?' He served me a mocking and unfriendly look that unnerved me.

I reciprocated and looked him in the eyes, and then quickly tried to change the subject. 'What was all that about?' I pointed back to where the altercation had taken place with pip squeak.

'Ahhh, the usual, a Vauxhall Conference side trying to fight a Premiership outfit, same shit son, just a different toilet, anyway who is the unlucky girl then you Kuta?'

My futile attempt to change the subject was shot down in flames. He was no greenhorn, exceedingly clever and not one to forget his line of questioning and train of thought. He searched my face for an answer to his question.

'You won't know her.' I said quickly, hoping he hadn't heard and trying to move on swiftly to another topic of conversation. 'What's her name?' Ranj crunched another peanut in his mouth whilst keeping his eyes firmly on me, he just would not let it go, the tenacity of a Pitball Terrier...why was he grilling me so much?

'Err...it is ....Kiran.' I said reluctantly, bitterly trying to deter him in any way I could. He stopped, his eyes widened and he smiled. He threw a peanut up in the air and caught it flush in his mouth, crunching it with satisfying glee. I noticed a change in his breathing. A suspecting shadow fell across his face. He knew something 'well, well, well, Kiran ey' he smirked. 'Yeh I think I know her, where's she from again?'

I gritted my teeth 'she is from Luton, you wont know her trust me.'

He stopped eating the peanuts and looked at me with his mouth wide open, 'go away, Kiran from Luton...no shit I went to uni with Kiran, yeh.'

He looked up as though deep in thought, while twirling a peanut between his forefinger and thumb 'bruv we used to go out at Uni, she was fit if you know what I mean.'

Dev chipped in 'look Ranj don't talk about her like that show some respect, she is not that kind of girl.' Ranj stared at him 'who rattled your cage? Dev looked away, mouth closed and just as worried and scared as I was. The tension in the air was tangible as we all looked at each other. The seconds ticked treacherously. I knew my dream was too good to be true. As I thought the worse, thankfully the silence was finally broken...

'Aaaa got ya, just kidding man, nah never heard of her.' He snorted loudly, sucking up phlegm violently from his nose into his mouth and then without hesitation spat it out onto the large floor standing pot plant standing innocently at the end of the patio, a distinct mark of disrespect and barbaric behaviour. He continued 'but I still reckon she has got a guide dog or something marrying a sorry arsed wetback and kuta like you.' They say the human body can absorb great pain, perform amazing feats and handle tremendous stresses. Right now, it was a culmination of these magnificent traits and attributes that prevented me from losing the plot with this nemesis of mine. This unwelcome guest. Patience, fortitude, machismo and tolerance, were amongst the pillars of strength that I needed to draw upon to extricate myself from my personal dystopia, the evil that had descended from the very squalors of hell to test me. Ranj then walked off and introduced himself to the other guests including my other friends. I could see most guests moving away as he approached and avoiding him like the bubonic plague. I too tried my hardest to keep my distance from him for the remainder of the evening. It would be hard, but essential to prevent any kind of scene from ruining the festivities, my sacrosanct occasion.

CHAPTER 13

— ⁓ —

Bop to the beat

The camera man had also arrived by now and was busy setting up along with his son, who was his right hand operator. He took a few moments to set up and then began filming anything that moved within a one inch radar of his lens. There was an air of excitement bubbling as some of the ladies were getting the props ready for the first traditional dance of the night before party. It was called *'jaggo'* - which means to wake the neighbourhood up to come to the wedding.

This dance is performed mainly by the ladies on the night before the wedding and is where the brides relatives dress up and literally shout *'get up'* to the town folk as they dance carefree through the village streets carrying pots called *gaggars or gaffers* on their heads. These pots would be decorated with candles and the actual jaggo songs were often meant as a bit of light hearted banter aimed predominantly at the elder generation. mum and a couple of aunties were on one side of the living room, as two or three other aunties were on the other side walking into the room from the hallway with the candle lit gaggars held carefully on their heads by steady hands. It is traditional for the *mammi (mum's brothers wife)* to instigate proceedings in the jaggo. In this case, it was the bumbling and cumbersome Gach-walpreet who had one of the pots on her head as she stumbled and fumbled her way into the room with all the grace of a dead bird falling from the sky. Auntie Balvir was meanwhile leading from the front holding a long stick with makeshift bells on them. The person in this role back in the homeland would traditionally lead the jaggo ladies through the village streets knocking on the doors, announcing the impending marriage. The traditional *'jaggo aaye'* Punjabi song crackled into life from the speakers. Everyone cheered and started clapping as the staged bride's side *(i.e. the pot carriers)* entered the *village' (the living room)* to wake up the *'villagers' (mum and the remainder of the forty or so guests)*.

The *'jaggo'* ladies danced around in a circle passing the pots to other aunties who fancied trying their juggling skills with the *'gaggars.'* After twenty minutes or so of *'jaggo'* enactment most of the aunties had stains on their suits or chunni's from where the *'gaggars'* had been tilted in the merriment allowing the candle wax to fall. The camera man continued to sadistically capture all the dancing and events as they unfolded, including the looks of complete dejection and horror as the wax unsympathetically stained their finest sequinned suits. In the other corner of the room there was a cue of guests having *mehndi* applied to their hands by Karina who was my mum's friend. She owned a beauty salon and in her spare time would charge a few bucks to come and apply mehndi at wedding parties. Mehndi is the art of adorning the feet and hands with a paste made from the finely ground leaves of the henna plant. The henna leaves are firstly ground, and the paste and powder can then be weaved into wonderful designs accentuating the wearers beauty ten fold. It is believed that henna and mehndi have been used cosmetically for thousands of years, and by all races. The mehndi would normally take a short while to dry and in-between the time from applying it to the pattern drying, all hands and feet with mehndi applied would be kept sterile and out of the way to prevent accidental smudging. The girls were walking about with their mehndi hands held aloft, above their heads and safe from violation.

Once the '*jaggo*' had concluded and everyone was resembling a Madame Tussauds waxwork figure, the ladies started the '*gidda*' which is a buoyant and energetic dance. At first the women gathered around in the centre of the living room all clapping and walking around conservatively in a circle, occasionally shuffling the feet back and forth without exerting too much effort. The older aunties started to sing boli's to each other, which translate as the Asian version of a rapping competition where the '*boli Mc's*' set out to curse each other with point scoring digs about bad teeth, dress sense and body odour. It was a kind of folk poetry but with a point scoring edge to it. If you were a greenhorn in boli cursing then you would get eaten alive by the true aficionado's of this sport. So it was best to stay out of the ring on such occasions.

As the aunties exchanged boli's (or known as boliyan) two of them, both on my dad's side, both darker skinned, dusky little numbers and each possessing a juicy throat cutting plat, swaying viciously from side to side, circled each other. They suddenly started hissing and puffing with their mouths, staring into the whites of one another's eyes, whilst the other guests clapped faster. As the hissing and puffing got louder the two of them lunged forward in dramatic fashion to meet in the middle of the circle tilting their heads from side to side and clapping furiously as though their lives depended on having the loudest hiss and claps. The rhythm and crescendo of the gidda and boli is distinguished from the hand clapping from the performers and these two warriors were certainly in character. They maneuvered around each other in sinister fashion still clapping, still hissing loudly, increasing the tempo and speed of the circling and hissing, but also making a strange '*wuuuu wuuuu, wuuuu*' sound with the accompanying chorus of '*wuuuu wuuuu wuuuu*' coming from the circle around them as well. Even the men had gathered in the room as everyone looked on laughing and drinking from their cups. The two of them, the dusky pair, then hugged after they had finished burning each other out on the dance floor, and we all clapped showing our appreciation for their sweaty, plat swaying efforts.

The evening was going well apart from the slight hitch with the arrival of Ranj earlier. I took a few moments and pondered how Kiran's night before was going over in Luton, she must have looked beautiful and I was excited to see her in the morning. I continued to drink and absorb the magical atmosphere of the party. A couple of the younger and fitter girls then clasped hands diagonally in the middle of the circle and performed the traditional '*kikli dance.*' This dance is generally performed by women in pairs where they cross their arms, hold each other's hands and whirl around singing folk songs. On this occasion the two cousins were not singing to each other but just spinning around at break neck speed whilst hanging on for dear life. It was like a white knuckle ride on the dance floor and again not for the weak willed. Some of the dad's had now also started to dance on the other side of the living room with slow steps in and out of the circle they were creating. They were tanked up on copious amounts of whisky and meat and were now in the mood to P – A – R – T – Y.

My dad was at the forefront and was dragging up everyone from Sharm to my eighty seven year old grandpa who was carrying around a dialysis bag strapped to his leg. He was getting carried away with the electric atmosphere and it was good to see him in such high spirits. Sharm was naturally jiving away to the bhangra music with the old time classic dance moves such as dancing with a bottle of Bacardi on his head whilst spinning slowly in a circle accompanied by shouts from the rest of the guys of '*hoi hoi*.' Bhangra dancing celebrates the harvest and is associated with the festival of Baisakhi in April when the mere sight of fields of golden wheat fill the farmer's heart with intense happiness. The farmers would be jumping and leaping around the fields with other villagers to the haunting and magical sounds of the dhols. Bhangra is now so famous that it doesn't matter who you are, it is performed everywhere from marriages, parties and any kind of celebration. Just the slight sound of a catchy bhangra track or a couple of beats of the dhol and you will have people tapping their feet, and men raising their arms in the air and passionately dancing to their hearts content.

The bhangra domino effect is superb in that you will see even the most reluctant person eventually succumb to the power of the beat as others around them get up to join the revelry. It is thought bhangra has been in existence as long as five hundred BC and it continues to fill hearts with joy around the world, as it was in my living room tonight. Inevitably I was dragged into the circle of guys by dad and immediately got stuck in with my bhangra footsteps and twirls. It was a great moment as everyone was now dancing in their own groups and letting their hair down in majestic fashion. We continued to dance to classic bhangra tunes without a care in the world, when I noticed Ranj drift onto the dance floor from the conservatory where he had been speaking to one of the uncles. On seeing him I tried to shift around to the other side of the room and hide behind the two dusky aunties who were still jiving crazily like a couple of X Factor wannabes. No such luck, he came towards me with his arms raised and jumping in tune to the bhangra music, his gold tooth glistening under the lounge chandelier. He then danced in front of me for a few moments as I swayed my body from side to side in a bid to placate him, entertain him.

After a second or two had passed without incident, I was satisfied that my subterfuge had worked like a treat, so I turned to escape Steve McQueen style, but before I knew it, the shadow of his massive grasping paw came hurtling over my head, descending over me like the shadow of a guillotine. He grabbed me tightly in a rear neck hold and dragged me backwards to him. He continued to tussle with me for a couple of seconds. I did not offer much resistance, I don't know why? I guess I was petrified that he might cause a scene, ending with my epitaph being read out tomorrow instead of my wedding vows. I played it cool, as cool as I could. He then released the sleeper hold and ushered me to one side of the room away from the blaring speakers and put his arm around my shoulder 'you said that you would keep in touch when we left school, and you lied, you lied didn't you?' He hissed drunkenly, his words slurring as he spoke and breathed over me. I could smell the remnants of at least four cans of fosters along with the anaconda like grip of peanuts, crisps and tandoori chicken coming from his breath and gripping my throat as he continued to pour over me. He squeezed me even tighter to his body with his arm firmly around both shoulders. I felt his brutish strength crushing my ribs as I struggled to breathe. 'Kam saab, I am going to make this Wedding memorable for you don't worry.' He said, snorting menacingly 'you will NEVER forget this day for as long as you live, that is a promise.' Ranj let go of me abruptly, he was evil, vindictive, and vengeful: He would have made a good Bond villain. He then walked off towards the garden in search of his next victim to terrorise, leaving me demoralised and shocked from hearing his jaundiced remarks. He had threatened me a night before the wedding! What was his god damn problem? He was nothing more than a thug, a complete waste of skin and sinew, and a walking, threatening disaster movie.

I knocked back my Bacardi and coke and quickly went upstairs to my room for five minutes time out, angry and frustrated; I just needed some space for a few moments. I locked the bedroom door and pulled back the carpet directly underneath the bed. I knew exactly what I was looking for and where it was carefully ensconced. Once the carpet was removed, I rummaged around with my hand and after a moment or two of sporadic fumbling, I found it, the Holy Grail. It was my *'last break glass for emergency'* bag of cocaine that I had always kept ensconced in my secret hiding place. I don't know why, I just did…It was one of the earlier bags that I had bought from Spanish. I held the bag in my hand and prodded the contents as I sat on the edge of the bed, pensive and unsure what I was doing? Tears streamed down my face as I gently threw the bag up and down in my hand. I resisted the urge to go to the dark side as I held the bag firm in my hand. This was not quite the diversion I had been hoping for to ease my troubles after the last few days, but right now, I was tempted, very, very tempted. All of a sudden there was a loud thumping knock on the door and I panicked. I did not have time to put it back under the carpet. Should I throw the bag across the room: No, bad idea! mum may discover it again, and that would be suicidal.

I scanned the room, my eyes like Action Man. My wedding suit jacket was hung up on the cupboard so I furtively slipped the bag in the inside coat pocket making a mental note to retrieve it later and put it back where it belonged under the carpet and out of sight. I opened the door and it was Dev 'what you doing bruv, I saw you going upstairs?' I smiled 'nothing really I just had to sort something out that's all, but its done now.' He looked at me closely 'you been crying?' I shoved him in the chest 'don't be a girl, cause not, now lets go hit this party hard.' We both went downstairs and continued to groove to the tracks with my relatives. Ranj was thankfully nowhere to be seen, maybe he had left? After all, he was punch drunk when he threatened me.

At around midnight the guests started to leave and I stood by the door shaking the guy's hands and hugging the women. I would see them all in a few hours in any case. Suddenly I saw the hulking figure of Ranj ambling behind some of the other guests. He was plodding past casually with his hands in his pockets, head down and looking jaded. His dark clothes, knuckle scraping shuffle and abstracted air creating an eerie atmosphere of somberness. He was walking out of the door disconsolate and lamentable: It appeared that the evening had taken its toll on him. Then unexpectedly he stopped and lunged forward grabbing me by my lapels mimicking a fake head butt, stopping inches before my nose and shouting 'I will see you Jimmy.' before laughing uproariously.

I felt impuissant, my stomach clenched and knotted for a second. I then felt my pent up anger building and rising close to boiling point as he held on to me, embarrassing me in my own house. He then let go of my lapels and playfully punched me in the stomach as he walked out of the door. The traumatic ordeal was all but over. I saw him blowing a kiss at my cousin Prity as she was getting into her car with her family. She returned the compliment by rolling her eyes and tutting loudly as she got in her car and escaped this animal. The devil had left the house. I shook my head and continued to say my valedictories to the other more respectful guests, all the time with a continuing and gnawing feeling of sickness tightly knotted in my stomach.

I walked back in and could see another incident threatening to spill over. Mum was grappling with Sharm. They were in the kitchen and were tussling over a set of car keys that Sharm was holding. Dad and Satwinder were also on the peripheries jostling for all their monies worth as well. The situation was transparent and was a usual occurrence whereby after consuming one or eight sherbets too many Sharm would invariably end up getting embroiled in a meaningless fist fight with someone over his insistence on driving home when he was always smashed out of his skull on booze. He would be having one for the road shots for the last three hours before he would try to embark on his journey home. I would often rebuke him as respectfully as I could and would hanker on to him how drinking and driving was dangerous and how he could end up seriously hurting someone through his ignorance or even killing someone including himself. On this occasion mum managed to man handle the car keys off of him and dad called him a minicab much to everyone's relief. We all retired to our respective beds apart from mum who seemed to have Duracell bunny type energy as she continued to beaver away getting last minute preparations for the Punjabi wedding of the year in order. Meanwhile I hit the proverbial sack and waited excitedly for the biggest day of my life. It was going to be memorable...

Chapter 14

A gathering

Finally the big day was here and I had made it un-scathed, well just about. I woke up looking and feeling like a living, breathing wide eyed zombie, the effects of only a few hours of decent kip had taken its toll on my weary frame.

Today was all about the ethnic weaving of two families, of our two souls and our individual fates and destinies, of love, honour, time and eternity. Our Indian marriage was an institution in itself, an indulgent world of traditional opulence, a loving union of me and Kiran, two lovers, symbolizing the giving and receiving of our love and commitment for each other throughout our entire married life. Your wedding day is the most important day in your life and it is every bride and groom's right to look the very best they can and I was not about to make an exception on mine. So I donned the classic cream coloured 'kurta pyjama' or 'veshti / dhoti' as it is known. This is a traditional Indian suit worn on such occasions of celebration. I also wore a pair of brown and traditional red sequined 'moojay' *(curled up shoes)* that compliment the attire so majestically.

Dad had spent an hour or so in the morning assembling my red *'bhugari' (turban)* that I was going to adorn throughout the ceremony. I sat in my bedroom, derriere in chair, as dad weaved the turban around my head and ensured that it fitted snugly. I proudly examined myself in the bedroom mirror and was fully content. I looked traditional and powerful as I stuck my chest out whilst stroking my forest like beard. Kiran would be enthralled at my transmogrification.

Eight fifteen in the morning, and a few minutes left to spruce my self up before we set off to the gurdwara. I followed dad down the stairs trying not to fall and break my neck by getting tangled in the curls of my moojay. I walked into the living room to rapturous clapping and cheering from the hordes of bleary eyed relatives and friends who had been waiting patiently for me sipping cups of *'chaa'* and eating samosas. I said my salutations to everyone. All the great characters from my side were their and I was pleased. There were uncles, aunties, mamas, mammies, massies, massers, chachas, chachia, nephews, nieces, pet gerbils – they were all there, resplendent and with bells on.

This was a great start I thought as I sat on the chair in the center of the living room in readiness for the *sehrabandhi ceremony.* Sitting next to me was my little cousin Joshua. He was eight years old and was my *sarvalla / sarballa (technical best man and meaning caretaker of the groom)* Kind of like your best mate when you are out on the razzle in town and you get pissed. Your best mate becomes a type of 'sarvalla' and scoops you out of your own pile of sick in the gutter and takes you home. His part was simple; he was to follow me around like a heat seeking missile for the first part of the day in his apprentice like role whilst picking up experience for the future when it would be his turn. Joshua was cool, and like any spirited sarvalla kept his head down and mouth closed whilst the oldies got on with their duties. Infact, truth be told, I did not even notice his presence through-out the day partly because he was about the size of Tom Thumb and very unassuming – just like any sarvalla worth their salt should be.

My grandma then tied a veil of flowers to my turban following the time held tradition of warding away the evil eye by screening my face with the flowers. Mum then applied some *surma (black eye liner)* to my eyes again and gave me some money. She used the surma pencil to put a black dot behind my ear to ward away any evil spirits who would be lurking with intent at the wedding ceremony and reception. It was like these spirits had nothing better to do then hang around aimlessly at func-tions waiting to snare the first victim they stumbled across without a black dot behind their ear. Once this was completed, I was given money and some *ludoos* by the guests. The money was tightly held in my *pulla (my red scarf)* and wrapped up in my hands to prevent any money dropping out. I clung onto to this scarf for dear life and it would take a national disaster to loosen my grip on it, that was a certainty. I looked around, excited and ebullient. Everyone is driven by notions of perfec-tion, of refinement and sublimity and this was rapidly becoming my PERFECT DAY!

Whilst the sehra ceremony was being performed the guests (boy's side) were all preparing for the journey to the girls side in Luton and I could see that they were all impeccably dressed in sharp suits and couture. The guys had all manner of suits on from two piece, three piece to

Miami Vice style jackets with wide collared shirts, all with the accompanying red rose pinned to the lapel of their suits, a traditional wedding gesture. The women on the other hand looked drop dead stunning, sexy and abundantly resplendent in their ensemble, the latest saris, suits, salwar kameez being worn expertly. Beautifully applied make up, sexy hairstyles and perfectly manicured nails, they looked scrumptious. The sari is a cloth which is wrapped around the body, either secured by pins or tucked neatly into the waistband. The salwar kameez is a long tunic worn over tightly fitting pants. It is worn with an accompanying duppatta as well. All in all we all looked mouth wateringly dapper and we all knew it. What a good looking family!

The two coaches pulled up outside the house and everyone started to get ready and make their way onto it. At the same time our white stretch limousine was parked across the street with the driver – the Greek Georgio, propped up against the bonnet complete with flat cap and a well turned out uniform. The limo was reserved exclusively for the immediate family of the groom and the order of play had already been arranged by mum and dad in the days leading up to it. The passengers were mum, dad, Sharm, Satwinder, grandma, grandpa, auntie Blossom, uncle Jarnail from Slough, little Joshua my sarvalla, dashing Dev and last but not least, me in all my glory.

In the truest traditional sense the boy's side are called the bhaarat and it is the bhaarat that gets to make the trip to the girls town whether the marriage is taking place here or back in the motherland. The bharat normally arrives at the girl's house amid dancing, singing and music. (Nowadays with time constraints for halls,

DJ's etc it is usually the gurdwara which becomes the official rendezvous point).

The coaches quickly stacked up with the jaded guests as the camera man followed them around with lines of long wires strewn across the garden path leading to the electrical supply from our house. I could hear unappreciative moans from some of my relatives as the cameraman felt compelled to zoom in on their faces with his camera, a cardinal sin at this time in the morning especially as half of the men were still nursing heavy hangovers from the shenanigans from the night before. The house was then locked up and the remainder of us took our positions in the limo as Georgia carefully pulled away from the kerb and headed off on our journey. Sharm was in fine fettle as he cracked Punjabi joke after Punjabi joke resulting in side splitting laughter from all of us. He was a great guy to have on board and as the jester of the pack knew how to ease tensions and lift the soul. Dad was sat there proud as punch as he continually teased mum about stuff. It was nice to see that despite many years of marital bliss that they had this unique and unparalled understanding and connection. It was what I wanted and knew that I would be the same with my wife, relaxed, open minded and humorous.

Mum fiddled with my sehra as she probed the cool exterior given off by my mirror calm surface. 'Kidda putt (son) are you nervous?'

I shook my head 'nah mum, I'm okay, just excited, I just hope she turns up?'

I laughed as the reality of being stood up suddenly became a choking possibility. This was enough to jolt my imagination as my mind raced for a second. What if she changed her mind after some of the rows that we had in the weeks leading up to the day? My mind began toying with me as my emotions swirled around inside me with the nagging doubts that this would certainly be a memorable day but for the wrong reasons. I had heard the wedding horror stories from over the years, the one about the girl who had a situation when her lehnga had fallen down in the reception exposing herself to the six hundred or so sniggering guests, or the one about the groom who was caught kissing the best girl in the back stage room at another wedding.

Thoughts of my wedding going down in the annals of history as the one where the groom was stood up were now pushed to one side as I looked out of the window and calmed my mind.

The coach drivers followed behind as we made our way at a leisurely pace up the M4, then M25 and briefly the M1 before arriving at the prestigious Luton gurdwara. There was a short wait before I got out of the limo with the rest of the family and I could see all of the bhaarat on one side of the car park outside the gurdwara, all with their heads covered out of respect for the customs when visiting the temple. On the other side were about three hundred folk from the girls side, all spread out and forming a crescent. It was like the biggest *kabaddi* tournament ever. There were some smart looking people from the girl's side with the guys donning sunglasses, sporting gold earrings – yes I said the guys - this was a fashion statement. They were all wearing some kind of head covering too. The women were looking divine and the very embodiment of grace and suaveness as they all stood to attention as well with their heads covered by chunni's. I got out of the limo and made my way to the centre of my side where I was greeted by the religious *giani (religious follower)* who worked at the gurdwara. He briefly explained the rules of engagement to dad and I as we braced ourselves for the ensuing *milni ceremony* that was about to take place. (milni basically meaning 'introductions').

The milni ceremony is where the bride's close male relatives give a warm and hospitable welcome to the groom's side following on from a religious Sikh prayer *'ardas'* from the giani. They normally give gifts including flower garlands, money and jewellery, and in some cases duvets and pillows. This is again called giving *shagun*. Whilst this was being arranged and prayers were being cited by the giani I noticed a black BMW Convertible pulling up outside the gurdwara. The driver got out of the vehicle, an Asian chap, around thirty years old, sporting an unruly shock of black hair and dressed in a smartly cut, black, Armani suit. He took his sunglasses off and folded them into his pocket before locking the car by depressing his key fob whilst aiming at the car. The bleep of the car alarm made everyone look at him as he swaggered over to my direction. I did not recognize him and whispered to Dev who was standing next to me 'who is that twat?' Dev looked baffled and replied 'don't know, looks a bit full of himself doesn't he? You would think he is getting married?' The guy then continued to swagger over to my side I could see him from the corner of my eye slowly snaking his way to the front of the pack to behind where I was standing. I ignored his presence whoever he was and instead got down to enjoying the milni ceremony. The order of play for the milni was ratified and the elder members started proceedings as they set off to have the first meet with their opposite numbers. The time old classic caper is to try hoist the other person up in the air after you have exchanged garlands and gifts. It is usually the fastest gunslinger that gets to have that accolade. This then leads to cheers and laughter from everyone as the conquering Roman general walks back triumphantly with his arms aloft to his legion of soldiers arranged behind him. One by one grandpa, dad, Sharm and others all went up to perform the honouary ritual. The best moment was when the quiet and non descript Joshua had a duel with his counterpart, Satnam, one of Kiran's cousins. After exchanging garlands Joshua went to pick Satnam up following instructions impeccably from Sharm, but he had misjudged his quarries obvious corpulence and ended up falling to the floor on top of Satnam much to the laughter of both crowds.

However more importantly he had won that duel with his attempt at picking him up and the groom's side was already up on the day - six points to three, in the picking up stakes. A decisive victory, as we all headed into the langar hall within the gurdwara to have houres d'ouvres before the wedding ceremony.

I turned to walk to the hall which was behind where I was standing when the black suited BMW guy crossed my path and '*accidentally*' barged into me causing me to stumble a step back. He done this innocuously and no-one else batted an eyelid as they carried on walking in. He remained stood in front of me for some reason and was just giving me a hard stare. I looked away and tried to move past him towards the direction of the others. He stepped in front of me again and hindered my access.

'Congratulations Kam.' He leaned in closer, patting my chest several times with the back of his right hand. 'You and me need to talk.' He looked me in the eyes.

There was something baneful about this guy, I could sense it. His look was menacing and I could see he meant it. Who the hell was this joker? I couldn't understand where he was coming from as I asked inquisitively 'sorry who are you?'

He looked to the floor momentarily and then fixed his gaze back at me 'who am I? You mean Kiran hasn't talked about me?'

My jaw dropped as realization dawned upon me, the BMW guy at my wedding, mingling with my family and friends and with access to firearms was...

'Listen MATE, I'm Jags and you had best make time to talk or you will be sorry, trust me on that.'

I had never seen a picture of Kiran's ex but had heard enough stories that kept me awake at night and here I was exchanging words with him before my wedding ceremony and well and truly gripped in the tentacles of fear.

I had heard that Jags was a guy who operated on two basic levels – kill and maim. He was a one shot, one kill kind of reprehensible individual, a pure manifestation of evil and criminality. He was too well connected for me to rebuff his suggestion and my pangs of despair were threatening to drown me in this sea of fear. It seemed to me that even the vignettes of jail were not enough to deter this grenade like and ticking time bomb.

The situation was unfolding fast in front of my eyes as my guts twisted, but thankfully on this occasion found its own natural conclusion as dad came running over with timely precision shouting 'come on son, we are running late, have some food before we start.' He took hold of my arm and gently yanked me forward as we set off into the langar hall leaving Jags looking expressionless with his hands in his trouser pockets. I looked back over my shoulder and could see him slowly following me into the hall.

We walked into the langar hall and filled in the empty spaces by the long white clothed tables. I could see such culinary wonders as samosas, pakooray, jalebees, barfis, rass malai to name but a few, delightfully laid out for us to devour. It was a true gastronome's paradise as we all tucked in heartily and with savoring aplomb.

My body was fuelled with adrenaline as I looked around the room anxiously looking for my nemesis.

I slipped two samosas, a jaleebi and some chutney sauce on my plate and nervously chomped away, being extremely careful not to stain my cream jacket and really top my day off in grandeur style. Dev was stood to one side with my sarvalla on the other side. We all continued to eat the sumptuous food and sip our tea, when I turned to look at Joshua the pee wee sarvalla, I saw him being yanked back forcibly by a huge hand which had firmly gripped him by the shoulder.

The samosa he was eating went flying in the air and was caught by the other hand of the perpetrator that had pulled Joshua back. The subject stood next to me and heartily ate the samosa as they nudged me hard with their elbow. It was the walking calamity Ranj, the sneering husk of a man. 'I've just been checking out some of the chicks here, bhanchod they are phat, I went over to one and said, kidda sweetie you had better get it then.' He took another bite of the samosa and continued 'she goes, I had better get what? I said your chunni sweetie cos you've pulled.' Ranj erupted in laughter, meanwhile the cameraman had captured this anecdote on film as he was walking around the hall and I could see him stifling his laugh.

I scrutinised the side profile of Ranj and realized at this moment that there was a good reason why I had made a conscious decision to lose touch with him from our school days. It just seemed that everything about this fellow was infantile. His ramblings continued while I searched the room for any signs of Jags, but I was unable to locate him. 'I tell you what Dev.' He reached across me and tapped Dev with the back of his hand, narrowly missing my cream top with the heavily chutney laced samosa that he was holding as he done so.

'Here listen, the women here are fit, one thing is for certain and that is I will end up with a sapno ki rani in-between the sheets tonight, it will either be that bird there.' He pointed to a good looking girl wearing a green suit from Kiran's side two tables across from where we were standing. 'Or if it is not her it will be, what's her name? Oh yeh Tina. She is hot, but failing all that my back burner is of course the lovely bride.' He winked at Dev and then snorted as he threw the remains of the samosa into his mouth and masticated. I looked away in disgust. The guy was a thorn in my side, an unwelcome and raffish bully.

'Hey, hello.' Ranj had caught an unsuspecting prey in his radar. He had just caught a glimpse of Dimple one of Kiran's friends, five foot four inches, slim, fair complexion and stunningly attractive. She was twenty five years old and a corker. Ranj was mesmerized 'kuta, does my tongue want to say hello to yours or what?'

He nudged me in the ribs. I took a deep breath and tightly clenched the napkin I was holding trying to keep a tight lid on my anger as it threatened to boil over. I refused to stoop to the level of the village idiot and get embroiled in a meaningless fight so I counted to ten and put on my best fake smile as the photographer snapped away in David Bailey fashion in front of me.

Ranj then walked off outside the hall for a few moments to answer a call on his mobile phone and I was not in a hurry to stop him. I caught him winking at Dimple as he walked out and surprisingly she reciprocated.

I turned to Dev and said disconsolately 'that bloke is a walking disaster, a complete waste of skin and sinew, what is he even doing here?' My hopes of an incident free wedding were increasingly being squashed like a bug as Dev cut in;

'Do you think he is going to cause trouble?'

'Well how is it looking to you Einstein?'

'Yeah I suppose, do you want me to try and get rid of him for you?'

'Mate you are a good bloke and all that but how, just how are you going to do that, he's here isn't he?'

'I don't know, I was just trying to help and all that?'

'Well I am not being funny if you do persuade him to leave, I will give you a cookie and a flaming rub down, hey what the fuck I will even throw in a frigging foot massage you crazy fool.'

'Nice one.'

'Bruv it is all going wrong, did you know as well as Ranj that Kiran's ex is here, he was showing his teeth outside?'

Dev looked stunned.

'Yeh he just threatened me outside that if I don't go and see him I will be in trouble or something, outside in the flipping milni.'

Dev whispered 'let me find out what he wants, this wedding is becoming a disaster what with him turning up and Ranj acting like a wetback, you okay, how you feeling?'

I could see claret in the tea leaves and I just wanted to run for the hills such was my feeling. I quickly pushed the thoughts out of my head and said 'look just watch my back, make sure Ranj doesn't get drunk and try it on with Kiran or I will fight him, I promise, nobody will do that to my wife, she is mine. You are the one person I can rely on, if you see Ranj or Jags coming give me some warning and that way I am prepared, yeh.' My voice was beginning to crack as I laid my instructions out clearly for my brethren to follow. Dev concurred and we turned back to the table and sipped our cups of chaa.

After we had all finished eating, Sharm came over to me and quickly ran over the wedding ceremony instructions once more to ensure they were suitably ingrained within my head. He was talking, but I was not listening as my mind was preoccupied with the presence of Jags. I had so many questions and not enough time to answer them all. What was he doing here? Sharm snapped 'are you listening?' I nodded in agreement to the instructions he had recited to me.

I then took my shoes off in the cloakroom and we all walked into the gurdwara hall whilst I continually looked over my shoulder. In the distance I could see Ranj harassing another female victim with his extroverted and annoying mannerisms. I just had to make it until the end of the day and then everything would be fine.

CHAPTER 15

—ᨦ—

'Knot' so fast

We all made our way into the gurdwara. This was a splendid big bricked building, ostentatiously built and casting an impressive and imposing figure on the land-scape, all augmented with a divine charm and elegance. There was a huge statue of Guru Gobind Singh (the tenth guru) positioned on his horse on top of the roof of the building and overlooking the car park in grandiose and majestic style lending an air of refined elegance and thought provoking splendour to the occasion.

Inside the guys all sat on the right hand side of the hall, whilst the women all sat on the left side, this was a traditional ritual seen around gurdwara everywhere. Everyone within the gurdwara were meticulously observing the rudimentary traditions and respectfully adhering to the protocol once inside, all heads covered with a chunni for the women or handkerchief, turban for the guys. On top of this nobody was sitting with their feet pointing directly towards the holy book as this is an automatic sign of disrespect and tantamount to treason, all legs were crossed or pointing backwards and tucked under the body. Then, for the infirm, disabled or otherwise injured, they were permitted to lean against the wall and point their legs to the sidewall, but never to the front where the holy book is positioned.

The kids meanwhile sat with either mum's or dad's whilst one or two from the school of bratz just ran amok at the back of the gurdwara whilst their dads grappled with them in futile attempts to tame their pestiferous behaviour. I walked to the front of the gurdwara directly in front of the *Guru Granth Sahib* and kneeled down to say my prayer and give thanks to my god, my forehead touching the floor out of respect. The Guru Granth Sahib is the holy book and main scripture of the Sikh religion as the Bible is for Christianity, the Koran for Islam and the Vedas, the Upanisads and the Ramayana amongst other scriptures for Hinduism.

I then sat down and waited for the arrival of my gorgeous bride. The gurdwara was by now full to the brim with all the guests from both the girls and boys side, and we all waited for the arrival of Kiran. The snarling dogs of self doubt were snapping ferociously telling me that she had stood me up, got cold feet, pulled the plug on me, and truth be told I was beginning to believe them.

All of a sudden there was excited whisper amongst the cross legged guests. I looked across at mum and saw her smiling and looking towards the back of the hall where the entrance was located. My heart fluttered for a second, my skittish thoughts and initial renunciation replaced with unbridled zeal. She had arrived. Even the staunchest of duffers out there knew full well that there was an irrevocable love between us, a bond so tightly woven you would have to be harebrained and blind not to see it. I looked over my shoulder and there she was.

Kiran looked sparklingly beautiful in her traditional red wedding lehnga (dress), consisting of a long red skirt and short red blouse with a dupatta (scarf) draped around her. It was embossed with amazing embroidery such as silver and gold stones, wires, intricate patterns, bead work and skilful sequences, all accentuating her fair complexion and divine figure. She looked like royalty, a true living doll with the stunning use of silk, lace, chaffron and red making the blood course through my veins. Red is traditionally worn by Asian brides on their wedding day as it is said to bring good luck and the couple lots of future happiness. It is the preferred choice over white as this is often thought of as the colour of mourning in other areas of the world.

Kiran's presence and natural beauty immediately lent a certain cosmopolitan veneer to the occasion and if I could have depicted how my perfect wife would look then she came right out of the wrapping paper. They say that the two occasions that your wife looks most beautiful throughout her life are, firstly on her wedding day and secondly when she is in the full bloom of pregnancy, and I could certainly concur with the former as she walked into the gurdwara with her entourage of little bridesmaids and cousin brothers. She kept her head down and behind her duppatta as she was ushered to the front by Jas her cousin brother from Manchester who had his arm carefully wrapped around her shoulders. There was a scintilla of nerves as she weaved her way slowly to the front with her entire *kandan (household)* traipsing in front and behind. She walked very slowly but still with such elegance and fervency.

I was sitting there with my legs crossed and getting bloody sweaty as the camera man and his henchman had insisted on keeping the camera light trained on me as they waited for Kiran to walk in throughout the preceding ten minutes before she did. As I was sitting there I could feel the pools of sweat squishing around in my underpants whilst I continued to give the camera man the evil eye. I was thankful when he trained the camera on Kiran now and not on my goofy and sweaty expression.

Kiran stood next to me. I felt a feeling of euphoria overcome me: Here she was my beau, moments away from being my wife. She was my goddess, the main artery of my life, a flowing river gushing through the previously baron plains of my existence, a true irrigational saviour and I knew I had won the lottery. I was a lucky guy, very lucky...

She exuded a certain eternal and irrepressible freshness as we exchanged a lingering, surreptitious look before she bent down on my left side with her lehnga skirt meticulously laid out behind her. Her twenty one *churra (bangles)* jangling together as she too knelt forward to give her thanks to god before sitting down cross legged and with her head bowed down throughout the ritual. I looked to my left and saw Tina sitting next to her and whispering in her ear and looking after her as the best girl. Tina looked fine in a finely sequined light blue Indian suit and chunni and was patently on course to be the eye candy for the day for the coach load of single, red blooded and hungry hounds that had traipsed up to Luton with me in the morning.

The wedding ceremony or anand karaj then took place as we both sat there with the camera man and photographer from both sides of the wedding parties taking their respective snaps and footage.

Anand karaj is the name given to the Sikh wedding ceremony, literally translated as *'blissful occasion.'* This ceremony normally takes place before noon and is in the form of four nuptial rounds called *'laavan' (four concepts)* where the couple circle the Guru Granth Sahib with the wife holding a red scarf (pulla) draped over the boys shoulder, with the remainder held in his hands. It is a reminder that the holy book and its teachings are the nucleus of their lives and that the principles are the very core of every individual. Throughout the entire ceremony and both before and after, the religious giani sitting at the front of the hall facing the worshippers recited the *'ardas' (Sikh prayers)* and some people joined in quietly whispering under their breath.

The four laavan were written by Guru Ram Das for his very own wedding. They are also referred to and known as *phere*. The first laavan is about commitment to ones own soul, family and community, the second to be committed to unconditional righteousness, the third to be on the spiritual path, and the fourth to communicate with the soul through spiritual practice. There are slightly different interpretations depending on who you ask, and what teachings you read, but the overall message is always the same. The embodiment of the concepts is all crucial beyond the semantics.

Prior to the first laavan I stood there and braced myself for the plunge. The first precarious steps into the shackles of matrimonial imprisonment were moments away. My last seconds as a free man, a libertine, were closing in on me like a hangman's noose. I was about to embark on the invariable green mile of married life, the point of no return. I smirked; I was a willing conscript and was ready to carry out my duties. One, two, three laavan later I had done it, happier, sweatier and increasingly more and more satisfied. She now belonged to me, well almost - my property, and my lover – MY WIFE!

After me and Kiran had been around for the fourth laavan, we sat down. The job was done and life was swell.

The remainder of the ceremony was concluded after this in timely fashion. Any fear, apprehension and uncertainty had now disappeared quicker than a hookers underpants. The hounds of doubt had gratefully vanquished from my mind.

That was it: We were officially married, with the small question of the token registry ceremony to be concluded afterwards, it was in the bag.

The giani then walked around and gave everyone a handful of 'karhah prasad' (sacred pudding) which was kept in a steel bowl. 'Prasad' is always offered at gurdwara's around the world and the ingredients consist of a certain type of butter, wheat flour and pure sugar. It is equally distributed to everyone regardless of colour, caste, style or appearance and thus fundamental to the value of Sikhism.

The deal was sealed and the guests began walking over and placing decorative garlands around our necks along with giving us gifts of money in a ceremony called giving 'shagan.' The average guest today was forking out ten pounds each, which was more than reasonable. The more extravagant punter was upping the ante by donating twenty pounds each.

I was getting suspicious when one or two guests would approach with a clenched fist and then shuffle around in the red scarf that I was holding to collect the money. They would use this stealth tactic to deposit a one pound coin or Scottish pound note. However in true Poirot fashion these imposters were normally sniffed out in subsequent video replay footage sometime after the ceremony. As they say the camera never lies so they would never get away with it and I would be ready to name and shame them at a later date. The tight fisted bastards.

As I looked around there was a swingeing cue built up behind us as guest after guest had their picture taken after putting a gold sequined paper garland around our necks, whispering 'congratulations or words to that effect' and offering some money. There was thankfully no sign of Jags, maybe he had said his piece and gone home I thought reassuringly to myself.

Each time money was being offered, the red scarf was brimming with notes and this was going to be our honeymoon pocket money, so I was pleased, more guests equated to more *'green.'*

The guests poured forward relentlessly when another guy leant in with his right hand going across my body. He put his empty hand in the red scarf and then unexpectedly growled in my ear 'didn't expect to see me here today did you?'

I was befuddled. Who was this? Before I could glance up to face this evil force. The mystery persons tone then became more sinister. 'You think you need all that money?' His left hand squeezed my shoulder hard. My heart stopped momentarily as the hackles on my neck stood on end.

I then managed to glance up despite the vast number of garlands partially obscuring my view. It was Spanish. He had found me, finally. The bounty hunter had fulfilled his quest and had me, his quarry very much in the palm of his hands. He was standing behind me looking as menacing as I had remembered him. He had tracked me down like the dog I was. 'I will see you later on for the money you owe me.' He leaned in a little closer 'and, if you don't you will be sorry.'

He squeezed my shoulder harder making my body jolt forward. He then walked off behind me, I looked around nervously. I was appalled that nobody had seen the threat. I looked at Dev and he was engrossed in conversation with my cousins, and all of Kiran's side were busy tending to her. I had just been threatened on my wedding day and there wasn't a witness in sight, things had just got bad, terrifyingly bad.

The gift ceremony went on for about twenty minutes and as soon as the donations had been given the women went off to get changed for the wedding reception where they would get a chance to show off another expensive suit and look soigné. The guys would generally go as they were.

Dad came over and escorted me by the arm and took me with him to the registry room downstairs where the official registry paperwork and ceremony would take place. As we were running behind schedule, dad informed me that this particular ceremony had to be performed almost at breakneck speed, a kind of *wham bham thank you mam* fashion. Dad walked me to the door whilst I started to take off the sixty or so garlands that were weighing me down like a tonne weight. I handed them to one of my cousins and kept a tight hold of the red scarf containing the money.

In the registry room downstairs we went for the ritual of pledging our vows to one another. Kiran sounded nervous and I was equally petrified, not from saying the vows, but mainly because of the appearance of Jags and Spanish on today of all days. After the vows were witnessed by Sharm on my side and one of her seasoned veteran uncles on her side we braced ourselves to leave.

I was now plotting my escape to a hotel that I had booked nearby – The Ibis in the middle of Luton where I could shave my beard off, take my turban off and slip into my designer suit. Dev came over to me as I sat there in the scrimmage of my thoughts 'Kam you ready to go in a minute? The limo driver is outside and said whenever you want to go, he is ready.'

I asked mum if it was okay and she agreed. Kiran and I stood up and exchanged a few words before departing our separate ways. At this moment as I was walking to the door, Preeto and two other aunties came up to me as I was wiping the sweat from my face with a tissue from the camera light being trained on me again. Preeto playfully slapped my face with her hand whilst tittering 'dekho moonday kul saap warga moo hai,' (have a look at him he has a face like a snake). She had a way with words, a true speechmaking technician. Well thanks for that I thought as I resisted the temptation to throw an insult back at her. The aunties all covered their mouths with their hands as they chortled at Preeto's stand up comedy routine. I looked around for the cauldron and broomsticks as they continued to cackle away at my expense.

However, I was in God's house and I was not prepared to stoop to her monosyllabic and scurrilous level. It was patently clear to me that she had taken an instant and unwavering dislike to me once she discovered that I had used drugs. Anyway what was she doing here standing next to me insulting me? Did she not have a party to go to? A black cat to tend to? I was becoming increasingly annoyed at her disrespectful attitude towards me. They then walked off in what was an otherwise dissatisfactory exchange. I looked at Dev quizzically and then continued wiping the remaining traces of sweat from my brow. What a flaming kushty?

I then tentatively followed Dev making my way to the awaiting limo outside. I walked cautiously, desperately trying to circumvent Spanish, making sure that I wasn't jumped and dragged off somewhere for a butchering of sorts.

We reached the door of the gurdwara and furtively snuck past a group of Kiran's cousins who were congregated by the men's shoe room chortling and expressing mirth with one another. They were pointing to me as I came closer, which was disconcerting and debilitating. They had exercised a traditional wind up which followed the anand karaj whereby the girls side (usually the under twelve's) would steal the groom's shoes after he had put them in the shoe room before setting foot into the gurdwara hall as was the custom before praying in the gurdwara. This joyful custom is affectionately referred to as *'jhutta chupai' (meaning hide the 'monkeys' shoes – alright I invented the 'monkey' bit just to add some extra 'masala – it just means to hide the shoe's).*

I could see the curled up moojay nestling under the arms of a young twelve year old lass who was goading me to pay her a substantial amount of money for their safe return. I snapped 'oh yeh, what if I don't want them back, then what?'

This young girl Simran, as sharp as a tack responded 'yeh, you want them back, cos if you don't, then what you gonna wear to go outside? Ha, didn't think of that did you?' The group of six or so young girls erupted in laughter. She was a tough cookie. Dev laughed too as I reached into the bag that Dev was holding and produced a pair of flip flops. I threw them to the ground near my feet and then sunk my feet into them smiling back at the group 'well I guess that is that problem solved, hope you get a bit of money for my moojay?' I sneered back playfully, not really in the mood for high jinks of any description. I started to walk triumphantly towards the egress when the little Simran launched herself in front of me with the pack following suit 'wait, so you are *'kanjoose'* *(tight),* you are not even going to give us any money, wait till I tell Kiran about this.' The group all stated gesticulating vociferously and I knew that my time was up. As the noise grew louder and the group more and more fractious, I quickly sifted through the red scarf that I was holding and whisked out a wad of ten pound notes distributing them to the baying mob that had snared me. As each rug rat took hold of the crisp tenner they fled for the hills. The last girl, Simran snatched her tenner and then threw the moojay towards my face as I ducked, before running off laughing, leaving Dev holding his sides and chuckling uncontrollably. I picked the discarded shoes up and followed Dev outside and into the waiting limo.

Our Greek driver Georgio was all smiles as he opened the door and let me and Dev in 'anymore Sir?' he said as he began closing the door. 'No that's it.' I said motioning with my hand to go.

The door began to close when...all of a sudden...it was flung open, and an all mighty figure came thundering in launching himself onto the back seats like he was in some kind of action movie. I cowered expecting heavy blows raining all over my body or the cold and icy thrust of a blade piercing through my kurta pyjama jacket. My thoughts ran amok, the indomitable Spanish had caught me at the last moment, he was wily and determined and his tenacity had proven to be my downfall.

'Room for a small one?' I looked up, my face still instinctively being covered by my hands and through parted fingers saw Ranj sat there grinning sadistically. He nestled into his seat making himself snug, closing the door behind him with a violent thud. I am certain that Ranj heard me sighing, as I slunk back into my seat. Ranj grinned at me. In a way I was glad, ad nauseum, that it was Ranj who appeared and not Spanish. It could have been a lot worse.

I looked at Dev dejectedly, while Georgia got into his cab after satisfying himself that Ranj was friend and not foe. He slowly set off for the Hotel Ibis. As we sat there Ranj let out a couple of farts in quick succession as he marked his presence in his usual unmistakable manner. 'Where we going then bhanchod'?' he said fidgeting in his seat. 'To the Hotel Ibis, I need to get ready for the reception.' I said in my most disgruntled voice. 'Nice one, you get yourself sorted and I will check out what delights await me in the mini bar.'

The limo driver Georgio closed the mid section window obviously annoyed with the loud, booming voice of Ranj being projected into his cab, as we continued the journey to the hotel.

I was desperate to tell Dev about my liaison with Spanish but felt uncomfortable mentioning anything in front of Ranj as he was yet another psychopath that I had to contend with, so instead I waited until we got to the hotel when I could give Ranj the slip before spilling the beans to Dev. The limo pulled away and I peered out of the window to see if I could see Jag's BMW. I looked out to the spot where he had parked it and noticed the car had gone. Where the hell was this loose cannon? My day was now spiraling into a night-marish abyss, a train wreck.

CHAPTER 16

—⁓—

Chauffer so good

We were making good progress in the limo with Georgio expertly negotiating the tough and unrelenting streets of Luton in his quest to get us to our destination in timely fashion. I had about forty five minutes to tidy myself up and get back to the wedding where the lovely Kiran would be waiting for me. As all three of us sat in the back of the limo, we chatted about the days events thus far. The conversation flowed surprisingly and without incident. Ranj seemed to have calmed down some what and looked rather relaxed. I noticed him staring at me, almost scrutinising me as we chatted about the day's events.

It was during this exchange that he turned to me with a look of suspicion plastered over his face 'so come on then you kuta, how do you know Spanish?'

I was stunned. I looked at Ranj and he was smirking back at me. What did he know? More to the point, how did he know about Spanish? These and many other similar questions were racing through my mind. In the silence I glanced sideward's at Dev for some inspiration but none was forthcoming as he merely sat there gawking back at me with his toothy expression, and not quite the leg up I had hoped for.

'Come on, how do you know him? You do fucking realise that this guy is bad news…he is like the *Gabbar Singh of Southall (bad guy in famous Hindi movie – Sholay)* and I am just curious what a drug dealing praa-chod (brother fucker) like that is doing at your wedding?'

'Ranj, geezer it is a long story trust me….you don't want to know man, it's messed up…' It was a can of worms that I did not want to open up. All of a sudden, the heart to heart moment with Ranj was shattered with an ear piercing 'oi, bastard, you are a son of a motherless goat.' The limo swerved precariously from one side to the other throwing us around like rag dolls in the back as Georgia continued with more profanities 'bastard, I kill you, I kill you.'

He finally seemed to regain control of the limo and whilst straightening up I noticed we were now travelling a lot faster.

I managed to make my way to the rear cab window and banged on it hard to get Georgio's attention as the limo continued to travel faster. Georgio opened it and I could see that he was concentrated on a blue Mondeo that was pulling away from him in the road directly in front of the limo. His eyes were squinted and his face red with dribbles of water over his chin as I attempted to speak to him. This was futile as he was focussed and hell bent on catching the Mondeo driver. I tapped him on the shoulder hard and said 'Georgio what the hell is going on? What are you doing? Will you knock it off? I have to get to my wedding.'

I noticed that his knuckles were now turning white from gripping the steering wheel, and despite his determination to pursue the Mondeo he let his foot off the throttle and luckily, he listened to me. The limo began to settle back into steady cruise mode as it was before and I saw him release his choke like grip from the wheel whilst letting out a puff of air. It was over.

'What happened bro, why were you chasing that car?'

He shook his head as he slowly continued to come down from his earlier impersonation of Captain Caveman 'these people have no respect, I am just doing my job and they insult me, I would have snapped him in two pieces if I caught him I tell you, I am Georgio, my dad was a wrestler you know.'

'Georgio, you haven't told me what happened?' I interjected as it was apparent that with the release of adrenalin from his body that he had begun to waffle, a common symptom known as the adrenal dump where it can cause you to babble uncontrollably. He assisted with an explanation 'I was driving along with my window open when this blue Mondeo pulled up on the side, the Indian guy opened his window and told me that I was a dead man and then he squirted some liquid over my face from a water pistol.'

Georgio paused for a second as he rubbed his hand over his face wiping the remaining remnants of the liquid off his face. He continued 'the bastard said that it was piss, and he kept squirting it on my face, and then he drove off.'

I examined his face for yellow liquid and could see incriminating smatterings of the offending fluid. I was not sure what to say 'that is fucked up man, listen we will get you err...cleaned up when we get to the hotel, what a fucker though, don't worry.'

I sat back and regaled the incident details to the other two and they both naturally fell to the seats laughing as Georgio closed the cab partition cover. It was clear that the other freak show of a driver, whoever he was, had clearly missed the road signs for Zippo's Circus. We laughed it off as Georgio could be heard mumbling under his breath. Ranj then nudged my arm and quipped 'you didn't tell me about Spanish, how do you know this guy?'

I don't know why but I felt compelled to tell Ranj everything with this given window of opportunity and without further ado, I used this as my cue to sing like the proverbial canary. Yes I poured my heart out, with the mix of the days significance and the 'incidents' with Spanish, Jags, my previous dealings with Sandhu before the wedding, my mother in law and even Tina's obvious disdain for me,. I found the floodgates well and truly opening up, I found the odd tear trickling down my face as I explained how I feared that my day was destined to be ruined. I was not ashamed, after all, it was only the three of us in the car, and at that moment the emotions were far too close to the surface for me to have any kind of strength to attempt to suppress them. I poured my heart out. Ranj's face dropped as he listened intently. He did not talk once, but just listened.

I was not convinced whether he was the right person to be talking to about this stuff? Was he really that inter-ested or was he merely killing time? He occasionally glanced out of the window throughout this ten minute outpouring of my grief and trepidation of the list of char-acters baying for a taste of my blood. It felt surreal, as I wanted to include Ranj himself on the list of clowns who were pissing on my wedding fireworks. That thought was quickly pushed to one side as for the first time in all the time that I knew him as a youth he was sticking to the communication protocol of listen having the same letters as the word silent as he sat ears tuned in and without so much as a squeak.

The limo eventually came to a standstill. A few seconds later Georgio appeared as he opened the passenger door. I could see that he still had yellow liquid streaks on the collar of his white shirt but I did not have the heart to tell him. I stopped talking as Dev put his hand on my shoulder and gave me a much needed, firm and reassuring squeeze.

Ranj curled his upper lip as if to say something and then for some reason refrained as he stepped out of the limo and walked off towards the hotel entrance. I looked at Dev as our phlegmatic friend sauntered off away from us 'well that was useful wasn't it?' I shrugged. 'I am glad I told him now.' I was taken aback by his dismissive, almost rude, and unsympathetic reaction to my woes.

I slid over to the open door as Dev did and we both got out. I followed Ranj to the entrance to the Hotel Ibis whilst Dev got the suit and my toiletries bag out of the boot and followed us in.

Georgio chipped in that he would be waiting in the limo cab when we were ready. He mentioned that he was going to freshen up in the hotel lobby toilets in the interim. I told him we would be less than twenty minutes. He nodded and we walked in.

We entered the hotel room. It had been pre booked by Dev in the lead up to the wedding. I quickly went into the bathroom and took my turban off, time was all important and any kind of set back would be frowned upon especially at this crucial stage. I then proceeded to shave off my beard. This was excrutatingly painful as the thick forest beard took several wild and hacking swipes of the razor to come off, bit by bit. The coarse bristles fought valiantly against the cold and steely decisiveness of the razor blades.

Ranj and Dev meanwhile sat in the bedroom chatting and catching up. I think Ranj was probing Dev for more details regarding my past but he did not let on as we never spoke about my problems again for the remainder of our stay in the hotel. I heard the clunking and clinking of bottles and glasses as the two were busy examining the delights of the mini bar in the room. After I had finished shaving, I walked back in the main room and slipped into my wedding suit, a two piece black number. My red tie adding the hot sauce and making me look sizzling and irresistible.

Kiran was a lucky girl I thought proudly as I cast a surreptitious glance at myself sideways in the mirror in-between chants off fat boy and roly poly from Batman and Robin sitting on the bed behind me. That was it, we were ready to go as we all raised our tumblers and shouted 'salud' and each gulped a shot each of Jack Daniels with a dash of coke inside.

'That was fucking good.' Ranj observed. 'Sod it lets have another.'

He opened another miniature Jack Daniels and before I could say *teri maa di (your mum)* he had sunk it completely and slammed it back on the table whilst running his sleeve across his chin with all the etiquette of a vulture devouring the carcass of an animal.

Once we had finished I chivvied them both back into reception so that we could start to make tracks. The limo was still positioned as it was and I could see Georgio's arm resting on the drivers window with his elbow poking outwards. Dev settled the bill with the reception staff as Ranj took the carrier bags of clothes and threw then onto the back seats of the limo and sat inside. I waited for Dev and then we both walked back to the limo and sat inside.

An inebriated Ranj shouted 'oi Georgio son – lets shake a leg then.'

Georgio started the engine and without wasting a second, we set off slowly out of the car park. I was determined not to be late; this would be embarrassing at my own wedding of all occasions.

The limo pulled away and I casually looked out of the window admiring the verdant grounds of the hotels enclosure.

It was a nice, warm day, the refreshing sound of birds chirping, the sunshine beaming brightly amid the cloudless blue skies it was swell, life was swell. I was on the cusp of the most amazing future with the most amazing wife, it was what dreams were truly made of. My heart was humming and I felt alive and in the moment. As I floated in this bubble of unabridged contentment, my eyes were suddenly drawn to something outside. I looked closely at what I had seen. Wait a minute, my tranquillity was smashed abruptly as I realised what I had seen. My attention was alarmingly drawn to a vehicle parked up.

I was taken aback as I saw the blue Mondeo parked in the far corner of the car park. It was the same blue Mondeo that had been involved in the incident with Georgio on our way here. I looked again as the limo made its way out of the car park. I was certain it was the same one and mentioned it to Dev. He looked as we drove further away from it and said that I was being paranoid. He was right, what was I thinking? It had already been a crazy day and my tendency to be paranoid was amplified ten fold after the incidents and visits I had, and so I sat back and relaxed. I put it down to being just an uncanny coincidence as we all continued to chat. I was feeling better as the Jack Daniels and nectar of ever lasting life was beginning to have an affect on my mood and sufficiently ease any tensions that I had.

I tapped on the window of the closed cab partition to tell Georgio to put his foot down a little. I tapped a couple of times but there was no response. 'Georgy boy put your foot down or we are going to get our arseholes ripped out.'

Georgio was most probably still fuming from the altercation before, so I was treading carefully in my suggestion and left it at that. As I waited, the limo started picking up speed and I sat back in my seat satisfied, 'he must have heard us, he is going faster.' I said to the others. We were all engrossed in conversation as Ranj confessed 'it's my turn next Kamster. I am looking for a missus to get married to, and to be honest I haven't found anyone close yet, someone I can settle down with.'

He then went on to say 'I am a tough nut to crack cos I am one fussy kuta, but watch this space in three months because that is when I am definitely going to pin some girl down and get married to her. Then my friends it will be the stag do to end all stag do's.' He spoke excitedly. 'It will be mental and one to remember when we are old and grey, sitting in our armchairs in an old persons home, wondering just why our bastard children put us in there in the first place, you had better come when I invite you?'

'No worries Ranj – I will try and make it.' I replied.

'Look you kuta, what do you need a note from your mum and a warm scarf: You had better be there. I am not asking, I am telling you, you will be there, it will be a true boy's holiday.'

'No worries paajee (brother) will do.' I said reassuringly.

We continued to chat away as I casually looked at my watch. We had been driving for a good ten minutes now and as I peered out of the window, I did not recognise any of the surrounding landmarks, not that I was conversant with it in the first place. It just looked unfamiliar.

'Guys where are we? Do you recognise any of these roads?' Ranj and Dev looked out of the window

'Nah.' they both answered back in chorus.

I was also now becoming aware that Georgio was unusually quiet in the front cab and tapped on the cab partition again to speak to him. There was no response as the limo increased in speed. I used my fist to tap harder and to get Georgio to open up but this was futile. The limo was now zipping down the road at a comfortable fifty mph, as I started to get a sick taste in my mouth. I don't know why but I was now in panic mode as I shouted to the other two 'something is up, what is going on guys?'

Ranj manoeuvred himself to the front of the rear compartment, no easy feat for a man giant like him but he managed it such was his determination. He too thudded loudly with his spade like hands but the limo careered along the forgotten terrain. Ranj moved back a little and it looked as though he had given up. He then took a firm grip of the sides of the limo and said 'get out of the way a minute' motioning for me to move aside for him. I therefore moved my body quickly to one side.

He then lunged forward with his hulking frame and launched his size ten boot firmly into the middle of the cab partition several times. He kicked away like a possessed demon, kick, kick, and with a series of deafening crunches later the partition didn't so much open as collapse and disintegrate around our feet as he dangled in mid air with his foot sticking through the open space. I fell back as did Dev who was crouching just behind Ranj and supporting him. I caught a glimpse of the driver's uniform as we lay there like wounded soldiers.

Ranj pulled his leg out of the cab hole and all three of us regained our footing when all of a sudden the limo spun around violently with a wheel spin causing us to smash into each other and ricochet off the limo walls with sickening bone crunching power. Ranj was instantly knocked out cold as his head collided several times with the sides of the limo like a pinball. He immediately slumped to his side like a car crash dummy, a sack of potatoes and across the limo seats.

Dev was bruised in various places as he was thrown around inside the limo like a rag doll. In the meantime, I had managed to steady myself with my feet on the seat in front of me and was able to come away from the violent turn unscathed. The limo had now come to an earth shattering halt. We lay there like wounded soldiers on a battlefield and the sickening taste of burning rubber wafting through into the back made me retch.

I looked up and saw the shadow of the driver through the blackened window moving around to the side of the limo. Where the hell were we? I was thinking as I tried to scan the environment for signs as quickly as my brain would allow me. I was baffled and did not recognise the baron and isolated car park that we had found ourselves ensconced. The passenger door was flung open and I heard 'get out now.' I could not make out the face of the driver as it was obscured by his cap. Was this a sincerely pissed off Georgio who was exacting his revenge after we made him wait a little longer than anticipated? I could not be sure. I looked at Ranj as he lay there in a dribbling state of unconsciousness and quickly at Dev who looked like a rabbit caught in the headlamps of a juggernaut. I tentatively edged towards the open door still checking for signs of broken bones or limbs hanging off on my own body. I was apparently okay thus far. I reached the door and I could see that the driver had moved away a little and not near enough to identify him. Who was it and what did this truculent person want with us? Dev was soon out of the cab with me as we both stood there like petrified and trembling gerbils. The driver removed his cap and revealed himself the phantom of the limo was none other than - Sandhu the pimp.

He spoke 'so you actually thought you could stiff me and get away with it did you?'

After the initial shock of seeing him had dissipated I looked down at the implement he was holding in his hand and tried to disguise the shock I felt in seeing a large serrated knife being twirled around sinisterly by Sandhu as he sized me up.

Surreal visions of me dressed up in a pvc suit with an apple in my mouth and being chained up as the gimp in the cellar in Dirty Sandhus's raced disturbingly through my mind.

'What did I say to you before, hey? I want the money you owe me! I am the sort of guy who will rip your fucking tongue out and fly it from my car aerial over five quid you owe me let alone the grand that is still outstanding. You see that is the way I do business.'

I was one twitch away from feeling the warmth of my piss trickling down my legs as I tried desperately to hold my shit together.

'Oh and to get you on your wedding day, well that's just the cherry on top isn't it?' He hissed at us. It was clear that he was trying to goad us into reacting. I could see it coming, we were veritable lambs to the slaughter. How were we going to escape this predicament? Even Houdini would have sprouted grey hairs in this pickle of all pickles.

I looked around quickly surveying the landscape, we were in the middle of nowhere, unfamiliar territory and unfamiliar enemy. This was as desperate as it got.

'I think you have a bag of money in your pocket for me, right?' He snarled looking at me.

The game was well and truly up as I put my hand in my pocket and took a firm grip of the red scarfed money that was nestling comfortably inside. My marriage money was to be for us, my wife and me, to set up our life together. What would I say to her, the shame? The time for reckoning had come; I stood here facing death or destruction, short term loss versus long term loss. My options at this moment had become limited if not non existent as I began to take the loot out of my pocket. This was it the moment of reckoning. One Amitabh Bachchan type heroic lunge for the knife could be catastrophic. The icy critique of the morgues cold slab was enough to make the decision transparently easy as I looked down at the serrated edge of the knife that was being twirled in sinister fashion under my nose. Similarly, as I did not have a particular penchant for hospital food I relented against trying my Bruce Lee flying kick move on him. I was faced with the moral dilemma of death, destruction, or surrender. I chose the latter. I paused for a second 'come on bruv, just let us go it is my wedding.' I pleaded, my voice quivered with trepidation and uncertainty.

What was I to do? I had two chances, slim, and no chance. The slim option was to beg him not to take my wedding money. This idea was scanned and rejected by my inner thoughts as it would have been shot down in flames by a predictable retort 'well you should have thought about marriage and families when you were shagging my girls, you bhanchod.' So I decided against my last chance saloon option.

Sandhu ignored my pleas and started to walk steadily closer to us as I produced the bag for him to see. His bulging bug like eyes lit up, he had the jackpot. He carefully disguised his euphoria by stifling his smile. He stood imposingly in front of us now, still armed and dangerous from the hunting knife in his hand. It glistened threateningly in the afternoon sun. Well that was that. I reluctantly handed the bag to him. He wrenched it out of my hand with his grubby little mitt and laughed, whilst feeling the weight of the bag. He then turned his back as he wrestled with the red scarfed money bag and put it carefully into his pocket. He turned back and faced us again trying hard to contain the smirk that was appearing.

'Hold on a minute what have you done with Georgio?' I asked.

'Who?' He snapped back at me.

'The limo driver where is he? What have you done with him?'

Sandhu smirked, his tongue prodding the inside of his cheek 'oh him.' He cackled loudly. 'I dispensed with his services.'

He opened his eyes wide in a bid to intimidate us and it worked.

'What you have killed him.' I asked fearing the worst. My anger was getting the better of me. Georgio was a diamond, a nice fellow doing an honest days work to put bread on the table for his family and this mongrel has thrown piss over him and then killed him, all for what? Knife or no knife, wedding day or no wedding day I was at boiling point – he was going to pay for this.

Sandhu had other ideas as he menacingly waved the knife under my nose. The eerie sound of desperation came thundering back to me. I was in a cesspit of resignation and surrender.

'Get back in your pram, and don't even think about it.'

Being stabbed through the heart on my wedding day was not my idea of fun. The very thought of something hideous happening to me: cutting me to the quick, disembowelling me. My day perpetuated throughout the annals of history.

A day recited as a spook story to scare kids with in the future: fervently handed down in Punjabi folk lore as the sucker who never quite made it to the gurdwara, too bad, so sad, next case.

It seemed the longer I remained in this quagmire, the longer I smelt the murky stench of impending death, the closer I felt I was becoming to meet my icy defeat.

I moved back to the limo door disgruntled whilst sharing a prayer and thought for the fallen Georgio. Dev remained staunch where he was and had not moved a muscle throughout this entire period. It appeared that he had frozen and was over awed by the incident. A kind of post traumatic shock had crept in as far as he was concerned. Sandhu pointed to the open limo door and said 'right now get that other idiot out of the back or you will all be joining Georgio on the slab, hurry up.'

His words echoed ominously and the accompanying baleful glare depicted his innate evil disposition. I turned to get into the cab and to comply with his instructions and to my amazement there was no sign of Ranj. I mean he had disappeared. I nudged Dev who also peered inside and was equally astonished at Ranj's amazing Marvo the magician disappearing act.

We simultaneously turned and looked at Sandhu who was hovering behind us with his knife

'What's going on? What are you doing? Just get him out...NOW!' We looked again to make sure but he had disappeared from under our very eyes.

'I am warning you two clowns, things are going to get nasty, get him out.' Sandhu attempted to peer over our shoulders into the limo but to no avail.

No sooner had he finished his statement, we heard the booming voice of Ranj appearing from behind the other side of the limo like a rising phoenix from the ashes 'now I have heard just about enough of this, you maachod.'

The fearless Ranj stepped forward and around the limo heading straight towards Sandhu 'haramzada, put the tooth pick away and let's dance the old fashion way, if you think you have drunk your mum's milk?'

I was astonished to see him and also very scared and turned to Dev 'I am not sure what's going to happen? This is bad news.' He looked back at me petrified. I continued 'I just want you to say thanks for always being there bruv.' I knew that we didn't have a mouse in a traps chance of surviving. I looked nervously at Ranj and Sandhu as they stood there for a moment sizing each other up again.

Sandhu looked pissed 'I will use this knife, I am telling you.'

'Look bhanchod, you are as about as intimidating as a pink fluffy rabbit, now release the tool.' Ranj undeterred retorted back sharply. It seemed that the Jack Daniels had transformed him into Superman. This guy had no remorse and was willing and waiting to swap some leather with Sandhu, even though he had a life ending blade in his hands.

'I don't know who you are, but this is between me and him (Sandhu pointed the tip of the knife at me) I have just come to get the money he owes me, that's it.' Sandhu's voice was full of trepidation.

Ranj had heard enough and went for the jugular 'course you have my darling.' He started to walk towards Sandhu, closer and closer.

'Wait Ranj stop.' I shouted. Was he so drunk or concussed from the limo incident that he did not register that Sandhu had a dirty big knife in his possession? This was suicide. 'Stop Ranj.' I shouted again. Dev piped up 'No, don't do it.'

Ranj stepped within an inch of his prey. Sandhu intimidated by the temerity being displayed by his adversary moved back a few steps and well away from the limo and us, his eyes widened in surprise. His challenger was a madman 'that is your last chance, move back or you will get it, I mean it.'

'Sounds like you live in a magical world where fairies dance at the end of your garden. Now you don't want to play with toys that might get you into bother do you?'

Ranj stood directly in front of him without batting an eyelid 'you see my old sunshine my years of being on the street has enabled me to identify those dogs who bark, and those who bite, and you bhanchod are in the former category, a little yelping puppy.'

Sandhu was playing the game well and all of a sudden did not seem phased anymore by Ranj's speech and continued to twirl the knife menacingly in his hand. Ranj remained close to him. In fact, too close for my comfort as I cringed and braced myself for the inevitable thrust of the blade into his torso.

They say the street is your best teacher. It makes you pay for bad errors of judgement until you get tired of making them or end up in a casket whatever comes first. I felt that Ranj had just picked himself some free flowers as he stepped up within slashing, thrusting, and dying range of the steely knifed enforcer, the angry steely knifed enforcer.

'What did your mum tell you the other day?' Ranj enquired. A weird question I thought, maybe he had softened up from his renowned bombastic approach: Was he crazy, stupid or a mixture of both? 'This guy has got a knife and you are going to die.' I looked on in anguished disbelief at the sheer madness I was witnessing.

Sandhu looked rattled and equally bemused 'What?'

WHACK! Ranj booted him flush in the crown jewels, doubling him over as he continued valiantly to hold onto the knife. He then smashed his boot football style into his head catching him directly on the nerve on the side of the chin, a popular spot where in most situations a direct knock out blow can be delivered decisively. Sandhu went flying across the desolated car park like a badly edited Chinese martial arts film. The knife in the meantime went flying out of his hand and in the opposite direction. Sandhu skidded on his backside on the car park gravel. He was instantly sprawled out unconscious on the gravel. Ranj walked over and stood above him for a second assessing his handiwork and then nodded his head, satisfied with his work.

Ranj then knelt down and rifled through his pockets. He threw the limo drivers keys at Dev who caught them immediately. He rifled some more and found the red money bag. He walked over to me triumphantly and deposited it into my hand 'he shouldn't be bothering us again the fool, anyway who is he?' He asked. I spent the next minute explaining how I had let this evil into my life with my shameful visits to the brothel, whilst Ranj eagerly lapped up every word. At the conclusion of my run down, he turned to Dev and chirped 'he is bit of a dirty kuta this one.' referring to my erstwhile brothel visits. Dev laughed nervously as I looked back at the flattened carcass of Sandhu laying there.

'His mum, do you know her or something?' Dev asked curiously.

'Nah that was what we call the brain engager.' Ranj then went on to explain how his distraction method had helped him over the years where he would engage his adversaries with a question to momentarily distract them and switch their brain off whilst he landed the finishing blow to them usually resulting in a clean knock out. 'The brain is working on answering the question and therefore not ready for the incoming strike.' He explained.

This was also a tactic used by some gangsters when they would ask someone if they wanted a cigarette. The victim would say 'yes' then WHAM, they would punch him in the mouth and break his jaw. This was a good tactic as it engaged the brain and secondly when the jaw is loosened it becomes easier to break than when it is clenched.

'Anyway how the hell did you get out of the limo?' I asked the big guy.

'I crept out of the other door when you handed the money over and he stupidly turned his back.'

Dev twirled the keys in his hand as we went to get into the limo and head back to the wedding.

'Hold on where is the driver?' asked Ranj looking around.

'Yeh what about Georgio?' I reiterated Ranj's concerns, realising that he was still missing. We looked around the car park from where we were standing, he was no where to be seen. What had he done with the poor fella?

'Wait what is that noise?' Dev chipped in standing closest to the boot. We listened in and could hear muffled noises and a soft, listless thudding noise against the inner boot lid. We all exchanged apprehensive and incredulous looks. We stood next to the boot and I opened it carefully. As the lid creaked open, our trepidation turned to relief. I was delighted as I saw the bound and gagged figure of Georgio lying inside, but alive!

We freed him from the tape around his mouth, while he let out groans of relief. We helped him out of the boot and back onto his feet. He was dazed and said that he had been hit around the head when he went to get something out of the boot and then the rest was a blur. He mentioned that he started to regain consciousness a few moments ago.

I handed the keys back to Georgio and asked him if he wanted one of us to drive. He said he was cool and we all went to get back in the limo.

We turned to go, when much to my anguished disbelief I saw the limping and wounded figure of Sandhu standing there spitting proverbial feathers. He had also alarmingly regained control of the hunting knife once again. He stood there shaking from the blow he had received only moments before and quietly glared at all of us. The knife blade for some reason looked longer and more cut throat then when he first produced it.

Sandhu was back in the driving seat and it was clear that he was no stranger to adversity or physical confrontation himself. He waited a moment, a moment that lasted for an eternity, and then without warning came rushing towards us, well towards Ranj in particular. He had a score to settle now. Ranj pushed Dev and me back with his other arm, out of harm's way. Sandhu meanwhile gained ground quickly, he was like a steroidal whippet, racing over arms outstretched, knife blade just a gnats pubic hair away from impaling the brute himself. Suddenly without any sign of remorse, Ranj side stepped and unleashed a flurry of vicious punches to the head of Sandhu. There must have been a succession of six or seven fast, unrelenting, and determined strikes, all landing with toe cringing ferocity and accuracy. Sandhu's pathetic lunge with the knife meeting thin air as he staggered and break danced his body. It looked like he was being machine gunned in a classic Bollywood movie as punch after punch landed with unerring efficiency. He then fell to the floor but Ranj was not done yet. He picked Sandhu up by the lapels tightening and twisting his grip and held him in the air aloft. This was unreal considering the size of Spanish. His legs dangled inches off the ground;

'Now listen you kutay di putt (son of a dog) my mate is a good geezer and his bride – the lovely Kiran is a special girl and doesn't deserve this bullshit on her wedding day you kunjar.'

'Mate I think he is out cold.' I cut in decisively looking at the dribble dripping out of the side of Sandhu's mouth.

Ranj had always had the heart of a lion, and with his middle name of Singh meaning lion in Punjabi, he was expertly personifying this valour and warrior spirit. He looked at Sandhu and then at us before dropping his quarry to the floor.

I was relieved, ecstatic that we had managed to survive this encounter but I was also painfully aware that time to congratulate my Kevin Costner bodyguard would have to be put on hold until later as I was already late for the wedding party. Without any more delay we saddled up and got into the limo – destination wedding!

I sat down inside and rummaged in my pocket to give Ranj a handkerchief to nurse a wound he had on his hand. I searched in my pocket and instead felt the small packet of drugs that I had inadvertently put in my suit jacket the night before in the bedroom. I took the packet out and all three of us looked at the bag and then at each other. What should I do with it?

My hand was shaking vigorously, not from holding the bag of drugs, but from the adrenaline that my body had released.

The shakes, hand wobble or adrenal dump was simply the adrenaline trying to settle down as it stampeded throughout my system from the incident with Sandhu. This was the main reason why my hand was shaking so much, it was simply because my body was now dumping the excess adrenaline that had been pumped in initially to attempt to cope with the fight or flight feelings when Sandhu was a gnat's whisker away from eviscerating all of us. I scrunched the bag of cocaine up in my hand and then quickly stuffed it down the back of the limo seat, out of sight, out of mind and out of prison. It was better off there.

Georgio meanwhile sat back in the driver's seat where I saw him satisfyingly discard the water pistol that Sandhu had placed on the passenger seat out of the window and onto the head of the unconscious Sandhu.

We then set off back to the hall with Georgio seeking the much needed assistance from the in built sat nav to get us back on the same day and in one piece. I felt my breathing begin to regulate once again and cogitated hard at what had just happened a few moments before. How lucky? It was only providence, and Ranj's street instinct, that helped extricate us all from such a nail biting and adrenaline fuelled dilemma. I was truly thankful.

CHAPTER 17

La 'dhol' ce vita

We entered the hall and I dashed up stairs and fought off the myriad questions that everyone from my mum and dad to the cleaner were posing about my whereabouts for the last hour or so. I raced into the room where my beautiful wife Kiran was and hugged her.

'Where the hell have you been? I tried your mobile but it was switched off. We have been worried.' I explained that traffic was the problem. Everyone bought my story and I took a much needed breather on the balcony outside whilst the guests continued to pour into the hall.

I stood on the balcony and took deep breaths. I felt my body only just beginning to relax from the limo incident. I looked down from my vantage position overlooking the reception hall and out of sight from the hoi polloi down below.

Kiran was in an adjacent room set aside for us with her girlfriends keeping her company and touching up her worst bits.

We both had a few minutes before we made our entrance to our reception downstairs. It was imperative that everyone got into their seats beforehand as it would have been a tad embarrassing to walk into a half empty hall, especially as our entrance was meant to be emphatic.

This was my dream wedding, an incomparable setting, a luxuriating venue stacked to the rafters with hordes of happy guest's hell bent on letting their hair down and enjoying the occasion with great verve and tenacity, such was the energy and exciting pulse that I was feeling even from where I was standing.

As I looked below I could see the guests starting to pour into the hall and making their way to secure one of the fifty or so tables that had been laid out by the catering staff who were stood by attentively and on hand to serve up every culinary whim that the horde of guests could throw at them. The hall was an amazing setting with a sensuous mélange of hospitality and refinement. A quality time with quality people.

Across the hall and on the stage the DJ and accompanying singer were in the throes of testing the acoustics of the sound system. I continued to scan the contours of the hall with great satisfaction and bonheur when I suddenly reeled back in horror. I gripped the balcony rail and leaned in closer to make sure my eyes were not deceiving me. I could not fathom what I was seeing as I looked on incredulous. There she was amid the guests standing there in her Indian suit sipping from her glass like she didn't have a care in the world, smiling at other guests and looking around the room curiously. My stomach churned disturbingly. This was all I needed on my wedding day, yet another obstacle and ticking time bomb, as if the others weren't enough.

It was none other than the hooker – Pam. It was an eye rubbing moment, I gripped the rail tighter, any tighter and I am sure I could have snapped it in two. After the initial shock of seeing her I resolved myself that I had to avoid making eye contact with her and go about my business for the day as there was no way on gods earth that she or anyone else were going to cause me anguish on my wedding day. I had just about had enough. A plethora of questions raced through my mind 'What was she really doing here? How was she related to Kiran's side of the family? Did she know this was my wedding? All these and many other crucial questions continued to cause me anguish as I saw Pam sidle over to a group of girls positioned by one of the long tables in the far corner of the hall. She took a couple of sips of the drink she was holding and began chatting away enthusiastically to her '*new found friends.*'

I turned and walked back to the room where Kiran and her friends were. Tina was sitting directly opposite the door and next to Kiran. I walked into the room and looked straight at Tina, she stared back for a moment before rolling her eyes and swiveling on her seat, turning her back and reassembling the multitude of bangles and coconuts that Kiran had dangling from her wrists. A clear act of defiance, and implacable hatred towards me. To be honest, I did not really care anymore. She was not important.

Meanwhile Dev also entered the room from the other door leading into the upstairs hallway and said that we should be ready in five minutes to make our entrance into the hall as the dhol players were in position downstairs along with most of our cousins. I grabbed Dev by the arm pulling him to one side and whispered 'did you know that the rundi Pam is here, downstairs in the fucking hall, mingling with the guests, what am I going to do?' Dev looked stunned 'shit, you sure, the little bitch, is she related to Kiran?'

I shrugged my shoulders 'I don't know, that is what I need to know. You know she is demented and will get drunk or something and probably tell someone. What do I do?' I said anxiously tying not to draw attention to our furtive discussion as Kiran and the others were preparing themselves on the other side of the room.

Dev reassured me 'don't worry - it will be cool.'

'How? She is here bruv, at my wedding.' I raised my voice as a culmination of Dev's apathy, being threatened by Spanish, the limo incident, Pam being here, Jags seen skulking about before, not to mention Preeto and Tina's unknown contempt for me all burning on my mind. Pam being at my wedding was far from cool. The girl was as slippery as a mazola covered snake and was here to wreak havoc and cause marital dysfunction at the very least.

'This is going to be a train wreck, an unmitigated disaster, I can see it, and I have to do something.' I said worryingly.

Dev looked at me casually and shook his head 'it will be okay, I think you are over reacting, she probably won't cause trouble geezer.'

His nonchalance and casual approach infuriating me. I went to give him a piece of my mind when Kiran's timely intervention saved Dev from a tongue lashing from me 'are you ready Kam?' She asked in her soft dulcet tone. 'I think everyone is waiting.'

'No probs let's go sweetheart.' I replied whilst casting a disappointing look at the apathetic Dev who stood there staring at Kiran as she stood up.

Punjabi weddings are simple but lively affairs and celebrated with a great deal of verve and relish. Today was like the Punjabi Mardi Gras, an occasion to beat all occasions. All over the hall there was an abundance of flowerlike sari's, resplendent Indian suits and wonderfully colourful turbans illuminating the reception like only a true Punjabi wedding could do so. It was the marriage of the visual with the feeling of quality that set the mood sublimely.

Kiran and I were now waiting outside the hall holding hands and laughing at the panoply of cousins and friends milling around in front of us jumping around, dancing and in great spirits. The two dhol players – Gurdev Singh and Kam Bansal – the veritable Godfathers of their trade were strategically positioned at the front and occasionally banged the side of the dhol with their sticks testing the authenticity of the sound. The dhol players were on hand lending an unmatched Punjabi flavour to the melting pot. The dhol is a large, high-bass drum, played by beating it with two sticks. The width of a dhol skin is about fifteen inches in general, and the dhol player holds his instrument with a strap around his neck. (The female dhol is called the dholik).

It was used in days of yore to communicate to villagers the marching of an impending army to the village through the use of different beats of the dhol representing different messages. It has been said that once you hear the haunting and rhythmic sounds of the dhol you will leave the world behind you as you step, bop and shazzam to the beat. The diversity of the music, the drumming of the sticks on the leather skin and the passionate dancing, enthralling people from all over the world.

I clasped Kiran's hand tighter as the dhol players furiously began playing the dhols. The beat immediately sent the entourage into a frenzy as the double doors leading to the hall were thrust open and the dancing and jiving groups marched forward triumphantly in tune to the dhol beats which were deafeningly loud. The DJ got in on the act by letting off all manner of props from firework type loud bangs, to pyrotechnic displays on the stage.

Dev, Ranj, Sanjay, Surinder amongst others were skipping forward with their arms aloft and moving their shoulders up and down in traditional bhangra fashion. The dad's were close behind also turning on the spot dancing and cheering with '*hoi hoi*' and whistles noisily projecting from the entourage.

Amazing, unbelievable, heart stopping rhythm – there simply were not enough superlatives in the English dictionary to sum up the mood. It was simply divine, technically organized, artistically presented and perfectly executed. Were we entertained? This was a resounding hell yeah all around!

The women including Tina, both mums and Kiran's cousins were less energetic as they walked in clapping in tune with the beat. It was sensational as we followed in behind the frenzied crowd heading gracefully towards the dance floor. It simply did not get better than this I thought as the place erupted. I looked around the hall and guests were standing up and clapping. Others were dancing around their tables. We felt like nobility and I could see Kiran and Tina smiling and acknowledging that this was a truly remarkable occasion. We made our way to the dance floor as the entourage all broke away into the open space and bopped to the beat. I led Kiran to the centre of the wooden floor as fountains of confetti exploded majestically above our heads along with the noise of loud fireworks continually sounding from equipment on the stage.

Kiran smiled at me as our family and friends danced away to the vigorous beat of the dhol. The dance floor was festooned with people celebrating, tapping their feet, and shaking their hips to the beat.

She looked stunningly attractive, like an oasis in the desert, her simple charm and heart stopping beauty captivating my senses. It had all been worth it. I could see the stacks of frisky young guys, young testosterone filled chicken choking adolescents out there scattered around the contours of the wooden dance floor all eyeing her up (thank God it wasn't me they were looking at). All fiddling with their trouser pockets, all straining their faces as their individual pillars of truth rose to the occasion. Kiran sexy, sassy and soigné moved elegantly past the sex starved drooling mob, stepping over their rolled tongues on the floor which were soaking her feet. Like a pack of hungry hounds their ears pricked up, panting and firmly fixated on her every twitch. They all wanted to fuck my wife. It was as clear as the day is long.

This was as close to nirvana as I was going to get despite the turbulent incidents that I had found myself in before.

The altercation with Sandhu was forgotten, the one off chance meeting with Jags her ex boyfriend was fading, and the fact that Pam was here did not even register as I moved closer to Kiran with my snake hips. I twirled her around with my hand and she responded in her usual elegant manner.

The dhol players played for a few more moments as swathes of guests swamped the dance floor to enjoy the delights of the dhol. What a hodge podge of people there was, a gathering of personalities from all walks of life, accountants, more accountants, some other accountants, oh and lawyers, more lawyers, and ah yes another gaggle of lawyers.

The wedding atmosphere was truly living up to expectations, served up with a master piece of sumptuousness and excess with an encapsulating Punjabi heartbeat thumping wildly throughout.

The mood was electric by now and was further exemplified in dramatic fashion with the grandiose announcement from the DJ *'congratulations to Kam and Kiran - the beautiful couple.'* as the groovers on the dance floor cheered and clapped raucously. The applause seemed to go on endlessly as Preeto came over and hugged her whilst patting my back in a token gesture giving us her blessing. There was a feeling of resentment being emitted from her every action when she was around me. Good, the fire breathing dragon didn't like me and she sure wasn't top of my Christmas card list either.

She then circled a ten pound note around our heads and put it on the stage for the DJ. This was another long held tradition and at the end of the evening's performance the DJ and their hanger ons would end up with a tidy sum in the shape of such tips along with their upfront fees for the gig. The DJ then announced that Kiran and me were to remain on the dance floor for our wedding song and instructed the other guests to skedaddle, which they did.

We both held hands and prepared ourselves for the brief yet glorious song that we had chosen to be the one that represented our love for one another whilst the patrons in the hall watched. I noticed the photographer and cameraman vying for the best viewpoint as they fervently propped themselves up on chairs around the dance floor to capture the imminent dance.

That was it, without further ado, the DJ played our chosen track '*Tera Saath Hai Kitna Pyaara*,' a classic melody from the Hindi film *Jaanbaaz (meaning how loving it is to be by your side)*.

As the tune crackled into life, Kiran and I moved in a little closer. We stood a hair breadth away from kissing range as we swayed our bodies left and right to the romantic ballad whilst our nearest and dearest friends and family took their positions on the peripheries of the floor clapping rhythmically all the time. I caught a glimpse of Dev as he put his right hand to his forehead mimicking an army salute before bringing it back down and smiling.

Standing near him were some of the others including Firoz, Surinder and then there was Ranj who was in the throes of chatting up Dimple, the girl he had fancied from the hall, both of them continued to playfully giggle together as I gently circled Kiran in tune with the music. I caught a glimpse of Kiran's dad. He had taken his jacket off and was drinking steadily from a pint glass. He raised the pint glass upon catching my eye and gave me a heart-felt smile. This was a timely boost and meant a lot to me. Standing near him and tapping the six toes of her foot to the beat of the music was Preeto the half witch, half trol-lop as she cackled like Grott Bag in tune with the music.

The music was gradually fading and I suddenly noticed the slapper Pam standing by the stage steps. She saw me looking at her and with her hand by her waist rubbed her fingers slowly for a few seconds as if to say that she wanted money from me. She smiled at me ruefully leaving me with a bitter taste in my mouth.

Kiran whispered 'there are a lot of people here isn't there.'

'Tell me about it; it is a great turn out.'

'Where is Tina by the way have you seen her?' she gently asked.

'Not sure to be honest.' Not that I could give a flying tutti where she had gone.

The song finished and the DJ told everyone to get ready for the cake cutting ceremony. The three tiered cake was wheeled in on a table by the catering staff and placed in the centre of the hall with all the guests huddled around. One by one photograph's were taken off us being fed pieces of cake by our mums and dads, uncles and aunties and cousins. As everyone took their turns to feed us a cake and take their snaps, the DJ chipped in by telling everyone that the starters were on the tables if folks wanted to get chomping.

He then went on to inform everyone that after the cake cutting then the dance floor would be available for them at any time. As the last of the cake feeding guests were slowly finishing off. I saw another hand feeding me some more cake. By this stage, I was stuffed and even the tiniest of morsels would have tipped me over the edge but I stood there politely and smiled for the camera. It is only when the cake was then pushed violently into my mouth that I looked to my side and saw the grinning profile of Pam standing there and wallowing in my fear. My eyes widened, swimming with anxiety, as I found it hard to comprehend the temerity she was displaying by standing there and feeding me cake on my wedding day. Was this ironic? I had no idea. Whilst we stood there posing for the cameraman she squeezed my butt with a pincer type grab causing me to jolt forward as Kiran looked on. After stuffing my mouth with the cake she walked off, and, without balancing the cake feeding ritual by also offering Kiran some as wedding protocol dictates. As she strutted away pleased with her contribution I grimaced as Kiran asked whilst covering her mouth with her hand in case the cameras subsequently picked up what she was saying 'who was that? She didn't even say hello to me.'

I replied 'don't worry sweetheart she is an old school friend but she has always been rude. Just ignore and she will probably leave soon.'

Kiran seemed to buy my smoke screened excuse, as the cake table was eventually wheeled away and the guests took their places at their tables.

I made my way to the head table with Kiran. I was trying to stay as physically far away as possible from Pam as possible. Did she not realise that her henchman Sandhu was lying in a pool of his own vomit and excrement in a remote car park somewhere in the city? The head table is normally reserved for the bride and groom along with immediate family and other members from the higher echelons of each family. The view from the table was stupendous as it was slightly raised off the ground on a makeshift platform and enabled us to have a complete overview of every contour of the hall.

I overheard Kiran asking one of her friends where Tina was again and sent them to find her. She looked concerned; it appeared to both of us at the time that her best girl had vanished without trace. I was secretly pleased but did not let on. I looked at each table trying to recognise the guests as Dev came and sat next to me. It was a collection of the best of the best. I gulped my drink down and looked at my watch. I still had several hours to go before I departed for the airport and my honeymoon. There was no way anyone was going to try something with me in front of so many guests. What were they crazy? I said consoling myself. I took another swig my drink just to settle my fluttering stomach. Mum and dad sat down at the table next to us and were all smiles as they chatted to Kiran and made her feel part of the family, she reciprocated, and the atmosphere was relaxed again.

Some of the guests slowly started to make their way forward to the dance floor with the music gradually intensifying in volume. Increasingly my hearing started to fade from the booming acoustics from the big based speaker sitting pretty a few feet from us. The constant ear splitting, booming, noise severely testing my mettle and resilience of my soon to be perforated ear drums.

Chapter 18

— m —

Swinging jamboree

As tradition has it the bride's family have the duty to host one meal for the groom's side and this is always the reception, where they lay on culinary treats and cordon bleu dishes and nibbles for the hungry hippos in attendance. Not only does this burden lie squarely at their door but they also have the delight in picking the entertainment, whether it is a DJ or a singing and dancing group, kind of old school songs more appreciated by the first generation mob. The hospitality provided by the expertly briefed catering staff provided a cultural experience as majestic as the venue itself. We were in the heart of nirvana and relishing every drop of it.

The starters were sublime - kheema samosas, delicious chicken pakoras, masala sauce, succulent chicken wings and fish pieces covered with oodles of mint sauce and pickle. These little fellows hit the spot as I indulged my senses and taste buds in heartfelt satisfaction. I offered Kiran some but she was somewhat preoccupied with the disappearance of Tina.

A giggling Ranj came up to the table 'kiddha, guess what? He paused. It was a rhetorical question. 'I am in, that girl, what's her name – Dimple, she wants my kittens man, and she is hot hot hot (he licked his thumb and pressed it onto the breast of my suit indicating that she was sizzling hot) I laughed and poured Ranj a drink.

We both clinked our glasses with Dev who stood up from his seat as Ranj toasted 'to our sweethearts and wives, may we always have a taste for them both.'

We all knocked back our drinks and Ranj left me with his parting shot before racing off 'alright Kamster, see you in a bit, I'm off to get my swerve on with her.' At the back of the hall I could see the petite figure of Dimple standing there looking around sheepishly waiting for her prince to return. Dev sat back down and focussed on his mission to devour as much chicken, fish and lamb as humanly possible from the array of finger licking starters. I could not blame him. They were mouth watering.

Finally, I saw the destitute and dejected figure of Tina slowly shuffling back to the head table from the other side of the dance floor. As she ambled over it was patently clear that she was distressed. She approached the table and hugged Kiran for a few moments. Her exhibitionist self pity was totally winding me up as I bit my lip. What was this kuti's inherent malfunction?

'What happened? Where were you? I was looking for you everywhere?' Kiran asked.

Tina gently pulled away from Kiran and held her hands, a look of deep grief filled sympathy and compassion plastered over her face.

'I am sorry, something just come up that I had to deal with, tell you later I promise, I can't talk here its too risky.'

She cast a repugnant look at me and said 'you okay? You look like that the cat that has got the cream.' She didn't wait for a reply and walked around the table to sit down. All that crying must have worn her out, the silly bag.

Her brutality revolted my sensibilities as I swigged another drink. What was her problem with me? I just could not put my finger on it the flaming kushty.

I patted Dev on the back and told him that I was popping to the loo as he continued scoffing the generous offerings of meat strewn on the plates on the table in front of us.

I walked across the dance floor heading towards the toilets and past the hordes of bhangra and 'gidda' dancing relatives who were in fine fettle. I performed a couple of cheeky moves en route much to the delight of Sharm who was instigating the most outrageous manoeuvres on the floor including the snake dance where he and another uncle were both facing each other on their knees with their hands meshed together to form the head of a King Cobra. They moved their hands around in snake like fashion in front and above their kneeling bodies as they leant back and forth as a King Cobra would do hissing and pretending to strike each other with their hands every so often. It was amusing and I eventually managed to escape to the toilets without being dragged into the snake routine. After I had finished I walked back into the reception hall. I could see the dancing was well under way with the guests piling onto the dance floor in droves. As I negotiated my way back to the table I was grabbed by the arm by Sharm and thrust into the heartbeat of the dancing. I lifted my arms ups and danced like a possessed Duracell bunny strutting my stuff in majestic fashion much to the delight of the baying mob who were now circling both me and Sharm with all manner of indecipherable, chirpy noises being shouted and shrilled.

Where the hell did he get his energy from? He circled me like a vulture occasionally flitting in and out of my personal circle of attack with his bhangra version of the running man. Oh how we all laughed as we danced feverishly and without a care. The warmth of the drinks I had consumed was satisfyingly warming the cockles of my heart. I swivelled on the spot and tossed my head side to side with much glee whilst casting a look over to my beau who was laughing as she remained sat at the head table. She was engrossed in conversation with Tina and her other friends.

Then without any prior notice, Sharm snuck up from behind me and tucked his head in between my legs as he hoisted me up in the air whilst grabbing my legs with his arms to steady me. I immediately had to duck as he almost decapitated me with the low hanging fan as it swished precariously above me. I had disturbing visions of the wedding photo's being spoilt with me standing next to my new blossoming bride in my finest couture, but with NO HEAD! That would not have gone down too well, and would have certainly spoiled the photographs.

Sharm, sweating profusely as he always did, and with body odour so bad it was enough to put a skunk in a life threatening coma then let me down from his shoulders. He stood there swaying, and whistling with his fingers in his mouth. I had to escape, he was big, drunk, and more importantly exuded the freshness of a tramps underpants.

In the meantime, the guys around me were becoming ever increasingly audacious with their dance moves and naturally more and more sozzled from the copious amounts of free booze that was on offer on all the tables.

Although boozing and dancing was the main draw for the guys, you would often see many patrons simply standing around and soaking up the atmosphere and revelling in the Punjabi flavour of the occasion. However even the staunchest of non dancers out there would be drawn slowly to the dance floor like a magnet over the course of the reception and the rest as they say is history.

Across the floor there were a group of guys performing their finest Mithun Chakraborty dance moves trying their utmost to woe the bedazzled bits of crumpet that were floating around seductively within drooling range of them. As they bopped and jived in synch with each other it was patently clear that these sad, knuckle scraping unkempt individuals had been up to all hours of the morning in a bid to perfect their infantile routine but with disastrous embarrassment.

Elsewhere you could see married partners sharing saucy and secretive looks with one another, trying in vain to keep their murky liaisons hush hush as their unsuspecting husbands and wives grooved inches away from them. This was the burning light of reality of today's modern society, it was just impossible to comprehend, but was the truth, the whole truth and nothing but...

After dancing for a bit I decided to get another drink and so skulked away surreptitiously without too many people snaring me as I tip toed off the dance floor. I cast a look back and smirked to myself as I could see the sweat soaked, body odour covered and dishevelled Sharm necking from a bottle of Bacardi neat before turning to the frenzied revellers and drumming the bottle like a Punjabi guitar as he caressed it endearingly close to his chest like a long lost son.

Elsewhere the children romped unpretentiously in the mini bouncy castle that had been ordered by Kiran's wedding planner ensconced at the back of the hall along with chasing the magician around who was busy entertaining the little blighters with his creative adroitness in making animal shapes out of balloons. The mums, aunties, and younger ladies used the occasion to catch up with each other with the trials and tribulations of their lives, to eat well, dance well, and live well. I even caught one or two distant aunties slipping a dash of Martini in their mango juice to lend some pizzazz to their day. Why not?

I sat back at the head table and held Kiran's hand. She smiled back. I could see that Tina was still looking teary and disconsolate but I thought better than to attempt to give her my token reassurance. I still could not work out what her inherent problem was on this day of all days. I mean talk about choosing her moments to be having a hissy fit and pissing on our fireworks.

'What's up with her?' I asked Kiran quietly. She looked at me for a second as though to say that it was not really her place to say and that I should really mind my own business. Kiran was loyal and it was clear that she did not want to break her confidence with Tina. Regardless, she whispered 'don't say nothing, but her boyfriend is here and she is having problems with him, but don't say anything okay.'

'Yeah cool, my lips are sealed.' Well at least that explained her mood swings, but now I was curious. Just who was this mystery boyfriend?

One thing was becoming more and more lucid I thought as I took a swig of my drink and sized her up sideways. I would have as little to do with her as possible once

Kiran and I had settled down and were getting on with our lives. She was just too much high maintenance and hard work. How the heck did Kiran put up with her? This was the sixty four million dollar question. I looked around at where Dev was sitting but he was gone. I looked back at the dance floor and the party was in full swing, but there was no sign of my brethren. Where had he slipped away to, the little bugger?

I quickly scanned the hall for a few moments but again there was no trace. Dev was a broken arrow. Where was my best man? I gently tugged at mum's arm 'mumji (slipping a ji on the end of mum was a term of endearment and was considered respectful) have you seen Dev' She looked so devilishly content and happy. She beamed back 'putt, he is helping dad take some of the presents upstairs into the changing room, he will be back in a minute.'

A few more minutes past and I saw a gaggle of Kiran's finest mates approaching the table. They came up to the table and after a little persuasion dragged Kiran and Tina off for a girly bop. Out of the corner of my eye I saw my dad and my father in law with other guys propped up by the bar area contently sinking pints of beer. The best place to be I thought.

I inspected the area closely but there was no sign of Dev. Strange I was told that he was helping dad with the presents. He may have popped out to make a call on his mobile, or gone to the toilet, or…well there was only one way to find out as I got up and walked across the hall to make my way to the upstairs changing room.

It was a welcome and temporary relief from the booming music in the main hall as I made my way up the stairs to chastise Dev who no doubt would be busy sorting and stacking the presents in the holding / changing room rather than enjoying the jamboree down below. As I stood at the top of the stairs, I heard muffled noises coming from the room next to the holding room. My heart sank. What had happened? I edged closer to listen. Were these muffled screams of help? I leaned my body tentatively towards the door and pressed my ear up against it. All I could hear were groans and the occasional muffled screech. Something sinister was going on inside and I needed to find out and quickly. I clasped my hand tightly around the door knob and held my breath as I braced myself for the grandeur John Wayne entrance. This was going to be messy. I could sense it and predicted claret in the tea leaves...What horror was waiting for me inside?

CHAPTER 19

---ᴍ---

Challenge

One…two, my heart was banging like a kamikaze tabla player. Then as I was about to thrust the door open to face my demons - I heard someone talking, screaming in ecstasy 'yes yes, you are the one. I said you are the daddy…'My hand released the door knob. I stepped back smirking as it dawned on me that these were infact muffled groans of unadulterated pleasure from a cavorting couple. This was a satisfying catharsis as visions of me stomping my foot on an assailants head and rescuing a damsel in distress drifted from my mind. I left the fornicating couple in their element as I walked to the contiguous holding room where Dev was meant to be beavering away.

The door was slightly ajar and I pushed it open and walked in still smirking about the near miss I nearly had walking in on the randy couple next door. To my shock and absolute surprise, I saw Dev sat down in a chair against the wall, doing nothing in particular but merely staring fixedly with a wide eyed gaze at my direction.

'What you doing mate? You shit yourself or something? I was waiting for you downstairs.'

I walked into the middle of the room and towards Dev. On the far end of the room, I could see the wedding presents stacked up against the wall. There must have been at least forty odd presents balanced precariously on top of one another. Dev remained mute and I immediately sensed from his pained expression that something was rotten. Like a good old fashioned horror movie I began to turn my body to see what was lurking behind me. As I did this the door where I had walked in began to close behind me as the assassin and Prince of Darkness emerged from behind the door and stood there staring at me. The assassin wore a heavy duty brown leather jacket, black combat pants, and brown Chukka Boots. His gait, depicting sinister, and evil intentions.

A cigarette hung loosely out of the side of his mouth. He took it out and exhaled through his nose in my direction and over my face. I watched as the smoke curled up in the air around me, like a hangman's noose. He came close to me, up to my face, it was his way of saying - he had won. He had finally nailed me, one on one. He took the cigarette out of his mouth and flicked the ash on my shoe, insulting me, before popping it back into his mouth. I feared he would make it to the reception and I knew the result of this would be catastrophic. Here he was the spectre of my nightmares at my wedding reception. It was Spanish!

Spanish then walked around me without uttering a word and stood next to the quivering Dev. He placed his hand on his shoulder and pressed it down whilst parting the bottom side of his jacket with his other hand displaying the handle of a 9mm colt pistol tucked threateningly in the waistband of his trousers. At this point and more so than any other, I could feel myself straining every nerve to prevent myself from falling to my knees and whimpering like a baby.

'Now, you thought you were smart, but you didn't take into account the shrewdness and cunning capability of me, your enemy did you?'

I was doomed. How the hell could I get out of this pickle with my limbs intact? The last thing I needed was to have a dust up with Spanish on my wedding day. This was a total disaster movie 'Look, Spanish bruv, I don't know why you have taken all this personally. I just don't do drugs anymore it is as simple as that. Why can't you leave it that? Come on it is my wedding day and all.'

Spanish took his hand off Dev's shoulder and snarled back 'shut up and listen carefully. Why do you think I am here? No-one, I mean no-one walks away from me. Ever since that night in the pub, I knew you would become my bitch you weak hearted tart. You with many others before you are my cash cows and always will be. That is what happens when you dance with a tarantula like me, I bite. I tell you when it is time to go clean, you feel me?'

He walked towards me menacingly, his scarred face looking just as forbidding and evil as I had remembered.

'Besides which, you owe me money?'

'What for? I paid for the gear I got?' My weak defence did not deter this wily brute.

He stood directly in-front of me and continued 'my calculations are that you owe me at the very least two thousand big ones from the free stuff I got you.' I looked bemused.

Spanish hissed and glared at me from under his scowling brows whilst stretching out his brawny hand 'now, the choice is yours, you either hand over some cash and I will go, or I will enjoy blowing your knee caps off, plugging your mate here and then taking your money anyway. What do you want to do son?'

The cogs in my head spun at break neck speed. This was too much to handle. I panicked and turned to run out of the room. I flung the door open. I needed to get some assistance to help to quell this evil and sadistic animal that had arrived on my wedding day to ruin my life. I had set one foot outside the door when from absolutely nowhere I felt a tremendous force push me backwards lifting me off the ground momentarily and thrusting me back into the room as I careered painfully into the presents scattering them like confetti around the room.

As I lay there letting out groans of pain and assessing my injuries, I pleaded 'please, please leave me alone, it is my wedding day...LEAVE ME ALONE! I shouted vehemently hoping that Spanish would be merciful with me.

I looked over to the door from where I had been projected from and there stood a six foot four inches, black henchman, with a shaved head, Popeye type arms and no neck. He was covered in tattoos and was a veritable monster.

He stood there like Goliath, a half man, half snarling, and frothing beast. He closed the door behind him and stood there guarding it like a loyal sentry. Spanish took his gun out of the waistband of his trousers and slowly caressed the handle whilst saying 'I am tired of playing games, it looks like you want it all to end here, TODAY, in this room...don't you?'

He walked up to me as I lay there bruised and battered and placed the tip of the gun firmly against my forehead. This was surreal I was about to die on what was meant to be the happiest day of my life, all for what? I had no idea! I felt this weird, warm glow engulf me as

I braced myself for the inevitable flash of light, searing pain and then death as I saw his finger inch steadily towards the trigger. It was all happening in slow motion. I could see it and was powerless to stop my imminent slaying. I wanted to live so badly. I loved my parents, I loved Kiran. Please, not now, when I was so happy. This cannot be happening to me, why me? My body was tense and I was shaking all over.

In situations like this when you are faced with a fight or possible death your brain switches to one of its modes and in this case, it is called the animal brain, or the right side of the brain. (It is called animal because all animals are one hundred per cent right brained, survival being their core functionality).

The right brain in humans is used for survival and is crucial as it analyses the environment for sounds and sights essential to help you survive an encounter. Due to the fact that it focuses solely on survival and the imminent threat, it also has the side effect of making you answer in monosyllabic sentences, one word answers as it precedes over the left brain which would normally be used for language and tool use.

Therefore, although I knew exactly what was happening, despite tunnel vision and everything appearing to happen in slow motion, my ability to communicate was dramatically stunned and would have amounted to mere grunts if I tried to speak. This was because the right brain had taken control of the reigns. This surge of adrenaline causes people to freeze in the face of adversity and to others it is the spark, which fuels you into action. I was frozen to the spot as the adrenaline, released from the adrenal gland was bolting through my veins like the Mumbai Express Train trying to prepare me for the situation I was faced with. I was now feeling the full force of this as my body quivered uncontrollably. I was cold and felt alone with the hollow and helpless feeling that precedes your doom.

I felt the cold barrel of the murder weapon nestling harder into my forehead as the tears streamed down my cheeks. It was time to say goodnight, my body, my feelings, my life, all over. What a waste?

Spanish hissed in my ear 'thought you could outfox me hey? You fucking loser. Nobody can get one on me, never.'

I squealed like a pig 'please, no please.' I could feel the padding of my casket as I clenched my butt cheeks in anticipation of the bang. I didn't want to die, not like this, all I had done throughout my life had led to this moment, it can't end like this.

I heard Dev sobbing uncontrollably in the background and saying 'no, no...don't...d ... don't do it.'

Spanish pressed the gun even more firmly into my head making my head jolt backwards when there was a knock on the door. Spanish quickly put the gun behind his back and looked up disturbingly towards the direction of the door, as did the black henchman.

I looked at Dev as he continued to sob and was incognizant to the visitor's timely intrusion. The door handle turned 'hello, here is the champagne that you ordered.' came the voice from behind the door. The henchman stepped back a few feet as the door continued to open. 'We have a bottle of champagne for your delectation.' The waiter continued to walk in wearing the white jacket that he and his twenty or so colleagues were wearing downstairs.

As the waiter came in, I sought this opportunity to start to stand up and dust myself down from my fall and near death experience. My legs were still jelly and my hands quivered as I dusted the arms of my suit jacket. I never looked up but tried desperately to gather my thoughts about what had just happened and think about my next move to extricate myself from this devastating dilemma. I heard Spanish chip in 'we didn't order any drinks now take then back down. We are having a family crisis meeting here, my brother and me. He pointed his finger at me with his other hand, with the gun still held tightly behind his back with his other hand. 'Now hop it and take the bottle with you.'

The waiter was not stirred by this outburst. He politely replied 'but I was told that you wanted drinks brought up, and you know what they say? When some-one offers you a drink, it is rude not to accept: especially on someone's wedding day.'

At this moment, shocked, I slowly looked up at the balls that this waiter was displaying in the face of adver-sity. I mean, he was the chief of waiters, the big cheese of professionalism. He had drinks to serve and he was going to serve them come hell or high water. This man was a legend, the very cradle of suaveness and efficiency, an inspiration to all mankind. If nothing else, he was an ideal candidate for promotion.

I continued to look up at this unsung hero, the picture became very lucid as the waiter continued to speak turn-ing to look at the henchman 'I think you, Sir, look like you need a glass of champagne, don't you?'

The henchman snarled back 'look just fuck off you squirt or I'll crush your bones into a thousand pieces.'

Dev made eyes with me and we both smirked wryly as the waiter took hold of a bottle of champagne that he was carrying and retorted 'now that is not nice is it? When you are offered champagne, you get champagne.'

WHACK! With that, he moved quickly forward smashing the heavy bottle of champagne with tremendous power and ferocity across the head of the henchman knocking him to the floor in an instant, ensuring he was sleeping with the fairies. I mean he went down like a ten pin, a felled tree, no questions, just out cold and dribbling unconsciously on the carpet. It was surreal.

Spanish stunned as we all were, reeled back in horror and I then saw him swiftly move the gun from around his back and towards the direction of the waiter. I gasped and froze on the spot. Dev stepped back and the waiter, none other than the Oscar winning Ranj in a white jacket looked towards Spanish, and we all knew our time was up. Spanish pointed the cold and soulless barrel of the gun life threateningly at Ranj's torso.

These were not exactly the happy and buoyant memories I had been planning for my big day as we all stood there whilst Spanish held the gun straight towards Ranj. We all knew what his intentions were and it was clear that within the next few seconds we were all going to suffer the grave consequences of allowing a mongrel like Spanish into our lives.

Spanish, his face was a mere blank canvas, expressionless and morbid, looked on menacingly. I looked at Dev, his face was deathly pale, and he was bricking it, no two ways of assessing that, he was an inch away from curling up in the foetal position with his thumb in his mouth. He simply didn't want to die on my wedding day, none of us did. It just didn't constitute his idea of fun, dying a grizzly death on your mates wedding.

This hair raising spectacle had just got more sinister and nightmarishly scary and I looked on through choke filled tears.

It was simply a matter of logic, the three of us were unarmed and scared, he had a gun, a track record of violence, and with the unpredictability of a typhoon, the situation was enough to loosen the bowels and wet the '*chuddies*' *(underpants)* of anyone. I was steadying myself for complete, uncensored violence, and a tirade of abuse, before we met our makers. It was inevitable.

Spanish held the gun steady in his hand and aimed at Ranj. He posed the biggest threat for him, this was patent. I could see the metaphorical visor lowering over his face as he prepared his body for the subliminal battle that had presented itself.

There was a deathly silence. No one spoke, we all just analysed. The henchman lay in his own vomit on the floor. He was about the only thing that was certain in this situation. Spanish started to move back, circling with his gun holding hand for Ranj to move over to where Dev was standing. As though, he wanted an overview of the situation.

Ranj responded, slowly. No one spoke. He motioned for me to join the other two by the chair where Dev was originally sat down. I responded in an instant, walking slowly around him. One false move, one twitchy trigger finger and this would be messy. Here he was judge, jury and hangman, and we were at his mercy. We had as much chance of surviving this ordeal as that of a cat smeared in pedigree chum and locked in a room of rabid and hungry Rottweilers. Basically - No chance!

I had already tweaked his ego, challenged his manhood and now Ranj had the audacity to do the same.

It was going to get messy. You could smell the imminent arrival of violence.

Then, as I was walking around him, I saw my chance, the window of opportunity was staring me in the face with a big red arrow pointing down towards it. Spanish stepped over the henchman as he went to secure the door. He cast his eyes away for a second as he fumbled with the door handle. I don't know why. I had seen enough for one day and launched myself at him with the determination of Dharmendra, the guile of Sunil Dutt and the unerring accuracy of Amitabh Bachchan. I thrust my hand out and somehow managed to slap the gun out of his hand and to the floor. The years of watching all those Bollywood movies had paid off, as the gun fell from his hand and into the middle of the room.

Ranj quickly reacted, stepping forward and kicking the gun away in the direction of Dev. Spanish tried to stand up but Ranj with the speed of a cheetah sprung forward and kicked him back to the floor knocking him flat on his back. Ranj towered over him, snarling 'stay down you kutay di putt.'

Ranj walked over to Dev, took hold of the gun, and inspected it in his hand, turning it over and looking through the barrel. He then lowered it downwards and straight towards Spanish 'watch this.' he grinned cheekily as his finger started to pull back the trigger. 'NO!...don't kill him; it is not worth it, bruv STOP! STOP!' I shouted.

Ranj was a loose cannon, an out of control maniac with an obvious thirst for violence, a man possessed as he pulled the trigger regardless, the gun still trained on Spanish as he lay there helpless. The sound of the clicking trigger as it was depressed made my blood run cold for a second. Murder on my wedding day, the cold blooded taking of another life, and all for what? It made no sense to me, none whatsoever.

I could see the front page news now. There was a deafening silence in the room as we stood there dumbfounded by what had just happened. Ranj laughed harder after he had done the dirty deed. Any hint of Spanish seeking the tiniest crumb of comfort, or remorse had just been shattered in one foul swoop.

They say fear has an uncanny way of giving you some hard perspective on things and right now, I was wishing that Ranj had never set foot in my life again let alone what was meant to be my big day.

Dev had already looked away in stunned disbelief as I stood there in utter dismay. My eyes slowly travelled downwards to see the screaming carcass of Spanish laying there with a hole plugged into his forehead. As I looked down, I was shocked. I saw him lying on his back looking up at Ranj unperturbed by his near death experience. I looked back at Ranj who was in the throes of tossing the gun to one side of the room.

'What happened?' I asked with my voice cracking, my mind desperately trying to piece together what I had just witnessed.

'Well what do you think? The gun is fake. It is just an imitation. I know that because I had one when I was younger. It says imitation on the side, it kind of gives the game away a bit, don't you think?'

Spanish smirked from his position on the carpet.

'How did you know we were in here?' I enquired.

'Well I was just finishing off with my girl next door and we were having some champagne when I heard a massive crashing sound, so I listened from outside. Then

I heard you squawking and saying something like, just leave me alone (he emphasized this with a more feminine tone) so I grabbed this jacket off some waiter guy who was going past and slipped him twenty quid to borrow it for ten minutes and that's that.'

The emotions overcame me and I gave Ranj a side hug. He hugged back. He had saved my life and I was indebted to him.

'Right let's get down to brass tacks here. I will sort this kuta out, you go and enjoy the party.'

Ranj then stepped forward and without a skip of the heartbeat booted Spanish as hard as he possibly could straight in the testicles deriving immense satisfaction as Spanish shrieked in horrendous pain whilst grabbing the wounded area with both hands and curling his body in the foetal position.

He lay there whining on the floor like a freshly castrated puppy, writhing around in agonising pain as Ranj dragged him sack like across the floor and dumped him against the wall at the far end of the room, panting with effort. Spanish was a sneering husk of a guy, big and strong and I was impressed. He dusted his hands down and turned to face me 'well this is some wedding you kuta, I am beginning to like you because you attract trouble and that means you are my kind of guy.' Ranj chortled 'Is there anything else you want to tell me about.'

'What do you mean?' I asked.

'Like, you know, are there Ninja assassins waiting for you downstairs with shuriken stars and blow darts? Or what about a hired hit man with a price on you head? Your probably worth about fifty pence, seriously what's the score, are there any other skeletons here today?'

'Mate what can I say, there is that rundi Pam I told you about, she is downstairs and then there is my mother in law but that shit I can handle, but she don't like me, then there is Tina who don't like me.'

'Is that it?' He laughed.

Dev chipped in 'what about Kiran's ex?'

'Kiran's ex, who's that?' Ranj asked.

'A guy called Jags was here in the morning. I told you about him in the limo, remember?' He used to go out with her and he approached me after the milni and told me to speak with him or I would be sorry or something like that.'

'Hold on a minute.' Ranj bellowed. 'This Jags character, has he just come out of prison, and drives a BMW?'

'Yeh that's him, do you know him?' I said sensing that if this was the case then Ranj could head him off at the pass and prevent my blood from spilling at his hands.

'Put it this way can I have your slippers after the funeral?'

'What?'

'No serious don't mess with that dude, he is too well connected. Jungle lore has it that he has got access to proper guns not these Mickey Mouse fake ones.'

'I have heard that and that's why I am shitting my pants.'

'Kuta, there is always a faster gun out there, it's the way the cookie crumbles, but all I will say is that I know he is a serious machi (fish) in the big scheme of things.'

'I have got a real bad feeling about this Ranj, what do I do?'

'All I would say is stay out of his way...anyway let me sort this situation out here. I will get some of my boys to get these two dumb fucks out of here and I will get a little treat ready for Pam so that she won't bother you after today.'

Ranj then reached into his pocket and took out his mobile phone and dialed a number before pressing it to his ear. He walked to the other side of the room and started to talk animatedly into the phone.

Spanish meanwhile continued to writhe around on the floor like a wounded animal. I patted Dev on the chest. We exchanged looks of relief as we vicariously felt each others anguish having escaped this snake pit of hostility.

A few moments later Ranj walked back, tucking his phone back in his pocket. He picked Spanish up by his collars and shoved him onto the chair.

'Now what is your inherent problem maachod?' Spanish kept his head bowed down. 'Is it because your dad still visits you in the middle of the night and tells you to keep it a secret ey?'

Spanish bruised and battered, then looked up at him, pain etched on his face and spat on Ranj's top. I looked on in horror, knowing full well that this would end with disastrous results. The phlegm trickled down his white jacket and dropped to the floor as Spanish looked on satisfied with his response. The fight and hostility had not quite been sucked out of him. If it wasn't, it was when Ranj punched him several times in the face, causing Spanish's head to jolt violently back and forth.

'You are probably beginning to realize who I am, but if you are in any doubt look me up on Google as hard, tough as nails bad arse from Southall. He punched him again several times in the head, breaking his nose and cutting his lip. 'Now when my guys collect you and take you home. You see my friend over there?' He pointed to me. 'Well you leave him alone from now on. If I even hear you mention his name in conversation let alone try to meet him again I will cut your tuttay off and force feed them to you with a flannel understand bhanchod kusra?'

Spanish nodded in agreement and then looked down sheepishly. Ranj was the all conquering hero. A man of unimpeachable loyalty and with every vestige of dogged determination aroused in his pursuit for honour for his brethrens. He faced me and said 'now, go back down to the reception and enjoy yourselves. I have got my team coming over, they will escort these two goons back to their lair and trust me they will not darken your hallway again, that is my promise and wedding gift to you Kam baby.'

I shook his hand vigorously. Dev handed the room key to Ranj and asked him if he wouldn't mind locking up after and depositing the key back with him. We then walked to the egress.

Ranj looked down on his snared and quivering quarry and snarled 'now I am going to thrash you like a disobedient kuta.'

I looked back and cast a truly thankful and apprecia-tive smile at Ranj who reciprocated back before turning and slapping the face of Spanish as hard as I have ever seen, causing Spanish to fall back over the chair and arse over head onto the floor. I gulped as I left the room. This was the way things were served up on the street, I guess.

CHAPTER 20

─w─

Sozzled sausage

Dev and I walked back down the stairs and made a quick visit to the outside toilets where we concocted a story about us being held up by some old acquaintances. We used this opportunity to straighten ourselves out as well, before we went back into the reception where the party was still in full swing. Once we had braced ourselves we headed back to the head table which was empty as everyone was dancing on the dance floor to an array of fast moving bhangra tracks. We sat down and poured ourselves a drink each and knocked it back heartily. This was the most needed drink of my entire life I can tell you. It went down an absolute treat and assisted immensely in settling my tumultuous nerves at this moment in time.

Meanwhile the food was strewn across the tables, a collection of tantalisingly scrumptious dishes including jeera chicken, chilli shrimp, fish pakora to name a few : the waft of rich herbs and spices, the smattering of garlic and freshness of tomatoes and chopped onions setting everyone's taste buds on code red alert. The tandoor dishes were amazing, awash with bell peppers, fresh chillies and a divine tandoor sauce with a collection of rarely seen or tasted herbs and spices. The robust delights of the curry eater's revolution was here to be sampled, savoured and devoured. This was a cordon bleu experience and the gladiators in the kitchen had done me proud conjuring up dishes to please and titillate the taste buds in emphatic fashion: no-one was going to be forgetting this wedding anytime soon, if not for the experience of the food alone.

I looked over at the stage and saw the dhol players picking up the mood with the finest rendition of dhol playing that you will see this side of town, while the crowds below danced passionately with a variety of bhangra moves. In the meantime I saw the drink weary frame of Sharm staggering up onto the stage from the other side as the DJ's were using this time to eat some food and have a few stiff drinks before resuming a little later.

From where I was sitting I could see Sharm tussling with one of the dhol guys. He was flailing his arms around and irritating the dhol player who was trying desperately to shrug him off. He continued to annoy him but had not accounted for the single mindedness of the dhol player as he staunchly drummed away regardless. I saw the dhol player, Gurdev Singh manoeuvre himself to the other end of the stage away from the pugnacious Sharm.

Sharm, his belly flopped over the waistband of his trousers continued to prance around at the back of the stage like a distressed giraffe, staggering and swigging from a glass he clutched in his hand.

The dhol players then slammed their last sticks into their dhols and the dancing crowd cheered and clapped loudly. They made their way back stage with the DJ crew returning suitably refreshed from food and booze. The DJ immediately set up the next track and the music blared out of the speakers.

However Sharm was still lurking with intent in the background and I then saw him stagger up to the DJ and say something. Although I could not make out what was going on I saw the DJ move his head back and motion for him to go back down to the dance floor. I could sense things were about to turn nasty and I elbowed Dev who was still in a state of shock from the earlier incidents of the day 'hey look up there, it is going to kick off, you watch, BSP is rat arsed.'

Sharm then stumbled over to one of the other bewildered members of the crew and yanked his head down into a headlock as he swayed back and forth like an inebriated oaf who had patently consumed one too many crates of whisky.

The main DJ looked back nervously at the carnage that was unfolding behind him as he kept the show going with a good mix of bhangra tracks. Sharm then returned to the DJ yet again and was seen whispering something in his ear. This time the DJ remained in his position without flinching as he waited for the music of the track to fade out. He then said 'ladies and gentleman we have the best man here for Kam who wants to say a few words to the happy couple, please remain where you are and the tracks will be on right after.' I looked at Dev and laughed, best man, since when? The audacity of Sharm in stealing Dev's thunder as the best man. 'Can you believe that he is purporting to be the best man? What a drunken joker!' I said to Dev.

'Well he might have saved me a job, cos I was piss scared about doing the speech, especially now after the shitty day we have had, seriously I am glad, let him do it.' Dev said satisfyingly.

Like a drunken phoenix from the ashes, Sharm sauntered forward to the front of the stage taking the microphone with him 'ladies, gentleman, I want to make a speech, so make sure you listen everybody.'

The music in the background was faded out and Sharm had gained the air time he was so valiantly fighting for only moments before. The guests looked on in quiet bewilderment at uncle on the stage as he held court.

A few sheets to the wind he rambled on 'I want to say that I don't know what a beautiful girl like Kiran, I mean very beautiful (I could see him moving his eyebrows up and down several times in quick succession) is doing with him? But...(he slurred)... I wish them all the best and especially her...she will need it with that monkey boy...' He laughed, his attempt at a joke being met with disquiet amongst the revelers.

Everyone laughed nervously and the DJ went up to Sharm in a bid to take the microphone of him but Sharm masked the microphone by his chest as his rant went on 'you know he used to do tutti in his bed until he was ten years old. I know ten years old, what is that all about I used to wonder? I know these things because I had to clean his tutti with my own bare hands, but now he is a good boy, he has been naughty about a lot of things, but now he is good.' I sat up and feared the worst. He was about to make some revelation about my drug taking or something, he was drunk and did not know where he was or what he was saying. He was dangerous when he was like this. He had to be stopped!

I could see both sets of mum's and dad's looking at each other nervously, praying and hoping for the proverbial hockey stick to yank him off the stage before he really landed himself in the brown stuff. I saw dad motioning for the DJ to take the microphone off of him before we ended up with blood shed on our hands. In the meantime I continued to squirm in my seat and prayed that he fell off the stage or something. The DJ was pushed back again as Sharm slipped and sloped around the stage evading him. I continued to wince as his rambled on with his sermon.

Then in a unique turn of events Satwinder who had clearly seen enough made her way up on the stage and was now standing next to him. Sharm forgot to lower the microphone as he fought off the futile attempts to get him off the stage from his ball and chain. His conversation was being amplified via the microphone to the entire wedding party in all its shameful and bad taste.

'I am not drunk, you always say that, all I hear is nag, nag, nag, maybe if you spent more time in the bedroom I wouldn't drink so much.' The crowd gasped in disbelief as the domestic raged on in full view, warts and all.

I could hear hecklers shouting out comments from below as their frustrations were gradually exacerbating at this side show 'oi sharabi (drunkard) get off, get off the stage.' Others were shouting 'put the music back on.'

Satwinder was now shoving and provoking him whilst on the other side the DJ was trying to wrench the microphone out of his grasping paws. Dad had now got up on the stage and was pulling Sharm backwards. It was like a scene right out of Fawlty Towers. This comedy scene went on and had the vast majority of the guests in stitches as they got their mobile phone cameras trained on the embarrassing situation that had developed.

More and more guests made their way to the front of the dance floor to seek out a better view. The gathered crowd, the hoi polloi, unanimous, laughing, jostling for better positions, cackling, jeering, it was a scene reminiscent from an olden day village where everyone had gathered to watch a hanging, a public flogging.

The tug of war and tussling carried on and somehow amidst the dissention Sharm's trousers suddenly fell down. They slipped down to his ankles and nestled there in a heap, exposing his hirsute and scrawny legs. He stood there for a second looking down and surveying the damage with his Donald Duck pants hiding his modesty.

We all gasped as the hall fell silent. Auntie Satwinder stepped back in shock. His legs could have been used as a stunt double for Chewbacca on Star Wars such was the hideous amount of hair sprouting out from every conceivable crevice. There were follicles growing off of follicles and I looked at Dev in absolute shock. He was one audition away from snapping up a role in Gorillas in the Mist part two. I had never seen anything so hairy in my life and not in captivity.

Sharm was standing there in all his glory still holding the microphone, casting a mulish look at the hordes of revelers standing beneath him. He was Caesar addressing his legions. The sense of fevered anticipation hanging in the air. What was going to happen now?

He then lowered the microphone as it appeared he was having a moment of clarity. A moment that all drinkers have when they are sozzled. He looked down slowly at his trousers again and then at the guests below, pausing for a second before muttering 'bhanchod.' Dad snapped out of the shock of what had just happened, he had now had enough, and quickly lifted his trousers up and dragged him behind the stage with his wife in hot pursuit frowning and giving him a sharp, indignant look as she scurried him off the stage with dad.

The DJ meanwhile took the microphone back whilst laughing uncontrollably whilst saying 'well folks, that was some show, so, if you still have the energy lets get this party moving again?' He carried on chuckling as he put the microphone down and let the bhangra tune kick in.

I could see all the guests feverishly talking about what had just happened, whilst others carried on dancing and still laughing about the debacle that Sharm had instigated.

While this was going on I looked at my watch and turned to Dev 'well anyway, only a few hours to go and I will be jetting off to paradise with my girl and hopefully will be able to put the incidents of this day firmly behind me, you know what I mean?'

Dev winked in acknowledgement and then looked over at Kiran 'mate you are so lucky, she is a stunner, and what a lovely personality. Why did a dog like you have to end up with her? I mean you are not exactly a catch are you?' He laughed.

He had said it in a jovial manner, but it was clear that the effects of the drink and associated demons were beginning to seep through his normally enshrouded persona.

I laughed too, but deep down I was a little offended by his attempt at humour but shrugged it off. Mates are allowed to say stuff to each other which if anyone else says it to you it could be construed as offensive. I used this ideology to seek a crumb of comfort that Dev did not mean anything by the remark. I could see that Dev was pouring more and more drink down his throat as we sat there which began to worry me slightly.

I was then approached by a waiter who leaned in closer to me and said 'sorry to trouble you sir but I have a message to deliver. A man over there (he pointed to the other end of the hall where the bar was located and where I could see the back of a guy. I could see him holding a drink and propped up by the bar) he asked me to tell you that he wants to talk to you outside. Something about best interests and future happiness.'

As he finished the sentence, the man turned around and looked over to us. He held his glass aloft and saluted me before taking a shot. It was Jags. He was back at my wedding and this was one adversary that even Ranj had warned me about. He referred to him as the devil, a man whose reputation preceded him and here he was baying for my blood, offering me outside of all things.

When someone clocks you, it is best not to ignore them praying they will simply disappear, and similarly it is prudent not to hold the stare for too long as this has the opposite effect where if they weren't going to pick a fight with you they will now.

I felt my body shudder and I nudged Dev under the table with my knee whilst pointing with my eyes towards where he was standing. Dev looked on and remained silent but alert. The waiter walked off satisfied having carried out his given instructions to the letter of the book, and no doubt trotting off to get his well deserved tip.

I turned to look at Kiran to see if she was aware of the presence of Jags and she was engrossed in conversation with Tina and was not even aware that her violent ex boyfriend was in the same room as her. She would have been petrified had she known and I was going to ensure that she did not get to find out as the memories would have come painfully flooding back to her.

I looked back at the bar where Jags was standing and he was gone, like an optical illusion he had vanished. I searched the hall quickly and could not see him. Where was he? When all of a sudden I noticed him disappearing back in to the foyer and out of the hall? What was he up to? More importantly was he lying in wait for me somewhere ready to ambush me when I least expected it? Why could he not let go of Kiran? She was my wife now and he had no business being here, it did not make any sense to me.

All of a sudden, I felt a heavy thud which caused me to jump, as Ranj sat in the chair next to me in dramatic fashion slamming the room key emphatically on the table.

'There you go, done, they have been picked up. Those fools will be back at home resting, and with a promise never to bother you again.'

Ranj then scrutinised my face 'what's happening Kam? You look as though someone has pissed in your *'lassi' (Indian milk drink)* is everything cool?'

'Well I have just seen Jags, he is back.' I started to panic. 'It is all over, my dreams, the wedding, my life. Why is this all happening to me on my wedding day? I just don't deserve this.'

'Koina, doesn't matter paajee. Where is he? I can't see him?'

Dev piped up 'he walked out that way.' Dev pointed towards the foyer 'a few minutes before you got here.'

'Look you have only got another hour of the reception and after a few more bits and pieces you will be on the plane to Butlins or wherever you have booked up.'

'I know, that is the only thing that is keeping me going.' I said semi triumphantly.

Ranj poured himself a shot and sipped it slowly as he tapped his foot to the music.

I looked across and saw Kiran looking so happy as it appeared that she had provided the sound advice that Tina was looking for as they both cried and hugged each other just a few feet away from me. Tina then came over to me and said 'how you feeling, you okay?' I looked at her in amazement. Hold on a minute this was Tina being nice to me, this was indeed a moment to savour. I replied with a slight but obvious tremor in my voice 'yeah I am having a blast.' I could not fathom for the life of me why she was suddenly being nice to me after all she had never been civil since I have known her?'

I put this down to boyfriend troubles, mused that she had probably had an acrimonious split with her boyfriend today, and needed a pick me up chat from Kiran to edify her again. Well it worked as she was uncannily nice to me. She offered to pour me a drink to which I agreed and then she toasted me and said 'here is to you, I wish you all the success in the world and just for the record I think you are a decent guy.'

There were not enough superlatives in the English dictionary to tell you how happy this exchange had made me. I mean this meant a lot considering this was one girl who had a major influence in our lives in the future bearing in mind she was Kiran's bosom friend. I toasted her as we clinked our glasses together; I took a satisfying swig before turning to Dev and Ranj with raised eyebrows. They both smiled back at me reassuringly. Finally I had a positive break on my wedding day and this was going to be my watershed when things were going to start to go my way finally.

CHAPTER 21

—∞—

Smelling of roses

The wedding reception was drawing to a close and was nearly unabridged. Most of the guests were tucking into the dinner that was being served including plates of chicken, lamb, and fish; all with accompanying roti / chapatti's and rice, not to mention the delicious desserts including rice pudding and kulfi. This was the place to be to allay your hunger pangs, as the succulent food drew you in like a finger licking magnet.

We followed reception and wedding day tradition as our mums and dads gathered around Kiran and me and started to feed us whilst the cameraman and photographer kept themselves busy getting shots from different angles. This went on for about ten minutes, as the usual suspects appeared to feed us bits of food from the steel plates that were on the tables in front of us.

Ranj and Dev stayed close by behind me drinking shots of Bacardi and coke as they doubled up and acted as my bodyguards in case Jags turned up guns blazing to turn this into the wedding day massacre. I felt a tinge of reassurance knowing these two troopers were on stand by just inches behind me as I kept on eating the food that was being offered to me. My instinctive feeling was to retch as I chewed each piece of food after it was placed into my mouth. I mean as a stickler for hygiene I was becoming overwhelmingly concerned that a small minority of people who stepped up to the mantle to feed me had grubby, unwashed, and grimy fingers. I had absolutely no idea what orifice their finger had just come out of as I masticated slowly, occasionally spitting the food out into a tissue when the cameraman was focussed elsewhere. Kiran meanwhile had not given this any thought as she chomped away unreservedly much to the occasional pitiful glance that I gave her.

Once this had concluded Preeto in all her sadistic glory inched towards me along with the accompanying Omen music holding a plate of 'ludoos' that at this moment looked as savoury as bird droppings.

I knew full well that from the mere evil look that Preeto cast me before unveiling the plate to all and sundry, that they had to have had a dash of jadu or similar witchcraft applied to them. It stood to reason, Preeto, black cat, and jadu, words synonymous with one another.

I mean I was so suspicious that I had an overwhelming urge to scoop Preeto up in my arms, run out to the lake outside, and throw her in to see if the cackling hag bobbed like a witch in the icy water. Failing that I was tempted to adopt plan B which would have meant sneaking up on her at night as she lay asleep on her nest of snakes and checking for the number of the beast – six, six, six after carefully cutting away tufts of her hair with a pair of scissors. This woman had a nasty streak of evil coursing through her veins and I could sense this. I don't know why? I just could. I was buggered after the day I had endured if I was going to be flummoxed on the

finishing line by a *jadu ludoo*. I turned to Ranj and whispered my concerns in his ear. He looked and whispered
back in my ear 'don't worry, stay cool it is your mother
in law, don't do nothing crazy that you will regret.'

Kiran looked at me confused and baffled as to why I
was slowing things down by chatting to my friends. The
poor girl had no idea about the sense of anguish I was
feeling at this moment. The redolence of a voodoo ritual
lingered menacingly above my head. As soon as I looked
back, Preeto was hovering next to me menacingly with
the ludoo plate in one hand and an incriminating ludoo
moving its way like a heat seeking missile to my lips 'eat
putt, open your mouth wide, eat....it is pyaar (love)
come on.' I resisted by moving my head back and saying
'no, please, no.'

Preeto's tail was up as she retorted, knowing the
surrounding crowd were very much on her side 'koina,
you have to have a bite.'

'No, no more mum. I am full from the roti, I will have
it later.' Preeto placed the plate of ludoo down and gently
took hold of the back of my head with her other hand
and moved both ludoo and my head along the same
plain. I was now a couple of inches away from becoming
a quivering and drooling wreck. Everyone meanwhile
chipped in with cries of support and 'come on putt it is
pyaar.' You fools I thought. You are witnessing
manslaughter, you are all witnesses in a potential murder
scene, imbeciles. I tried to move my head back. I would
rather have eaten a ghoulash containing pieces of
congealed ear wax, peeled bunion skin, nail clippings
and belly button fluff from a down and out tramp, all
washed down with a helping of rats piss then eat this
satanic ludoo.

Just as the edge of the jadu ludoo touched my lips Ranj
swept forward and took hold of Preeto's hand and said
playfully 'auntiji, no. It is a new young generation tradition that the mother in law eats the first ludoo.' Then
without wasting another second he bent Preetos's arm in
a goose neck manner and stuffed the entire ludoo in her
mouth pushing her chin upwards to ensure she bit into it,
which she did. He did this innocuously and playfully, and
in doing so did not raise an eyebrow at first. She was
stunned and gob smacked as we all were. This was a first.

Everyone laughed. I looked around and noticed that
Manjit (Kiran's dad) had a look of absolute shame and
disgust on his face, as did Kiran. If I could have high
fived Ranj I would have but instead I shot him a cheeky
knowing smile as he patted my back before returning to
his position behind me. Preeto meanwhile had no choice
but to pull out half of the ludoo and with the cameraman
and photographer trained solely on her, ended up eating
the remaining ludoo that had been stuffed in her gob. She
was not happy but kept on smiling pretentiously as she
gulped down the last piece of ludoo. Her evil, demented
bunny look had now been replaced by a limp and
defeated bunny look as she slipped away making some
excuse about getting something. The ludoo ceremony
never got started again and the crowd around us
dispersed. I turned back to Ranj 'so mate that was playing it cool was it?' we both laughed.

Ranj pointed to the back of the hall, there were people
clustered around the tables at the back, talking, drinking, and eating. I could see Pam standing and talking to
another guest looking smug as she looked over in my
direction. 'Check this out; I just got a text from Rosebud
she is coming here any moment now. I have told her

where Pam is standing, what she is wearing etc. She will do the rest mi amigo.'

'Who's Rosebud?' I enquired

'You will see kuta, don't worry.'

Pam chatted away without an obvious care in the world as I focussed my attention on the door immediately behind her and saw a visually stunning girl walk through in a seductive fitting green Indian suit. She walked past Pam and then stopped and turned back to speak with her again.

Ranj tugged me by the arm 'that is Rosebud. You are going to want to see this, come on.' I followed him towards where Pam and Rosebud were engrossed in conversation. As we were getting closer he stopped by a nearby table and pretended to fiddle with some cutlery as he pulled me in next to him 'listen to what she is saying, she is always a treat.' We were sufficiently at an angle for neither Rosebud or Pam to clock us as we eavesdropped on their conversation.

Although we had joined the conversation midway and had missed the opening salutations and pleasantries, I had a feel for what was happening. I overheard Rosebud saying 'yeh I have to say that Kam messed my sister about too, and I think it is right that we teach that bitch a lesson don't you think. I mean that is the only reason that I am here today to get revenge for my little sister.'

Pam was nodding excitedly and unbeknown to her was being snared as every second ticked by, the dumb truck.

'So come with me and I will introduce you to my sister who can tell you more about that arsehole, come on.'

Rosebud took hold of Pam's arm and led her outside into the car park as we both followed furtively behind, dipping in and out of the shadows every time Pam looked around innocently.

'Is Rosebud a friend of yours?' I asked Ranj as we continued creeping up on them.

Ranj stopped me and explained 'she is always the first one I call when I have problems with other girls or whatever. She is like the enforcer and will sort out any shit I have without any problem. She knows I will do the same for her.'

'Welcome to my world.' Ranj was now in full flow 'these days too many people go on about you are my brother, you are like a sister to me, you are my brethren etc. Excuse me if I yawn…that is bullshit and what counts is stuff like this, when it is going down. I mean it is no good brothering my arse with words and pussying out on me when I need you, that is not what calling someone bruv or brother is all about in my eyes. You catch my drift kuta?'

We carried on using the building line as we followed the girls into the car park and supposedly to see Rosebud's sister in a parked car. Ranj continued on his soap box 'brother, brethren is meaningful and strong terminology to use and without the minerals and substance to back it up with actions it becomes nothing more than bullshit and empty words.'

Ranj was emphatic in his description, and I could feel the vehement passion and convictions of his words ringing in my ears. The conviction and passion that he had for his friends. This lesson was now increasingly and abundantly clear for me as I had witnessed that he was the sum total of his words and actions throughout the day when he had saved me on numerous occasions and acted like a true 'brother' to me.

We trotted over to the car park but there was no sign of the girls. Where were they? Ranj motioned for me to follow him which I did. He then walked around to the shed where the motor bikes are parked up and motioned for me to be quiet. We both peered around the corner and I could see Rosebud in full flow as she drilled a low punch firmly into Pams stomach. Pam clutched her stomach and keeled forward grimacing in pain. Rosebud sniped 'yeh, and if you ever show your face around here or give my Ranj anymore grief then I will visit you again and you will wish you never crossed my path.' She then helped to stand Pam back to her feet and steadied her 'now I want you to say thank you very much for that lesson, I enjoyed it very much.'

Pam looked confused 'what?...I can't.' BANG...Rosebud landed another devastating punch in her stomach and she repeated the previous steps by falling to her knees whilst holding her stomach. Again Rosebud stood her up and after steadying her again said 'now life is all about respect and discipline. There are rules that we all have to adhere to and this one is simple, you are here causing problems for my brother.' I looked at Ranj and the penny dropped. So this was his sister. It all made sense to me now.

Rosebud continued 'and my brother doesn't need any problems cause he is a nice guy.'

Pam nodded her head in agreement and without hesitation.

'So we ready to leave the wedding and drop you off home?'

Pam weakly mumbled 'yeh.'

'Okay now repeat what I said about you enjoying this encounter and this way I am satisfied that this will

stay ingrained in your brain.' Pam repeated the requested sentence word perfect and they then turned to
face us.

Ranj took hold of my arm and yanked me back
behind the wall. We ran back to the reception hall and
were just about to enter the foyer when I turned to him
and said 'hey, I just want to say thanks for everything
you have done today, I really appreciate it.'

'No worries, I can see how much she means to you
and couldn't stand around and let these wasters spoil
your day.'

'Bruv, she is like my life, you know. When I am with
her I feel complete, alive and full of energy.'

'I can tell with that mushy, I am in love look plastered
on your face bhanchod.'

'I just can't fathom why these guys would want to
spoil my big day, this stuff is like sentimental shit, you
know sacred cow stuff.'

Ranj shook his head 'listen I am from the street and
one thing I have learnt at an early age is that no-one out
there gives a crap about your feelings, desires, ambitions,
or anything about your life but you. The sooner you
grasp this way of thinking, then you will really begin to
understand the need to be a little bit selfish and ruthless
in life as far as others are concerned, you feel me.'

I was momentarily stunned as I began to see the
deeper complexities and substance from my newly found
best friend's character as his profound statement
resoundingly hit home.

'Listen I was going to ask you something. How close
are you to Dev?'

The question confused me. What was his sudden
curiosity for my relationship with Dev?'

'Err, well he is like my best buddy, we are tight...why do you ask?'

'No reason.'

'No, no come on what's up?'

'Well, to be honest. I don't like the guy, never have. I tell you straight. I think he is a kuta and about as trust-worthy as a four pound note.' Ranj's words stunned me. I had no idea.

Ranj spoke on 'I see the way he looks at you. He has the green monster coursing through his body, and like my mamma says a mate who is consumed with jealousy is a weasel. They are never truly happy for you because there is too much poison and hatred stopping them in their worm like body.'

'Serious, but he has always...'

Ranj cut over me 'look I know you two are like two sperms on a stick and you grew up in the sandbox together, but.' He prodded his finger to the temple on the side of his head 'you have got to trust your dumaag (brain) in situations like this, he is a jealous bhanchod in my opinion, period.'

'Ranj I hear what you are saying but the guy has always done stuff for me, bent over backwards, been flexible lots of times. I don't kn...'

Ranj cut in again 'course he is gorgeous. Flexible...it is easy to be flexible when you have no spine, look what do I know? I just follow my street instinct, and sometimes I do get it wrong, but not often. Let me ask you some-thing, how do you think I knew it was your wedding?'

He bamboozled me with that one and in honesty I did not have a clue 'don't know, how did you find out?'

'Dev somehow managed to get hold of my mobile number and text me and then called me on your stag night saying that you were getting married and stuff and that I should turn up. He said that he thought it was out of order that I was not coming and not to say anything, blah blah.'

'You are joking right?'

'Nah, he knows that I have got a reputation for being a bit leary when I have had a pint and he thought that you not inviting me might have caused friction between me and you, and to be honest it almost did, his plan nearly worked.'

'Nah you have got that wrong, he is...'

'Look there is something going on, I don't know what but his plan back fired on him the kuta, cos I get on with you even though you never contacted me or invited me to the wedding.'

I studied Ranj's face, he was honest and lucid with his opinions and his sincerity was appreciated. I had no idea the under current of hatred he had towards Dev and this was eye opening stuff.

'You can't trust anyone these days. Keep your circle of trust tight, and those who are true friends will definitely stand the test of time.'

'Thanks man I appreciate it. Well everything you have done today basically.' I reached out and our hands collided powerfully in the middle in a solid and meaningful handshake cementing our newfound respect and relationship with one another. He patted my back 'you are an okay bloke Kam. I have time for you, but keep in touch in the future, not like last time.'

'One hundred per cent bruv.'

"When those idiots wake up from their slumbers you will be long gone, so everything should be cool now."

'Oh yeh, you best make sure you come to my wedding and stag do in a few months. I think Dimple could be the one. I mean she took me to another level up there.' We both laughed and made our way back inside the hall.

It was ironic and paradoxically surreal. He was previously the one guy I had despised being there and now I was thankful and blessed that he had actually been there fighting tooth for tooth with me. The walking, talking Agatha Christie mystery waiting to be solved was now my new found brethren and guardian.

We made our way back to the table. I turned to Ranj 'bruv, that was your sister then hey?'

'Yeh she is my sis, told you she would sort it out.'

I was trying to comprehend whether their mum had injected steroids into her colustrum when she had breast fed them as these were two warriors, vigilantes of the Asian circles. Two scary individuals that you did not want to cut up in your car and get into a road rage incident with that was for sure.

CHAPTER 22

~m~

Mobile Danger

We both sat back at the table and I could see Dev chatting to Kiran. I noticed that his hand was placed rather disturbingly on her knee. It looked innocent and maybe it was innocent but it made me do a double take as I nestled back into my seat. Dev had not seen us return and carried on talking with his back to us. I was sure that even Kiran had not noticed that his hand was on her thigh especially as the lehnga she was wearing was heavily cut and so not that sensitive to pressure.

I stared at his hand and it did not move for at least two or three minutes of my observing. This was wrong, disconcerting and a boot in the knackers for me. I was bracing myself to say something when Ranj nudged me and said 'look who's coming.' He pointed across the hall with his finger and smirked. I looked up and reeled back in shock at what I had seen. It seemed as though my luck had just evaporated for good.

'Your goose is cooked son.' Ranj chipped in mockingly.

I looked in absolute horror as Pam was walking towards the table. There was no sign of Rosebud. I thought the situation was rectified, mission accomplished. Had she got the better of Rosebud when her back was turned and dumped her body somewhere? No way, she came closer and closer to the table. I looked at Ranj in a desperate attempt for an eleventh hour interception, a lunging rugby tackle, a sniper to pick her off with a bullet through the eyes, anything, something, but nothing was forthcoming as he simply sat back in his seat and sipped from his tumbler. My smile was fading and heart stopping. Dev's tactile hands were the least of my worries. Pam was ready to spill the beans with my wife sitting inches away from me. This was it. My mind was in emotional and capitulating turmoil.

She approached the table and stood in front of me. I felt the sickening taste of bitter defeat and culpability as she bowed her head and spoke 'I am sorry if I have caused you any trouble. I am leaving now, please forgive me. You will not see me again Kam, sorry for everything.' With that she averted her eyes from me and scuttled away the same way she had come.

I could only look on in stunned disbelief. What had just happened? I had no idea. I let out a histrionic puff of air as I glanced at Ranj, who was tapping his hand on the table and laughing raucously. It seemed that he had more faith in his sister Rosebud than me and it appeared that this was Rosebud's way of concluding the matter once and for all; the icing on her cake.

Kiran meanwhile looked over Dev's shoulder and back at me 'what did she want?'

Dev turned quickly and whisked his hand back hoping that I hadn't seen him, but he was obtuse. My eagle eyes had already clocked him. What was he up to? Why look so guilty? These questions were circulating with incriminating malevolence in my head, and the vast amounts of alcohol in my system were lending an even more sinister edge to my thoughts coupled with my inherent paranoia, Dev was now very much in my sights.

However, he was a mate and so in the grand scheme of things, I just put it down to his drunken state at the time and knew that on occasions he had a tendency to be over friendly with people. Still, I was now weak with relief, the Pam situation was a close one, she had been hanging over me like a thick black cloud all throughout the reception; like the Sword of Damocles and now, as they said in Oz, *'ding dong the Wicked Witch is dead.' (well gone home anyway).*

'Don't worry Kiran – you wont see her again, she is no mate of mine.' I said as I looked at Kiran and then at Dev.

Dev looked away and knocked back a half empty glass of Bacardi that had been left on the table. There was something not right about the situation and I continued to grapple with what it could have been.

Dev's behaviour was becoming all the more peculiar the more alcohol he consumed and he then got up to walk away.

'Where you off to mate?' I asked trying to gauge his reaction and delve into his strange behaviour.

'I am err…ermm…just going toilet, back in a minute.' He walked off as the DJ announced on the microphone

'Folks, get yourselves on the dance floor as here are the last songs before we wrap things up here today. You have been a rip roaring and fantastic crowd – well done – now *'chakk de phattay' (a Punjabi phrase literally meaning go rip up the floor boards with your dance moves).*

All the guests from every nook and cranny of the hall all leapt up and made their way onto the dance floor.

They seemed to appear from everywhere, from under the stage, abseiling down on ropes, being zapped in like the crew of the Star Trek Enterprise and so forth. Kiran and her other cousins were letting their hair down on the dance floor, as was Tina. They were making the most of the last few songs for the day. I spoke with Ranj in the meantime while the dance floor festivities raged on.

'You know you mentioned your team of boys. What are they like mercenaries, vigilantes or something?' They sort out other peoples mess?'

Ranj replied 'no, they are just loyal friends who will back me up when there is a call for help. They are doers not sayers.'

'You know what you said about Dev outside to me, well what did you mean?' I don't know why but I just wanted to ask Ranj what he thought about him touching my wife's leg and whether or not I should mention it? So I carried on probing him with my finely tuned questions.

'What's the point? He is your friend remember, devious Dev I used to call him at school. As slippery as a snake; but hey you get on well with him don't you?'

'Bruv seriously, what is your honest opinion of him?'

Ranj studied me 'you want the truth?'

'Yeh well of course or otherwise this conversation is pointless if you tell me what you think I want to hear' I quipped.

'Firstly why are you asking me, has something happened between you two?' he asked me suspiciously.

'Well, yes and no. Nah nothing really.'

'Look you are talking about being straight and already you are holding stuff back, what happened?'

That was the cue I was seeking and the flood gates opened, as I blurted out my suspicions 'I just saw him with his hand on my wife's leg and she didn't seem to mind and then when he saw me he shit his pants, look even now he has been gone for ages, There is something going on, he has always acted strange around her, but I have taken no notice of it until now, today, that moment. Am I just been my usual paranoid self?'

'I am not surprised. I don't want to say I told you so but I think he is a spineless worm, a blood sucking leech. The kind of guy who when you are not looking would slam a blade into your back rather than see you be happy and prosper. I worked that shit out when I knew him at school. Once a bhanchod worm always a sneaky worm.'

Ranj was far more descriptive than I thought he would have been. It was obvious to me at this time that there was some previous history between the pair of them. At this moment, despite taking Ranj's scathing and jaundiced comments about Dev on board, for some reason I decided to give him the benefit of the doubt. I mean I was not about to give up a long standing friendship for something as trivial as what I had seen today, and with drink involved; It was ludicrous.

In fairness I strongly believed that Ranj had got his assessment wrong. Dev was far from perfect and had his faults but in all the time that I had known him and the moments gone by he has always been there for me.

I quickly tried to make light of the brewing tension and jokingly quipped 'flipping hell, he is not that bad bruv. Has he pissed you off or something? What you gonna do call the team to sort him out, ha ha?

Ranj looked at me, his face deadly serious 'it has been arranged.' He looked away, his byzantine expression momentarily emasculating me.

I sat up concerned. 'Hold on..err...what has been arranged?'

'Well you know, the team you joked about, the fact that I don't like him very much...well they were waiting for him in the toilet...and right now (he looked at his watch) he is probably being carved into a thousand pieces and scattered across a field close to this hall, the kuta, good riddance.'

My jaw hit the floor. Maybe I had got it all wrong and didn't know Ranj as well as I thought, his hair trigger temper, his icy cool stare in the heart of battle were all part of his make up. The man sitting next to me was a steely and ruthless killer.

I looked around and could not see Dev anywhere. I asked anxiously 'you are joking right?' I studied him closely, this was a wind up for sure, I prayed. It had to be, he was not going to kill Dev, why would he?'

He stared at me, no emotion at all, but I could sense his feeling of hate towards Dev had become an all consuming passion that had made him do what he intended.

'Ranj, tell me you are joking...right?' My voice cracking slightly, maybe I did not know him as well as I thought. This was no wind up. This was the culmination of his objective for the day. He had treated Dev with contempt and disparagement all day. There was still no response, just the cold and ruthless glare that any would be serial killer would be proud of.

They say that violence begets violence. All day he had fought with pure spunk, a confident manslayer and now the beast had been triumphant, he had snared his true quest; his quarry was captive and probably hacked to death as the thoughts churned disturbingly in my head.

Ranj, malevolent, gloomy faced and lordly reached out and touched my arm with his hand 'don't worry, it will be ok, he felt no pain when he went.'

I stared at him, still in appalled shock, not sure what to say or what to do. All I recall is an empty, hollow feeling in the pit of my stomach. Why?

After a few awkward and eternal moments of silence his serious face broke into a cackling howl. He had wound me up a treat and knew how easy a target I was with the concoction of drink and paranoia combining unremorsefully as my achilles heels. The sense of relief was palpable as I once again relaxed into my seat. I poured us another drink as the bhangra music played on sublimely.

After a few moments and changing the subject I asked Ranj 'have you seen Jags floating around anywhere since last time, do you think he just got fed up and left?'

'Yeh I think so, you are just too small fry for him. What is he going to do with you? I think he has scared you enough and he will probably be waiting at the airport for you as you board your plane, that's all.' Ranj looked away after delivering this crushing blow.

'What?' I sat upright.

'No I am just yanking your chain you kuta, he was probably curious to see who she was going to marry that is all. I bet he is sitting at home now, in his slippers watching Songs of Praise or something, trust me.' Ranj was a funny guy, a character and I liked him.

I looked around the table to where Kiran had been sitting and noticed that there was a mobile phone lying there.

I recognized it as Dev's mobile phone. There was only one way of testing the mettle of Ranj's suspicions about

Dev and that was to have a quick trawl through his text messages. I picked it up and unlocked it. So without further ado I scrolled down and read some of the messages that he had sent some mutual friends and others that he had exchanged with me. They were all there, saved in his inbox. I looked around and the dance floor was jammed, Ranj was busy talking on his mobile phone and crucially Dev was still not back from wherever he had disappeared to.

Then I struck gold. There it was the message asking Ranj to come to my wedding, sent on my stag night. The snake had gone behind my back. I flicked the message off and went to put the phone back on the table. I had seen all the evidence I needed in this case, but then a felt an overwhelming compulsion to see what photo's he had saved on his phone too. I don't know why, I was just mildly curious and suspicious.

I then opened his folder containing the camera photos and scrolled down through the eighty five photos he had stored.

I scrolled down and there were some funny and memorable occasions stored and I found myself smirking at them. Then I continued to scroll, when one picture caught my eye. I toggled the button to get back to it and opened it up.

I looked closely. Oh my God! I almost dropped the phone in disbelief, my heart stopped for a split second. I looked up anxiously and saw that everyone was busy enjoying themselves as I raised the phone up to my face for a better perspective on what I was seeing.

It was a photo of Kiran at the restaurant in Slough when we had met some time ago. I remembered him taking this photo and was under the impression at the time that this was meant to be a group photo and not an individual one of Kiran.

I scrolled down to other photos and every single photo depicted a picture of Kiran with the vast majority of them from the wedding reception. I looked at the dance floor at Kiran bopping away with her friends.

This was surreal, a nightmare. She was cheating on me with Dev, the hand on her thigh, the continual worrying before the wedding; the secret looks that I would see Dev giving her. It was all making painful sense to me as my stomach churned sickeningly, the deep emotional pain you get when someone you trust stabs you in the back. I was facing up to what was now becoming a tangible and ugly truth. My suspicions, Ranj's suspicions were all true.

I scrolled down some more, and a lot of the photos were of Kiran sitting, posing at the head table as Dev had snapped away every time my back was turned.

The treacherous Judas had been drinking the water from my well from under my nose and making a fool out of me in the process. How could he have done this to me? The bastard! I clenched my fists, shook my head and gritted my teeth. I would kill him, I would kill her, they had played me like a fool and I was the only sucker in town who didn't know the reality of what was happening. Ranj in the meantime walked off onto the dance floor and I saw him dirty dancing with Dimple, the girl he had been seeing, cavorting with and fancied the knickers off of. She was one of Kiran's friends.

My blood continued to boil as I went down to the earlier photos and then saw the picture that repulsed me more than any of the others, the one that made me slam the phone down on the table in furious anger and loathing.

I steadied myself and slowly looked at the picture again to make sure. It was the picture of me standing outside the brothel and the one that was posted through Kiran's door days before the wedding and what nearly cost me my marriage.

I had been set up, I had been a mug. Both Kiran and Dev had tried to damage my reputation, but why would they do this?

The brothel photo was now the final straw that had broken the camels back for me as I put the phone back where it was on the table. I would beat him to a pulp when he returned and then we would be even. No, I stopped myself as thought after evil thought raced through my mind. No, I said, tough seldom wins over sneaky and nasty. I would pretend I knew nothing and then try to catch them in *'flagrante delecto' (red handed)* and with the smoking gun in their hands, catch them in a passionate embrace or something; the deceitful and duplicitous bastards.

What would I do with her? I was not sure. Was she really involved? I saw Dev walking back towards the table, finally.

He had been gone ages. As he approached the table, my thoughts suddenly switched. I was going to set about him and find out at exactly what stage the trust, loyalty, and goodness had been sucked out of him. I needed to know, and I wanted the answers now.

Dev reached the table he chirped 'oh thank God, there it is.' He pointed to his phone and placed his other hand on his chest in relief. 'I have been looking everywhere for it, that was close.'

I smiled trying to disguise my ruthless demeanor 'yeh, you don't want to lose that do you, then you would be in trouble wouldn't you?' I squinted my eyes at him whilst treating him with total disdain. So here I was calm and restrained and going with the flow. The more I looked at him, the more my blood pressure rose, but I went with the flow, still nice and calm...

In a sudden paroxysm of unrelenting fury and red mist I could take no more, there were simply too many unanswered questions. Sod this I muttered under my breath, '*only dead fish and sheep go with the flow*' as I leapt over the table and dragged Dev by his lapels over the table and onto my side clattering and knocking the chairs over. The music cleverly disguised the commotion and only a handful of guests turned to see what was happening and rushed over to us to break up the dissension. I helped Dev to his feet and told the others that Dev had just slipped over and that he would be okay and to leave us alone.

They all moved back and carried on their drinking and merriment. I was now harbouring dangerous, sinister thoughts and now I had Dev's attention I would get to the bottom of this sordid affair once and for all. I had learnt some valuable lessons from Ranj. He had been an adept teacher. Dev looked at me worryingly as I pushed his chest into the chair; he sat with a thud and knew full well what was coming. Now I had lost my sense of humour; Dev was in a big puddle of shit without the shoes to cope...I just felt like plugging the fucker...

—⁓—

CHAPTER 23

Snakepit

There was no way Dev was going to come away from this situation unscathed. I had made my mind up. The biggest mistake you could ever make is to mess about with your mate's girl full stop, but on his wedding day, well that was just suicidal. At this moment in time, my blood was bubbling over and just the look of this sad and pathetic excuse for a weasel sitting in front of me was infuriating enough.

The venomous thoughts oscillated in my head amidst the chaos of the dancing and festivities surrounding me and I knew that the way to really get to the bottom of what was going on and to drill down to the nub of the matter was to talk to my so called buddy on a level. I pulled up a chair and sat down next to Dev.

'So tell me what the fuck is up, mate?' I could feel every fibre in my body straining not to land a fist straight on his jaw and put him to sleep.

This day had taught me some valuable lessons and none more important than realizing that you need to look beneath the surface to truly see what substance is there, the show, the façade that you see being portrayed is superficial and what really counts is what principles, morals that person is really made up of. Above all street loyalties are fickle and can change in a whim as was painfully transparent right now.

He said nothing and just stared at me. I could hear the cogs in his head churning and thinking up an excuse for the sordid affair. My silence finally compelled him to talk, as he feebly mustered a reply 'bruv what's happened?'

'Lies, fucking deceit, back stabbing...being a SNAKE!' I couldn't resist the temptation to enunciate the word snake through gritted teeth as Dev looked on contemplating his imminent fate.

'Kam...don't do this, seriously I don't know what is going on?' His face was scrunched up in a question mark and he genuinely looked confused. I leaned in closer, my breath now on his collar, my fists clenched and the ever pressing urge to rip his head off not far from my thoughts. There is one thing I detest more than anything, when you have tried to make a fool out of me, mistaken my niceness for gullibility and you don't have the guts to admit what you have done, face up to the snowball of facts stacking up against you. This just insults my intelligence.

'Okay, you little rat...just tell me why...why you have got a photo of me standing outside Sandhus...on your phone, fucking explain that then?' I had caught him mentally disarmed with my question.

My sudden paroxysm and relentless use of profanities jolted an elderly couple who were ambling past the table heading up to the dance floor. They exchanged nervous looks with one another but carried on regardless. I smiled back and took a swig of the half empty tumbler sitting in front of me to steady myself, buy some thinking time as I returned my steely gaze back on my snared quarry. I was studying his eyes, the windows to his soul. Dad had told me when I was growing up that everything you ever wanted to know about someone were all revealed in the eyes, fear, sincerity, humility, excitement, lust, and in this case downright treachery. His eyes were over flowing with back stabbing perfidy and snake like betrayal.

Dev's face dropped in horror; he leaned back in his seat, the cheap smell of betrayal etched evidently on his forehead. How would he get out of this cesspit? I was intrigued.

He remained seated in silent trepidation, just looking, studying my reactions, scared, fearful, and not knowing exactly where this confrontation was leading and the ramifications that were lingering ominously around the corner.

'Again bhanchod…do you want to tell me about the photo? Come on Dev, don't be afraid; tell me how the photo of ME standing outside Sandhus got onto your phone?'

Dev looked appalled. A combination, of his stupidity for leaving the photo on his phone, and guilt for having betrayed his friend.

'Why did you do it, that's all I want to know?' I asked again.

Finally, he broke his muted silence and uttered a few words 'look bruv, it is not what you think.' He could not look me in the eyes, a good indication that someone is lying to you or they are bricking it. He was a fiery combination of the two.

I looked to my side and could see my *'wife'* walking back to the table with her entourage of Tina and a couple of her other friends tailing behind her, dancing and all looking effervescent. She looked happy, full of verve and had no idea of the toasting I was giving her secret lover. She simply had no clue.

She approached the table and she sat down. Our eyes met, I smiled, reassuring her that everything was just fine, all was rosy in the garden…but it was far from rosy.

The truth being, things were far from being fine, they had just got dirty and I was surreptitiously plotting my revenge. There were alot of unanswered questions, things that needed clarifying before I knew exactly where this situation was heading.

I grabbed Dev by the arm, digging my claws into the arm of his suit jacket pulling him closer to me 'last time, the photo…why?'

He looked up to the ceiling pensively and back down at me as he reached out slowly for the bottle of Bacardi unscrewing the cap and pouring himself a generous shot. He sipped from the glass, his hand shaking and his brow damp with sweat.

Then he hit me with his excuse, his earth shattering revelation 'Tina asked me to do it. She called me a few times out of the blue…and…then one night when we were talking, she was asking questions about you.' He took a sip of his drink, his hand unsteady as the rim of the glass met his lips. I did not mind, he was drinking truth serum, I knew that drink has the ability to loosen the tongue of anyone. Make the staunchest and most pious individual magically loquacious.

He continued 'she said that she had heard this that and the other about you, you know that you did drugs and you were checking out other women. She then said that she didn't believe me when I said that you had left that life behind you; the life of drugs and stuff like Sandhu's. She still didn't believe me and said that I was full of bullshit.'

At this juncture dad came over to the table 'come on son, this is the last couple of songs.' He tugged at my arm.

'Dad, I have got stomach cramps, I need to sit down for a few moments.' He bought the excuse and made off back to the floor.

I motioned for Dev to continue as he was and he responded 'she said that if that was the case, you know you leaving the brothel life and all that behind you; then to take a photo just to prove it. So...even when I took it I felt like a prat, and don't know why, I just wanted to get one up on her.'

I shook my head deploringly as his continued with his outpouring. I always knew that Dev was gullible and easily led but he had shown as much gumption as the winner in the donkey derby and even by his standards, this was criminal. I just knew what was coming and braced myself.

'Bruv...I even told her over and over that evening when I phoned her from the car that you had told Pam where to go and that you hadn't seen her since you started dating Kiran and she was cool with that...I am not stupid...I know how it looks. I did ask her why she wanted me to take a photo.'

I looked at the buffoon sat in front of me and contemplated what I was hearing.

Dev drank some more and slurred 'she said that it was just to prove to her that this was the final visit and it would reassure her as Kiran's best mate. She swore to me that she would not mention anything to anyone about this. It was between me and her, like a pact. I saw this as a way to bridge a gap with her.'

'What?' I could not resist the temptation to show my disbelief and interrupt his flow.

'I know I have fucked up, but I had no idea she would use the photo or anything...that she was...well that crafty and evil.

I found out she posted the pictures anonymously through Kiran's door the next day.' His speech became fast and erratic.

'Why would she do that then, did you set this up or not?' I had him on the ropes and was going in for the knock out punch.

'Baba di sohn (swear to God) I had nothing to do with this bruv.'

'Yeh, so let me get this right, I then get a call from Kiran when she received the mystery photo and Tina is there miraculously to console her, you fool.'

I looked over at Tina, the pestiferous cow and gritted my teeth. She knew that the photo evidence had the potential to cause the marriage to break down, but done it anyway. I can see it now...she is nothing but a cold hearted bitch, a marriage breaker.

The vast amounts of alcohol in my system was distorting my thoughts, making me angrier and more and more vengeful.

'How did she get a copy of the photo?'

He paused and looked at me ashamedly 'I sent the photo later that evening. I sent it on with a message *'Kam has told that Pam girl where to go, here is proof, now do you believe me?'* He fumbled through his phone and showed me a message from his inbox reflecting exactly that message. He was right, there it was, proof.

'Why would you send the photo in the first place, are you insane?' My mouth lathering with frustration and bile.

'I am sorry bruv, I didn't mean to do any harm.' I could visibly see his spirit packing its suitcase and leaving town on the last train, his legs buckling under the burden of guilt.

'Tina must have then told Preeto about me doing drugs then, kunjari, marriage breaking whore.'

'Yeh she is the one that fucked it all up.' Dev chipped in.

'That night, when I tapped on the window of the car, were you speaking to her on the phone?' I asked the cretin.

'Yeh, I felt guilty and just called to say I had got the proof she wanted. That is when she demanded I sent the photo, so I sent it later that evening.'

The pieces of the jigsaw were fitting into place. I knew Dev was gullible as he had proven to me over the years, and had done the most ridiculous things, but this one had just taken the biscuit.

I looked across at Tina, Kiran and Preeto as they were engrossed in conversation. Preeto was looking down trodden and doleful as she sat at the end of the head table drinking copious amounts of water. She had had her wings clipped from the previous incident with the ludoo feeding escapade with Ranj. The mere thought of her contemplating the damaging effects that her own curse would have on her was amusing, if of course, she had cursed the ludoo as I strongly suspected, and in the realms of plausibility, I was certain she had.

Kiran sat and chatted with her as the DJ made his final announcement of the reception, last song, last dance and my final encounter with the drowned rat sat in front of me who was now shaking and metaphorically licking his wounds, yearning for salvation and some crumbs of comfort from me, that were not forthcoming.

I sat back and took a moment to look at the situation in perspective. What about their sordid affair? This was the big one. The secret I really wanted to rumble.

I could see Tina laughing and joking with Kiran as she adjusted her bangles on her arm. It looked like she didn't have a care in the world. I could not understand how and why she would be so malicious to try to break my marriage up.

She was a cold hearted bitch who could not bear to see someone else be happy, a soulless creature who had poured scorn on our relationship from the very first day. I blamed myself for a moment; maybe I should have got to know her better.

I was in a state of perplexity as I struggled to regain my composure and prevent myself from breaking down and losing emotional control. Was she the victim of a bitter childhood? Had she broken off acrimoniously with her boyfriend?

Had something happened so terrible in her life that caused her to focus on wrecking my one chance of happiness with a girl I worshipped?

Normal people are just not so vindictive; unless they have a motive and I had worked out that it was down to her own life being so bitter and twisted that she did not want to see her friends happy. The same minerals and credentials as the creature sat on the chair in front of me, as Ranj had accurately described him, a filthy little worm.

I focussed my attention back on Dev 'did you invite Ranj to the wedding, yes or no?' The questions were coming in thick and fast and Dev had nowhere to hide his Judas type treachery.

'Yeh I did.' He replied sheepishly and hanging his head in shame.

I knew exactly why he had done this and moved swiftly on containing my disappointment for a moment. I wanted to knuckle down to the real issue burning a hole in my mind, causing me the most anguish and fear.

I looked back at Dev, he stared back at me blankly 'so why did you have your hand on my wife's leg before?'

I asked him outright. No more games, no more fencing with him. I just wanted the truth, the day's events were taking their toll on me, and my disappointment was fluctuating between physically hurting him and launching an invective assault.

My thoughts lost in a jumbled up murky and depressive abyss.

Dev lowered his eyes to the floor and clasped his hands together. The bunny had been caught in the headlights. This was one predicament that he would not wriggle out of, worm or not, he was under the spotlight of interrogation and had better come up with the right answers.

I repeated myself 'The hand on her leg, what were you doing?'

I was praying that there would be a plausible explanation; I was searching for this small crumb of redemption, a tiny shred of dignity after the tumultuous day and week that I had endured.

'I'm sorry Kam, really sorry man, please try and understand.' He spoke with the hint of reluctance and pity.

'Understand what?' I asked inquisitively, almost hoping and praying that he did not offer me the answer that I knew was coming anyway.

He clasped his hands together and looked shaken, as if he had been rumbled. He spoke apologetically 'what do you want me to say…ever since I first saw Kiran…I fell in love. I tried to stop but it was just too hard.'

It was surreal, this is my wedding day, and here I am having a conversation with my so called best mate about him falling for my wife. The taste of bitter condemnation swirling in my mouth, the knavery, and disloyalty was consuming me as I felt my face flush with anger.

He was not finished 'I have always loved her. That is the truth. I think she is an amazing person, just something else.'

He looked at me with his snivelling features. I felt winded, this self confessing vermin was laying it on the line for me, and painfully…

'So you fucking kuta, you stabbed me in the back, treated me like a piece of shit, all the time carrying on with her behind my back, right.'

'Bruv, I messed up, I messed up.'

The enormity of the situation hit me straight between the eyes. Dev slowly started to stand up.

'I know you probably hate me right now, but I did not mean for it to get this far…'

Amidst the music in the background, there was a deathly silence between us as I scrutinised what he had just said to me. 'What do you mean this far, how far? What is that supposed to mean? You mean…you slept…with my wife?'

I stood up and moved the chair out of the way, moving myself forward to face him. Eyeball to eyeball. They say you can't strengthen the weak by weakening the strong, and right now, his words and actions were fuelling my burgeoning strength and hostility towards his weakening demeanour, this carcass of treachery stood there.

The vital and integral ingredient of trust in a friend-ship was lost in the ether. I envisaged gratuitous violence and spilling of the red stuff as I stood a gnat's whisker away from his face, growling and puffing like a satanic Rottweiler.

'Sandhu, Spanish, I thought it was them, the ones that were trying to ruin my marriage, interfere with my life, but the fraud, the cheat was right under my nose all along...YOU...driving the stake through my heart, I don't believe it.'

Dev looked at me incredulously as he stepped back and out of my fighting arc, a very wise move.

'You are crazy. I would never do that to you...'

His story had more holes in it than a slab of blue cheese, I could see it, and he could sense that the net was closing in.

It was only a matter of time. I poked his chest with my finger and asked again 'did you sleep with my wife?'

'I swear, baba di sohn, I would never disrespect you like that. I can't help the way I feel about her. She has no idea. I just know that she loves you bruv and that I have to suppress my feelings that is all.'

'You fu...'

'Look you have to believe me. I am drunk and don't even know what time it is let alone whose leg I am touching. I mean I could have touched you up.' He smiled and offered his grubby hand in a gesture to say that it was all okay.

BANG! I could take no more of his insolence as the red mist not so much descended as came crashing down in front of me.

I stepped forward and punched him with ferocious and unrelenting power in the stomach. If I could have mustered up any more physical power then it would have been nothing short of a miracle as he slumped to the floor in an instant clutching his midriff in excruciating pain. As he writhed around on the floor groaning in agony I looked around the hall, no-one had clocked me such was the speed of the delivery, not even Kiran and the girls, as they were too busy in their own world.

The timing of the blow was impeccable as the DJ announced the end of the party and the dance floor revellers started to collect their belongings and head south.

I looked down in disgust and disappointment at the injured vermin on the floor beneath me. All the lines he had fed me previously about me calling the wedding off, scaring me with tales of Jags, sending the photo, and trussing that up with a bullshit story about how he was doing that for my own good. He wanted my marriage to fail, to break down and then for him, the back stabber to step in and woe her instead so that he could fulfil his sick lust for my wife. I saw through his games, his deceit. What a bhanchod of bhanchods!

The hall was emptying fast as the guests saddled up and were heading home or to the girl's house for late night drinks.

My immediate family were heading back towards me including mum and dad. I saw Sharm sat nearby and sobering up by drinking from a bottle of water. He seemed well on the road to recovery. His trousers were also crucially pulled up at this stage. I checked once more and the coast was clear as I scooped Dev up by his arms and attempted to place his curled up body on the chair. He resisted as I tried to straighten him up so as not to attract attention, but my attempts were futile as he sat foetal like in the chair squirming all the time. The pain, no doubt, searing through his body, and shooting to his brain.

The previously consumed alcohol mildly numbing the kidney malfunctioning, and throbbing liver failure pain that he was no doubt suffering from.

Tina and Kiran walked over to where I was standing, as did Preeto and Manjit oblivious to the sucker strike that had felled Dev only seconds before. They continued to chat fervently as Dev remained seated looking plausibly like he had been the hapless victim of over indulgence in his drinking. My parents were not far behind as we all gathered our accoutrements before beginning to leave the hall. Dad took the room key from me and was busy arranging for my cousins to collect the gifts from the room upstairs and load them up in his car.

Traditionally the bride and groom march on to the girl's parents house where her parents officially give her away to the boys side in an emotional and heart wrenching ceremony. The sorrow and sadness can be so consuming in these moments that you would think that someone had been murdered with loud banshee type crying and histrionics from close relatives. Thankfully, I had carefully planned for us to escape into the sunset by cunningly booking the '*only*' flights that I could get a mere few hours after the reception had concluded. This was met with jaundiced and excoriating comments from both mum's and dad's in the planning stage, but I had managed to smooth it over with great cunning aplomb and chicanery.

Moments before we were about to walk out of the hall Kiran reached over and wrapped her arms around me hugging me tightly. This took me by surprise and I immediately reciprocated by putting my hands around her and squeezing her back.

This immediately discarded any thoughts that I had previously of her cheating on me with Dev. It was patently obvious that this had been a one way crush and definitely not reciprocated by my wife. Tough love as they say. At least I had unearthed this harboured secret from my erstwhile best mate. It was hurtful, but I was glad that I found out now.

'What's the matter?' I asked more relieved than she would ever understand.

'Nothing, I just want you to be happy…I want to …'

All of a sudden and before Kiran could finish off what she was saying in our romantic interlude - Ranj appeared with his usual impeccable timing as he draped his oaf like and sozzled frame around both me and Kiran.

He moved us both back and forth as he spluttered 'just want to say I wish you, no, I mean we wish you all the best.'

He moved off us and pulled his young suitor 'Dimple' forward from behind him 'we wish you a happy marriage.'

Kiran smiled and winked at Dimple. They were already acquainted and good mates having gone to University together. Dimple then congratulated Kiran as I spoke with Ranj for a second.

I turned and hugged him. He had been a stalwart mate to me throughout the day and in many ways I could not have made it to the end without his commitment and loyalty as a true brother. I hugged him tight 'thanks bruv, I owe you one. Keep in touch and I will see you in a couple of weeks when I get back from my honeymoon.'

Ranj smiled back 'kuta, you're going on your honeymoon, what about me? (He winked at Dimple) I am going for my 'suhaag raat' (wedding night) in a minute.'

He took hold of Dimple's hand and punched me in the chest with the other, laughing all the time.

He turned to Kiran '*bhabhi (sister in law – a term of endearment)* respect and good luck with him, your going to need it, ha ha, no seriously you are both a great couple and we are really happy for you both.'

Kiran smiled back as I saw Tina float behind us, lurking with intent and like a bad smell. Ranj looked down at Dev who was now beginning to straighten up and slowly stand to his feet 'what's he been drinking, bhanchod?'

He poked Dev in the chest 'oi shaarabi you with it? I'll see you around.'

Ranj then turned back to me and warmly smiled…

'I am off then, take care bro, remember, don't be a stranger, you have my number, call me sometime - we will hook up.'

With that, he led his girl away, hand in hand, and out of the hall.

We left the hall. I checked my pocket and ensured that I had the red scarfed money bag comfortably in my inside jacket pocket. It was there in all its glory. I could smell the holiday spending money.

As we stepped into the foyer, I casually glanced to the top of the stairs. I was immediately stopped in my tracks by the sight of Jags standing there with his sunglasses on. He looked every bit the Mafioso hit man as he glared back at me taking his sunglasses off so that I could see the whites of his eyes.

I shook off my sudden shock and looked around me where I was surrounded by a ring of steel of friends and family. I sought solace in the fact that only a fool would try something in such circumstances. Jags started to walk down the stairs slowly in my direction as I scurried towards the exit catching up with the others. I could see Dev limping tentatively out of the door and into the crisp Spring evening air.

I was still scared as I caught up with Kiran and looked back worryingly. Jags strolled through the foyer heading out into the open air and towards me. What was his major malfunction? Was this just one big intimidatory exercise for him so that he could see me piss my pants, buckling under the pressure of his non verbal threats?

I was so near to getting away and nothing was going to stand in my way, absolutely nothing.

We made our way to the limo as I tried to resist the urge to break into a jog. Dad was busily loading our holiday suitcases from his car to the boot of the limo with the assistance from Georgio whilst the pesky photographer insisted on taking a photo of us outside the hall. I mean what was the matter with him? He had all day to take photos and he chose this moment to take a snap.

Kiran then took a hand full of puffed rice from Preeto and threw some over her shoulder behind her several times as was customary. This was to convey good wishes on her parents and I hoped secretly also to cure Preeto's sadistic penchant to poison every fucker with jadu within a ten mile radius of her and her black cat.

As Kiran threw the rice she almost took my grandma's eye out as a granule whizzed perilously past her head. Thankfully, despite being elderly and infirm, her Matrix type reflexes and rear bent body swerve saved her from visiting Moorfields Eye Hospital, either that or she just broke her back as I did hear a sickening crunching sound as she cowered.

Once we were given the all clear, I darted for the limo, without making it obvious that I was becoming intimidated.

Georgio was standing by the rear doors and as we approached him, he duly opened the door letting me fling myself inside and into the sanctum of the rear cab. I let out a huge sigh of relief as Kiran stood outside the rear door waiting whilst I shuffled over to the other side and let her sit inside next to the open door.

The endorphins skipped around my body as I squeezed my fist triumphantly next to my thigh in utter contentment. I sat there in quiet jubilation when I felt a loud tap on the rear passenger window next to where I was sitting. My body jumped and I looked nervously expecting a ski masked fiend or barrel of a gun pointing at my head. It was thankfully just the cameraman seeking every opportunity to get a better perspective for his filming shots. I depressed the electric window down and the camera lens poked through as I leaned my head back onto the headrest taking in some much needed breathing time.

I looked back through the rear window and could see Dev standing with Firoz looking deflated. I looked some more and saw Jags appear behind the limo. He walked around the back peering inside and shaking his head. What was he doing so close to the boot, had he planted something? There was a reason he had made the effort to come today and I was about to find out. He carried on walking and stood on the pavement opposite the limo just staring at me, scrutinising me. His hand stroking his jaw, something was definitely up. I knew he had access to guns and was not afraid to use them. I smelt the fear. I was going to be gunned down in the limo next to my widowed bride. What a way to go? This situation was now as real as it had got all day...I was a dead man, it was just a matter of seconds!

CHAPTER 24

—≈—

Emasculation

I sat in the back tapping my foot impatiently hoping that the next fifteen minutes would whizz by magically as the time held tradition of wailing loved ones said their farewells to one of the daughters of the family.

This was heart stopping stuff especially when the elder uncles and aunties who would normally be composed and assured in the trials and tribulations of every day life would suddenly become quivering and drooling wrecks as they were dragged kicking and screaming like possessed demons from the limo.

Kiran was crying hysterically as guest after guest poured through the open door. She sobbed into their chests whilst clinging on to them like a leech. The groom's job at this delicate juncture was to do one thing, and do it well for the sake of future matrimonial bliss, and that was to look bloody concerned and empathetic as the nearest and dearest loved ones said their goodbyes. Another good strategy was to occasionally shake your head, and touch your wife's shoulder with a reassuring squeeze and pat. This all went down sublimely in the subsequent viewing of the wedding DVD. In this moment of high tension, I managed to work these strategies to perfection and was a definite contender for a Bafta award through cutting edge, emotional drama. I rocked.

The next guest was the fire breathing dragon herself, Preeto, in all her sadistic glory. She lowered her head into the car to hug her daughter, I visualised the metaphorical snakes hissing and slithering on top of her head akin to Medusa. Her face was a picture waiting to be taken as she glared at me momentarily before wrapping her talons around her girl.

Both Preeto and Kiran remained stuck together for a few minutes as they let the emotions and tears run freely. The camera man was feverishly zooming in and out, occasionally blinding me with the bright hand held light that his son was hoisting precariously above his head and between a small crack in the open limo window.

After Preeto had said her goodbyes, she was literally dragged embarrassingly from the car by another guest, hissing snakes included whilst letting out screams of desperation and longing. Kiran looked on sobbing. Her make up was running and I could see her shaking and continually blubbing. I used this moment to hold her hand and gave it a gentle squeeze. She moved her hand away slowly and dabbed at her face with a tissue, soaking up the streams of tears running down her cheeks. This was entirely understandable, this was a painful, and heart wrenching moment for her, saying goodbye to the family that she has lived with for twenty two years. I know I would find it difficult, but as a bloke, it is hard to comprehend.

The next one in to say goodbye was her dad – Manjit. He leaned inwards and just placed his hand on top of her head and hugged her briefly. That moment was for me the most poignant and pithy for many reasons. Manjit was a man of few words, terse and profound, my kind of fella. His feelings were expertly encapsulated within that fleeting moment and I saluted his professional approach, a man after my own heart I thought. He then moved his body out of the car as the blundering and hulk like beast in the size of Sharm came clattering in. He was still clearly a few sheets to the wind and decidedly squiffy as he blubbed like a baby.

Once he had his couple of minutes of fame in front of the camera, it was the turn of Tina, the marriage breaking kuti.

She leant in and tightly hugged her best friend. As they embraced I heard the muffled sounds of Tina whispering reassuring words in her ear and gently stroking her back. It seemed to do the trick as Kiran was visibly calming down. Tina then kissed her on the forehead and exchanged an icy stare with me. Once again, for some bizarre reason there was definitely no love lost between us, despite our earlier mutual drink and toast. She then paved the way for the next wailing crony for their two minutes of fame.

This charade continued for another ten minutes. During this short time I looked out of the window and dreamt that in a matter of hours we would be canoodling romantically by the warm azure waters of the Caribbean, getting warmed by the late afternoon sun. These thoughts were just the aphrodisiac and pick me up that I needed and assisted in lifting my flagging and tired spirit ten fold. As I wistfully drifted off I could actually hear the soothing murmur of luke warm water cascading down from the majestic water fountains in our hotels garden terrace.

The feeling of unbridled harmony and tranquility radiating throughout our fatigued bodies as we lay their entwined on the sun kissed beach, a quiet retreat away from the hustle and bustle of this day. Not long, not long to go now...

After the last auntie said her valedictory, the limo door was gently closed and Georgio nestled into his seat and started the engine. I knew this as I could see him through the splintered and damaged inner partition that had been destroyed before. He smiled back 'ready?'

'Oh yes, never been more ready. I said excitedly 'straight to Heathrow Georgio, do not pass Go and do not collect two hundred quid.'

Georgio looked at me confused 'two hundred what.'

'Never mind, we are ready.' My humour zipping over his head.

I cast my final look behind me and could see that Dev had his hand aloft as he said goodbye. Nearby Jags was talking to another guest whilst Tina was crying on one of her friends shoulders. Preeto was being held up by Manjit and was a lost and bewildered wreck.

I had made it, we had made it. What a day it had been. I had managed to escape this badly spun web of despair, near death beatings and what ifs. I was feeling physically and emotionally drained, totally emasculated.

The journey had been arduous, full of pit falls, road blocks and oil slicks but my determination and over whelming desire had got me to the finishing line, unscathed.

I could have screamed for joy as the close relatives of both our families pushed the limo from behind to send us on our way following wedding tradition, along with vast amounts of copper coins being tossed in the air raining down on the standing guests. The youngsters thought Christmas had come early as they raped, pillaged, and throttled each other to get to the loot, resembling determined and hungry frogs in a fly field.

Georgio carefully cruised along the car park travelling at less than five mph heading towards the exit and our ticket to paradise. Normally the bride's brother or close male relative would also accompany the bride to the groom's house for the first night but as we were going straight to the airport, I did not fancy one of her cousins sharing our honeymoon suite with us, so we decided against this.

The car inched along the gravel, I looked back again, my paranoia kicking in, just to make sure everyone was still standing as I had seen them, only ten seconds before. I saw the forlorn figures of Dev and Jags standing amongst the other guests in different positions. What a bunch of suckers I thought as we moved slowly further away from them all.

I looked at Kiran and she was staring out of the window sniffling but with a concentrated and wistful look emblazoned across her face. I thought better than to disturb her, we had plenty of time to talk over the next couple of weeks. YESSS! I had negotiated the snares, near death incidents, but here I was a rooting tooting surviving groom, with my prize sitting right next to me.

We were midway along the car park and the relatives who had been pushing the limo all moved back and let Georgio cruise along. I looked back and they all laughed and joked with one another as they made their way back to the crowd. I waved goodbye and then turned my body and sat back in my seat, it felt so much more comfortable.

I glanced across at my bride, yes my beautiful bride and was slightly perturbed. Kiran was now staring at me; she said nothing just stared at me. Her face was a blank canvas, a pitiful hue spreading across it as I studied her closely for a reaction of sorts.

'What's the matter sweetheart?' I touched her arm gently.

Her soft beautiful features were full of anguish and torment as she continued to look at me, through me. She was deep in thought, something was bothering her.

'STOP! JUST STOP! She screamed at Georgio catching me totally by surprise. Georgio who had seen his fair share of action for one day immediately complied by slamming on the anchors. The limo came to a shuddering halt.

'What is it, have you forgotten something?' I asked her trying not to panic too much, it was probably something innocent, a handbag, some jewellery or something plausible.

She remained silent; her brow furrowed and bottom lip now trembling. Something was brewing and I did not have the faintest idea. My heart was doing palpitations just at the thought of something else ruining the getaway especially as we had made it thus far. I turned to face her in the back of the limo. I could see Georgio's concerned expression as he poked his head through the partition gap.

'What, what's going on?' I asked her softly.

'It's too hard.' She said her lip quivering and in a defeatist tone.

As soon as she had said that, she fiddled with the limo door handle and then jumped out of the car. I tried to grab her hand but she managed to evade capture and no sooner had she sprung from the passenger side of the limo, she begun to flee towards the gaping crowd hitching up the bottom of her lehnga as she scarpered away, not responding to my desperate pleas for her to come back.

I was aware that it requires discipline, grit and fire to stay strapped in the harness of marriage and was inconsolable with Kiran's weak willed decision to throw in the towel so prematurely. I needed to find out why she had relented so soon?

I got out of the limo from the other side and gave a short chase catching her by the arm, as she was mid way down the road. I pulled her arm back and she fell into my arms. I did not mean to use such force to stop her but she jolted backwards from the force and her head landed on my chest. We both tussled for a brief moment before she released her wrist from my grip and pulled her body away. She took a step back and stood in front of me. Defiant and speaking through choke filled tears. 'Kam, no I can't do it. I will be living a lie....I don't, I....don't....love you!'

My world came crashing down around me at that moment, the sledgehammer blow slammed crushingly into my body, the words cut me to the quick, wounded me like no other incident had managed to do so for the entire wedding day, in my life.

How would I learn to live without her? The perpetual sadness and longing would be all too consuming. A life time of anti depressants, and other such happy pills pulling me towards their spiralling quicksand of misery.

I had reached my nadir, the bottomless pit of self despair and helplessness. My one way ticket to the heartbreak hotel had been well and truly reserved.

'I love someone else, I always have, it is just that it has taken me today to realise that my heart belongs to that person.'

I shook my head repeatedly.

'Please Kiran don't do this to me. I will do anything to make you love me, we can get away from all this bullshit and start afresh somewhere nice.' My words stuttering and desperate 'you will never want for anything for the rest of your life, please don't do this to me today…not today after what I have done to get to this moment, please I am begging you, darling, please.'

I was pleading with her, the tears and yearning for my wife to stop this nonsense and fall back into my arms were my last hopes. She was just having cold feet, and the last minute u turn was par for the course with many newly weds, albeit this was the first time I had ever witnessed a scene like this. Her emotions were merely toying with her and I had to make her realise that this was a natural reaction.

I glanced over to the crowd through my watery eyes and could see Dev standing to the side. He was expressionless and just stared towards our direction. All around there were mouths still ajar with shock, watching at the drama unfolding.

Kiran saw him too, I know as I saw her looking at him. I felt like doubling up in pain as Dev stepped forward an inch, he had slayed me ceremoniously and in a way that only someone who you trust implicitly could. Dev was the guy she wanted to share her life with and he had stolen my girl from under my nose.

Dev, the past master of guile and deception, was finding it hard to curb his enthusiasm as he stood there taking his hands out of his pockets and slowly rubbing them together. All the lies he had fed me, the fact that he was my best man was the hardest and most bitter pill to swallow. He had stabbed me through the heart so dramatically; his rank betrayal and flagrant violation of our brotherhood disturbed me to my core. It was conspicuously reprehensible. I wanted to kill that bastard, rip his arms off, bust every bone in his treacherous body, but at this juncture, I simply had no fight to offer. The life force and energy had been sucked out of me.

Kiran stood there at the cross roads of her life, crying and in a state of doom laden delirium. I saw both mums and dads looking on in disappointment and abject horror. A little further along were Sharm and Satwinder, both standing gob smacked and rooted firmly to the spot. I could see Firoz, Surinder and the boys also looking on in amazement. The whole situation was surreal.

Kiran took a deep breath 'I am sorry, so sorry…it's my fault, not yours.'

She fed me the classic line, the words that signalled the death knell of any relationship. My ability to detect bull crap had been honed over the years and I was not that gullible to fall for a time held classic line like that. I searched for answers but nothing was forthcoming. She then turned and walked over to the crowd leaving my heart heavy and hanging in my mouth. Who was responsible for snatching away my happiness and stealing my girl from under my nose?

I fell to my knees hitting the ground in a weakened and dejected heap.

Kiran looked back, paused, but then continued walking forward towards her beau. Who was he? She stopped a few feet away from both our families and friends.

The excited whisperings and mutterings continued amongst the crowd. I remained sunk to my knees as I saw Kiran moving her head towards the guests to meet up with the chosen one. Dev stepped further out from the side and into view. He walked a little closer towards Kiran where he stopped 'Kiran.'

The crowd gasped and I felt physically repulsed as the truth was threatening to lurch up and elbow me squarely in the throat. I tried in vain to control my devastating sorrow and despair from spilling over. I sat there looking through tear soaked eyes, whimpering to myself and weeping like a pathetic sobbing mess that I had become.

They looked at each other for a moment and then Dev broke into a smile. His ferret like features burning me up inside every moment that ticked by. He had been setting the bait for some time now and he was ready to pounce. He had hooked his big fish and all I could do was look on with disgust.

I could feel myself rapidly replaying my relationship with him through my mind, frame by sickening frame, all those shared moments, the heart to hearts. I was devastated, did anything he ever say, have even a granule of truth? I was lost for words and feeling mortified.

My comic book of a life was exploding in my face in grandeur fashion, as Dev was mere moments away from the back stabbing sweet taste of victory. I looked on in desperate anticipation. There was a commotion on the other side of the car park as someone was gently pushing and parting guests as they made their way to the front of the pack. I desperately searched for the courage to push through my anger and tears. I simply could not fathom how I had become entangled in the myriad lies and deception. Why me? All the answers to my questions were sequentially being displayed to all and sundry. The meat was firmly nestling on the bones as my life was being ripped apart lucidly.

Kiran directed her eyes away from Dev leaving him standing there. She, along with everyone else, inspected who this fearsome warrior was, negotiating his way through the jungle of people standing in the way of his prize. The mystery person continued to hack their way through, parting the final two aunties at the front and standing there valiantly.

I stood to my feet and walked slowly forward so that I was now standing a whisker away from the treacherous Dev and with a side profile of Kiran. I looked at the newly emerged person. He stood there like Satan himself, a consummate phoenix rising from the smouldering ashes that my wedding day had become. My heart somersaulted repeatedly with continual sharp spasms of pain as the gut wrenching reality of who it had been all along woke me up from my wallowing self pity.

—⚁—

CHAPTER 25

Coup de gras

It was none other than Jags, the guy who had been surreptitiously skipping in and out of the shadows all day waiting for this moment to resurrect his relationship. His sheer determination and tenacity was laudable but heart breaking.

I looked on despairingly as my paranoia kicked as it often did in high octane situations like this one.

I battled to come to terms with the fact that Jags and Kiran were meant to be, and that they had never stopped loving one another. The letter that I had discovered in her bag in the restaurant was from him; maybe he wasn't in prison after all. The cogs churned rapidly, she kept the letter because it meant something to her. I mean after all was said and done, her lover had made the effort to come to the wedding day. The threat he had made of needing to talk to me after the milni was again painfully replayed in my mind. I felt like a prize donut, as smart as a door knob as I looked at them helplessly.

He wanted to warn me off his girl, tell me that his feelings for her were still burning like embers in the fire. I was just the unfortunate sucker caught in the cross fire of cupids firing arrows. How stupid have I been not to see this coming a mile away?

It was now becoming clear that he had passed on a message to her, perhaps via one of her friends that he was at the wedding and was willing to take her back and let bygones be bygones. It was all fitting into place, making sense to me, My nightmare had now become his dream and fantasy as he smiled at me mockingly before fixing his gaze on his lover.

There was a deadly silence as the four of us stood there at the last chance saloon, like hired guns in the stare down.

The trouble is that the last chance saloon always attracts dangerous gun slingers and the town pillaging bad guy was definitely Jags who was coincidentally also dressed in all black.

The crowd noise, the incessant chattering, the high jinx replaced by unnerving silence, the crescendo of lively banter waning into emptiness, you could hear the proverbial pin drop, a fucking grenade pin as the situation threatened to explode in our faces in dramatic fashion.

Some guests continued to whisper furtively amongst themselves, attempting to decipher exactly what was going on, who was with whom, and what was going to happen next.

They greeted each other with smiles 'Kiran, you look nice.'

'Thanks, you made it then.' She spoke quietly.

I felt powerless as the lovers shared this intimate interlude in front of all of us, rubbing my nose shamefully into the brown stuff as they went on.

'I thought I would see you on your BIG day.' Jags spread his arms in front of his body emphasising the word big.

'You look different.' She responded.

'I know I thought I would make the effort...now are you sure you want to do this...I mean really sure?' Jags asked her before they set about this new chapter in their life.

Kiran looked at me tilting her head sympathetically, before looking back at Jags.

'I have never been so sure about anything in my entire life. I am going to follow my heart for the first time and come what may.'

'So you still feel the same as you did back then?' Jags clarified.

'Yeh, my feelings are even stronger now.' Kiran was sure.

'I am not surprised, your feelings were strong then, and it looks like it is meant to be judging by today's performance.' The foundations for their relationship being ceremoniously laid out before my very eyes.

Jags moved forward and gently placed both hands on Kiran's face. I could see dad being restrained by Sharm and a couple of uncles from Kiran's side. I moved forward instinctively to stop the inevitable from happening as my guts twisted and churned inside. The fat lady was just metaphorically beginning to sing as the curtains of my marriage were about to come thundering downwards in death defying fashion.

Jags said 'good luck.' Kiran took a deep breath and sighed 'thanks for the support.'

Jags then leant forward and kissed her tenderly on the lips. Dad shouted 'kuta, kamina, who do you think you are coming here and doing this to my son? I will not leave you in one piece.' Sharm was doing a remarkable job of containing dad's flailing arms and legs and keeping him tightly leashed and away from the scene of the illicit affair unfolding on this miserable day.

Jags concluded by saying 'now, you have made your mind up, go and do the right thing, enjoy your life, be happy.'

'Thanks Jags.' Jags stepped to one side as Kiran moved forward gingerly, trying not to make eye contact from the disapproving looks the aunties were giving her. The signals and smell of anger were clear for all to see including and especially Kiran.

Kiran strolled up to where the manipulative son of a monkey Dev was standing. She stopped and then shook her head as she walked past him and into the crowd. Dev dropped his head as the humiliation hit him full on. He felt and looked worthless and this single act of defiance edified me in otherwise what had become the most harrowing, heart burning and soul destroying incident I have had to endure...EVER!

Kiran walked through the slowly parting crowd and into the foyer of the hall with all of us slithering up behind her like the regular, professional ghouls and rubber neckers we were. I quickly made my way to the front of the herd so that I could be the first to witness the charade my wedding day had become. I wanted to see the mystery guy, the champion of my girl's heart so that I could size him up as my next meal or not. I got to the front as the others languished torpidly behind dragging their knuckles across the carpet of the foyer. Kiran stopped as did the crowd of guests. There sitting on the bottom of the stairs was...the ONE!

Tina had her head in her folded arms and had been sobbing. She looked up at the scene in front of her and took a moment to survey the situation before smiling at Kiran 'Is it true?' Tina probed.

Kiran smiled back as she now stood inches away from Tina who was slowly starting to stand up now.

'For real.' Kiran spoke with her soft dulcet tone. Tina's smile was beginning to spread across her face as the pair were patently oblivious to the hordes of popcorn eating onlookers that were scrutinising their every muscle twitch.

Kiran reminisced 'you promised that one day we would be together…well today has become ONE day.'

Tina fell into Kiran's arms as the pair embraced passionately.

'I really love you and always have.' Tina spluttered the words out as they echoed around the foyer. I held my heart and shook my head in utter shock. All this time I had no idea, not a shred of doubt that they were…lovers!

'Now we have come out in the open. I just want to be with you. We can do what we want and when we want. I just could not spend another day away from you.' Kiran's outpouring and declaration of love nailed the final rusty nail into the coffin of my marriage as they kissed passionately on the lips.

There was uproar in the crowd on one hand and gasps and fainting on the other. Some shrewd operators meanwhile had the footage safely captured on their mobile phones and were already in the throes of sending it on to their acquaintances. The cameraman was also filming the carnage as it unfolded blow by blow.

They parted with their lips and stood gazing lovingly into one another eyes as I disconsolately walked up to them and mustered up a granule of energy 'how long has this been going on for?'

Kiran turned to me 'I am so sorry Kam, you have to understand that I tried to make it work for you, for my parents, for the god damn community, but the truth is we have always had feelings for each other and that is the bottom line. It has just taken me this day and that moment in the limo to face up to the fact that I am in love with Tina and no-one else.'

I looked at the pair of them as they held hands. They were no strangers to intimate physical contact that was for sure. No wonder Kiran had known such intimate details about Tina's penchant for red lingerie as we had laughed about in the car one time, the duplicitous bitch.

'So this was all a cover up? a sham was it, the crying in the wedding hall, the chat by the head table was that all about scheming to run away now? I raised my voice

Tina interjected curtly 'we are sorry you found out this way, but there was no other way. I don't want to live life with any regrets, you only live once and all that. Our love is too strong. I am tired of sneaking around to spend time with her, suppressing our feelings for the sake of everyone else's insecurities and perfect lives. She motioned an inverted comma's sign in mid air when she said the word perfect. 'Still it is better you found out now so that you can move on with your life as we can too.'

I plucked up the strength to ask one final question to Tina 'the love letter... was that from you?'

'Yes it was from me.' Tina did not hesitate in giving me the facts, no remorse, and not a care for my feelings and broken heart. She was ruthless to the bone.

I looked at dad's face and he looked lost. Mum was crying and being consoled by auntie Satwinder. Preeto's parents were similarly doleful as they stood there still reeling from the shock of what they had witnessed.

Tina broke away momentarily and I overheard her arranging with one of her friends to give them a lift. She returned to Kiran's side and held her hand again 'we have got a lift sorted, shall we go?'

I was looking straight at my ex wife through hazy and water filled eyes, a breaking heart and gut wrenching pain.

Kiran leaned forward and landed a peck on my cheek 'sorry, I am going to go now...when you are okay to talk, call me and we can sort out the wedding paperwork. You will find someone one day who really loves you, I promise.'

She turned and apologised to her parents, who turned their heads in disgust at the shenanigans they had painfully witnessed. The lovers then left the foyer holding hands with their getaway driver close behind.

The waterproof dams fighting back my tears were creaking and threatening to flood. I had done so well up to this moment to keep the flood gates sealed firmly shut. However, as she turned her back and walked away from me holding the hand of her girlfriend I felt the pressure intensifying as she walked out of my life for the final time!

The water dams all of a sudden burst emphatically as rivers of tears stated to gush down my face soaking my shirt.

I stood there breaking down, really falling to pieces as my world had crumbled around me leaving me with nothing.

My dignity had been stripped from me and the hollow solitude of the situation was suffocating me like a veil as my body begun to shake from the adrenal dump. The combination of the adrenaline running amok in my system and the ferocity of my crying. It felt as though I had lost a loved one. I may as well have, the pain was undoubtedly the same. Sharm took me in his arms and squeezed me hard. His warm bear hug helped pour the much needed oil on my troubled waters. This moment of respite was short lived as I took several quick deep breaths to compose myself. The overwhelming whiff of his armpit and stale booze snapped me out of my suicidal frame of mind for a split second as I let all my tearful anguish out.

He remained staunch, rock like, as he clung on to me with all his might, cooling the flames like the trooper he was.

I then heard one of the guests muttering amongst themselves that Kiran had now left with Tina. The surreptitious lovers were off to seek out the path they had chosen.

I felt nothing less than resentment and bitterness towards them, as they had ruined not only my life but also that of both our parents. They had made my wedding day the talk of the community and a lasting folk lore story that will be recited and embellished around the world for years to come.

Therefore, I had become the discarded few, the superfluous loser in the game they call life, my heart continued to burn inside. They say that having your heart broken is like paying taxes, death and wetting your pants as a child: totally unavoidable.

Sharm moved me away from him 'are you going to be okay son?'

'Yeh yeh cool, I just had a moment. I am going to go and sort myself out. I will be fine, thanks for everything.'

Sharm softly slapped my cheek and joined my anguished parents. I walked over to my parents and told them that I was going to get away for a bit, to collect my thoughts, and pick up the pieces of my shattered life. They understood my need for privacy at this earth shattering moment and hugged me telling me to be strong and the usual edifying advice that your parents would offer in similar circumstances.

I walked through the crowd of friends and family and was completely incognizant to the pats on the back and supporting comments that were being thrown at me as I bumbled past them. My fog cloaked brain not registering what had happened. As I walked out into the freshness of the evening, I suddenly caught a glimpse of Jags walking towards me. His arms were swaying by the side of his body as he came closer and closer to me.

I stepped back up the steps expecting the chatter of an AK47 rifle drilling me full of lead or the tip of a Luger pressed into my back, such was the reputation that preceded him. Instead he pulled me back by my arm down a step so that we were now on the same level. I stumbled in front of him and looked on. I was hoping my wet nose and sad puppy eyes were enough to distract him from the merciless beating that he was no doubt preparing to dish out to me.

'I have been trying to warn you all day about her. I knew she would never change.'

'What do you mean?' I said stunned by his approach.

'Why do you think we broke up geezer think about it, I caught her in bed with what's her face...Tina...yeh she was sleeping with her behind my back, can you believe that shit, a good looking girl like that?'

I felt the metaphorical sinking of his fangs into my neck as he carved open my gaping wound even wider.

'You knew this all along?'

'Yeh, why do you think I was here? Firstly I couldn't believe that she had changed, and secondly I wanted to warn you and to prevent a scene like this happening.'

This was the final brick in the wall of insanity that this day had become. Situations like these in days gone by had driven our brethren to drink and suicide. I felt myself leaning towards the latter, disembowelled, depressed, and alarmingly suicidal.

'So...so, she was with Tina even when she was with you? She told me you used to beat her down and stuff, is that true?'

'Nah nah, do I look like I would hurt a woman, you shitting me or what? We used to row all the time. Guess what? It was always about her burgeoning feelings for Tina and it just got worse after I caught them in bed together. Yeh, she made some excuse about experimenting and drinks but I knew the score. A bit after that I done some time for drugs possession and that was that.'

'Let me guess did Tina detest you from the moment you started dating, right?'

'Yeh she did.'

'Right, that is why Kiran went along with all this marriage stuff. It was because of her parent's pressure, especially her interfering old bag of a mum. She would still have seen Tina even though she was married to you, trust me. Those two are inseparable and passionate lovers (he raised his hand up) all this would have been a pretence, a show, a double existence to keep the old dear off her case.'

The dagger in my heart just twisted for the umpteenth time today. I was grateful for Jags being so frank with me, especially now that I was relieved that he didn't want to cut me a new arsehole for marrying his former girl-friend.

I had one more question left in the tank and went for it 'what is this about you having access to guns and all that?'

Jags laughed 'that is all just rumour control. I got to know a few guys in prison. They are the ones with the reputation, definitely not me. It seems like the jungle drums and grapevine work properly around here. I like to live a peaceful life.'

'Right, okay.' I was unsure what else to say.

'So no hard feelings hey, but I did try to warn you about her.'

Jags then shrugged his shoulders and patted me on the back as he walked away leaving me with his thoughts.

The significant events throughout the day were all lucidly clear to me now. I looked up and signalled to Georgio to crackle the limo into life as I made my way over to him. I felt so alone and empty as I made my way over to the open door of the limo dragging my heels with apathy.

'Kam, wait.' I stopped. I knew who it was and this was not the best time to speak to me as I turned slowly to face him.

'Can we talk bruv? I just want to sort things out with you before you go.'

Dev, the pariah, must have had a death wish, as he stood there with one hand clutching his torso from my earlier assault. There are few problems or situations, which cannot be solved through a suitable and timely act of violence. I wrestled with this ideology as this martyr of double crossing stood shamefully in front of me.

He slowly moved his hand out to me, pathetic and desperate 'I am sorry mate, let bygones be bygones. What's happened has happened and I still value you as a friend.'

There is an old saying that your friends are like parachutes, if they are not there the first time you need them then in all probability you will never need them again. This was the icy cold truth as I was seeing it. The sanctuary of friendship had been dealt the cruellest of blows when he had deceived and lied to me. There was no turning back; never would he darken my hallway again...

We both knew that if I were to extend my hand out and reciprocate with a handshake then this would absolve him of all the guilt and betrayal that was hanging over him like a cloak.

The misery he had caused me was too great for me to brush off. I am a man of principle and what this arduous journey had taught me, is that in this world you will meet a lot of Dev's, people without any substance to their existence, players, time wasters and tricksters seeking to exploit you at any given opportunity. Don't let them, or you are the true fool.

I looked down at his out stretched hand and pathetic attempt at salvaging our once platinum selected friendship; I knew that this was the end. I shook my head deliberately and disapprovingly. I looked him in the eyes. Somewhere, someone had sucked the goodness out of him; caused him to do the one thing you never do, betray your true friends, your inner circle of trust. This was a doomed and eternal cardinal sin and seldom with no road to recovery.

This cretin was one generation removed from a

vermin with his rat like personality and actions. I decided the time for laying the truth bare to him was right;

'YOU... offer me your hand in friendship. With what face can you do that? You are a sum total of your actions and you will never meet a more loyal mate than me ever...even in another lifetime. You messed up, and you will have to live with your betrayal for the rest of your pitiful life. I never want to see you again...EVER!'

His face remained still, the shock and scorn of my words rocking his world: and with that, I walked away from him as tears rolled down his cheeks. I turned and walked the lone green mile to the open limo door and nodded to Georgio to get in.

I flicked open my mobile and made a call.

I sat in the back, and gave Georgio details of the address of where I wanted to go. I then made a couple of calls on my mobile, one to Heathrow check in desk to request a name change on the plane ticket and the other to someone else. (An address thirty minutes away) I left the pain and misery of the contemptible wedding behind me as the limo careered out of the car park.

Thirty minutes later the limo screeched to a halt outside my chosen address. I again flipped open the mobile and pressed redial. The call was answered instantaneously 'are you ready? Don't forget your passport and toothbrush.'

While I waited, I put my hand down the back of the seat and rummaged around for a bit before pulling out the previously discarded bag of cocaine. I retrieved the bag, and tossed it slowly, up and down in my hand feeling the texture of the white substance through the bag. I had left this world behind and taken the righteous path but where had it got me I questioned myself?

I sat there and replayed the day's events in my mind. My marriage was devastatingly doomed from the outset; there were no ifs and buts. My wife had been harbouring secret feelings for her best friend for some time now and no matter what I did, I didn't have a ghost in hells chance of making her love me despite my best efforts. What realistic chance did I have?

Hey , *'c'est la vie'*, they say shit happens in life but the real test of character is how you respond to it.

Do you curl up into a ball as the metaphorical boots fly in from every conceivable angle or do you get back to your feet and wade through the pervading snake pit of dejection and despair to live to fight another day? This was the true litmus test. When the curtain of doom falls down on you, hold your head aloft and you will see that the pain soon goes, the disappointment soon fades, a new day, a new beginning, a new quest...

My relations with Dev and Ranj throughout the day were a mixed bag of emotions. Well they were eye opening to the say the least and I remembered a famous analogy that helped me put today's tumultuous friendships into some perspective.

It is the one about the cow, the cat, and the bird. The bird is eating seeds off the ground one day when suddenly it started to snow heavily and before the bird knew it, he was trapped under a pile of snow. He was freezing and about to die when a cow walking past him looks down and shits on him. The warmth of the cow dung helps the bird get some sensation back and melt the snow. The bird feels great as he sits in the cow dung merrily eating the remaining seeds and singing to his hearts content. Meanwhile a cat walks past and sees the noise, so he digs the bird out of the dung and eats him.

The moral of the story being, not everyone who shits on you is bad and not everyone who digs you out of the shit is your friend. The person I initially thought was shitting on me throughout was Ranj, and he actually turned out to be my saviour in some perilous situations; whereas Dev was supposedly the guy who was always there for me digging me out of situations, but was the one who had the sneaky intent and let me down so dramatically in the end. This analogy helped to assuage the disappointment and slake my perspective on the events that had unfolded.

I cogitated further, delving into the depths of my mind and frame of reference. I look around the world and see people dying of cancer, heart attacks, and disease. I see injuries, poverty, famine, accidents and life changing events every single day. Life is nothing short of a lottery, a roll of the fucking dice, some days you are the statue other days the pigeon. Who knows when your time is up? When death taps on your window?

I now equate life as being on a battlefield in the midst of a bloody war with bullets strafing and whizzing past your head. At any time when your luck runs out you will be struck down with a bullet and be paralysed, injured, disabled or dead whatever comes first.

Therefore, in context, my marriage is over, my reality cheque has bounced, but I am still standing, licking my wounds, feeling beaten up and wounded but nevertheless still here.

With this in mind and the realisation that there is a time to create and a time to evaluate, I felt that now was the time to do both and to travel rootlessly. It would be good for my heavily battered soul.

As I was wrestling with my inner thoughts the limo door opened on the other side and the first thing I saw were the longest and most seductively tanned legs you will ever see. The long legged temptress sat down next to me closing her door behind her. She kissed my cheek with her luscious pouting red lips and then sat back. I could see that she was holding a small bag containing the bare essentials for a trip abroad. She placed the bag on the seat in front of her.

I tapped out two lines of cocaine on my hand and inhaled them both swiftly as I offered the bag to the temptress, who repeated the drill on her hand. She flung the empty packet to the floor of the limo...

'Kiddha sohni kurriye.'

'So your marriage broke down ey? You are a fast mover.'

'That's life.'

'So where you taking me?'

'Been to the Caribbean before?'

'No...but I am looking forward to it.'

'Well I promised you that day in the garden when we exchanged numbers that I would stay in touch with you in the future.

I am so glad I did now. Let's go and have some fun...'

She smiled back sexily and reassuringly, just the tonic I needed.

I tapped on the roof of the limo...'Georgio, vamos...'

So, in the dying embers of the day, as one chapter ends, another one starts, this was my...

Masala Wedding...

୧୦୨

∽o∾

'Naughty Indian Affairs'

∽o∾

Read the second Book by
Sonny Singh Kalar
in the Masala Book range!

www.masalabooks.com

Lightning Source UK Ltd.
Milton Keynes UK
01 February 2010

149420UK00001B/16/P